LARKSPUR

A MYSTERY

Also by Sheila Simonson:

A Cousinly Connexion
Lady Elizabeth's Comet
The Bar Sinister
Love and Folly

LARKSPUR

A MYSTERY

Sheila Simonson

St. Martin's Press

NEW YORK

Library of Congress Cataloging-in-Publication Data
Simonson, Sheila.
　　　Larkspur : a mystery / Sheila Simonson.
　　　　　　p.　cm.
　　　"A Thomas Dunne book."
　　　ISBN 0-312-04338-4
　　　I. Title.
　　PS3569.I48766L35　1990
　　813'.54—dc20　　　　　　　　　　　89-70259
　　　　　　　　　　　　　　　　　　　CIP

First Edition

10　9　8　7　6　5　4　3　2　1

I got the letter from Dai Llewellyn in June, when the locals were still coming to my bookstore out of curiosity and the tourists had not yet found it.

Ginger Gates tossed the bundled mail at me and I fielded it left-handed. I was waiting on a customer. He bought Joseph Wambaugh's *Lines and Shadows*, then fresh in paperback, and a field guide to the High Sierras.

I chatted with the man for a while, handed him a flyer that described my book-ordering service and map inventory, and smiled at the twelfth reference to the heat wave since 9:00 A.M. It was four in the afternoon. Only three of the twelve customers had bought books, but all of them had given me a free weather report.

"Hot out," Ginger shouted from the back room.

I contemplated homicide.

"Tam starts work today."

"Good." Tam was Ginger's daughter, second string guard on the junior college basketball team I coached during the winter. Tammy was spending the summer guiding white-water rafters. I hoped she wouldn't break her long legs.

I picked up the mail—two sweepstakes brochures, a coupon offering a free soft drink for every two cheeseburgers purchased, the electric bill, and a letter in a heavy bond envelope with my name, Lark Dailey, and the store's name,

Larkspur Books, in black ink and a rather crabbed hand. Below that another hand had written in the rest of the address.

I turned the envelope over. The initials EDL were embossed on the back flap, but there was no return address. One of my players, I reflected, had decided to get married and chuck basketball, and her granny had addressed the wedding announcements. It was that kind of envelope.

Ginger stuck her head around the partition that separated the storeroom office from the shop itself. "How's business?"

"At this rate I'll file for bankruptcy before Christmas."

Ginger chortled as if I'd said something witty, gave her mouse-blond perm a pat, and picked up the feather duster. Books accumulate a lot of dust. She began whisking the feathers over the revolving science-fiction rack.

I tossed the junk mail into the wastebasket and took the bill and the heavy envelope to the back room. My brand-new PC gleamed. When I had entered the amount of the bill, written a check, and stuffed it into the return envelope, I opened my mystery letter.

My dear Miss Dailey,

I have just learned from my friend, Lydia Huff, that you have opened a bookstore—a real bookstore for the selling of real books—in Monte, California. Forgive an old man's impertinent curiosity, but why? How? Are you in earnest? If so, I hope you will join the house party I'm assembling at my little fishing lodge for the Fourth of July weekend so we can talk it all over.

Lydia and Bill, Win D'Angelo, *la belle* Denise, and a handful of other congenial souls have agreed to keep me company. Because I always spend July at the lodge, I find I need a literary weekend at the beginning of the month to sustain me through the sheer earthiness of the rest. Do come, and bring a guest if you like. Your mother and I are old friends, as you probably know. But even if we weren't, I'd still look forward to meeting another Literary Pioneer.

Yours faithfully,

Dai Llewellyn

P.S. Four days—Thursday through Sunday, if you can spare the time. We have swimming, canoeing, fishing, and Lucullan food in addition to the stellar company. EDL

I ransacked my memory. Ma had a lot of old friends. I had met Bill and Lydia Huff. Bill published the local weekly and a great deal else, being sole proprietor of a rather famous small press, the kind that prints high-quality chapbooks and regional histories.

Old Bill was a bit folksy for my taste, but I liked Lydia and I'd cultivated the connection in a desultory way. The only real bookstore and the only real press in the county ought to coexist in harmony. I wasn't sure I could put up with four days of literary chitchat, however. I had better plans for the Fourth. Or did I?

I brooded. The annoying little bell that rang when a customer entered my shop bonged, and I went to the counter. Ginger peered at me around the s.f. I shook my head, 'I'll get it,' and moved forward to greet the woman who had come in. Lydia Huff's large light-gray eyes lit when she saw me. We embraced after the fashion of people who have drunk cocktails together, and I mentioned the invitation.

The hundred-kilowatt eyes beamed. "Oh, do come, Lark darling. We're apt to get all reminiscent and inky when there aren't any fresh faces. You'll like Dai. He's a dear."

I was about to say, "That's nice but who is he?" when memory kicked in. Of course. A major minor poet. A distinguished teacher. My mother's mentor, or one of them. E. David Llewellyn—poet. My heart sank.

"Uh, Jay and I . . ."

"Is that your lover?"

When older people use the word *lover* they make me uncomfortable, as if they were popping me into a mental gilded cage. "We're friends," I muttered.

"Bring him!" Lydia made an expansive gesture emphasized by the flowing sleeve of her heavily embroidered lilac tunic. Lydia supported all the local arts and had once been a weaver herself, so she was apt to look expensively homespun. "Bill's daughter will be there—and Dai's grandniece, Angharad. Do you know her?"

I nodded and she went on with the guest list.

I knew Angharad Peltz. She taught English part-time at the j.c. and considered women's basketball an appropriate activity for nonverbal ectomorphs and lesbians. She didn't say that, but that's what she meant.

I'm a little paranoid about basketball because my family is hyperintellectual and they did not look upon my selection to my college varsity basketball team as they would have say, regarded precocious publication in *Poetry Magazine* or the *Journal of the American Historical Society* (my mother is a poet, my father a history professor).

By the time I made the Olympic team (via Ohio State) they were almost reconciled to having produced a sport in both senses of the word. Unfortunately, the 1980 Olympic team was sacrificed to the gods of politics. If I had come home with a gold medal, or more likely a bronze, I think they would have understood my enthusiasm, but my basketball career fizzled like a damp firecracker. So there I was, five years later, coaching part-time and running a bookstore on the wrong side of the Rockies.

Lydia had paused.

"It sounds nice." I hoped that was a suitable but noncommittal response.

"Oh, it is. The lodge is pure 1930s rustic—lots of peeled logs and paneling—but Dai has transformed it into a kind of high-class hotel. Not that he rents it out." She laughed, ho-ho-ho. I deduced that Llewellyn was a fat cat. If he owned a lake, he had to be.

Lydia was enthusing over the amenities, which included a Filipino chef. There was a private dock, canoes only—no motorboats or speedboats, my dear, he doesn't like noise—and so on.

Eventually she wound down and I said I'd think about it. She had come to check out our display of Huff Press books, naturally, not to buy anything. She rearranged a couple of titles, said she was satisfied, and left.

"He's an old goat."

I jumped. I'd forgotten Ginger. "Llewellyn?"

Ginger waved the feather duster almost fiercely. "Dennis took me out there last year. It's a fancy place, okay, but who wants to be sneered at by eighty-year-old faggots?"

I wondered whether "faggot" was local parlance for anyone from San Francisco who didn't crumple beer cans with his bare hands or a more precise metaphor. "He must've been pretty hard to take."

"He was." She whacked the dust from a row of Penguin mysteries so hard the rack revolved. We had mysteries and science fiction on specially constructed wooden racks. The real books reposed on real bookshelves. "He looked at me as if I wore polyester pantsuits."

"Patronizing," I guessed.

"Yeah." Ginger brooded. I suspected she had a polyester pantsuit in her past, but she was now strictly natural fiber. She was also, belatedly, going to college, having married at eighteen, divorced at twenty-two, and hand-raised a pair of kids while waiting tables. College was very disturbing to Ginger's assumptions. I was fond of her, maybe because her assumptions were disturbable.

"Does Dennis like the old man? He's a distinguished poet, you know."

"Maybe he is, but he treats Dennis like the chauffeur." Dennis Fromm, Ginger's whatchacallum, was a forest ranger. She snorted. "Worse than his own chauffeur. The old guy has this pretty-boy Mexican kid to drive for him, and they flirt."

"Oh."

"Well, they do. Dennis had to take his mom out to stay at the lodge, so I went along. I was glad when we left."

"I suppose Denise likes the old man."

"Oh, you know Denise. She fluttered all over him." Dennis's mother, oddly enough, was a dancer. That is, she had been a dancer in the Isadora Duncan mold. She was now in her sixties, still graceful, still dramatic. How such a haunting, romantic type had produced a son like Dennis was more than I could figure out, but, hey, my mother produced a female basketball player. Dennis was dumb but sweet. I had reservations about Denise.

The longer I thought about it—and I brooded for several hours—the less I liked the coincidence, Lydia Huff just dropping by in time to abet Llewellyn's invitation. I began to smell a conspiracy.

Whenever I succumb to paranoia I go to the source. My mother was home—between writers' conferences—and she sounded innocent.

"You're sure you didn't set me up?" I took a bite of taco salad, tipping the mouthpiece of the phone up around my forehead so I could chew corn chips and listen.

"Set you up? What do you mean, darling? I've known Dai forever, of course, but I haven't talked to him in, oh, it must be months now." The line crackled. Thunderstorm. I missed New York thunderstorms.

"And you didn't just happen to mention my bookstore to him . . ."

"I probably did," Mother said cheerfully. "It's not a secret, is it?"

I ground my teeth on another chip.

"What is that noise?"

"I'm eating dinner."

"I always forget the time difference. We had brook trout."

"Dad's been fishing again. Canada?"

She described my father's end-of-semester escape to the wilds of Quebec. Nice but beside the point.

I said, "Give him a kiss for me. Now, about this invitation . . ."

7

"The lodge is supposed to be fabulous. Dai wrote 'Siskiyou Summit' there. You ought to go."

Clearly I was supposed to recognize the import of 'Siskiyou Summit.' I didn't. I speared a chunk of cheddar. "The weekend of July Fourth will be my first big tourist rush. I should stay with the store."

"That's probably true . . ." A burst of static intruded. ". . . say you'd found a reliable clerk?"

"Ginger." I craned around the door of the office for a view of the shop. Ginger was waiting on an elderly couple who looked as if they might actually buy a hardback. "She's pretty good." But not literary.

"Why don't you have, er, Ginger hold the fort? You could drive into town from the lodge a couple of times to check up."

"Expensive."

"I'll underwrite it, darling."

I chewed vigorously.

"Really, Lark, you're in business now. You shouldn't overlook the advantage of having connections."

She was right. When it came to books, I had connections in a big way. The idea of using her name to sell things didn't sit well with the taco salad, but there were a lot of things about my bookstore setup that bothered me. It was financed by a loan on the family trust fund—one kind of "connection." And now this.

My mother will probably never win a Pulitzer for poetry, but she may take the National Book Award one of these years, and she already has an impressive list of secondary honors. Why pretend I don't have literary connections?

"Tell me about Llewellyn," I said, sighing. "Is it true he's gay?"

"Yes, and a great blow it was to us at Bennington when we first found out." Mother chuckled. "There we were, the entire senior-lit contingent, ripe for Meaningful Liaisons, and he wasn't interested."

"All-women's schools are a perversion." I had attended Ohio State over Mother's protests.

8

"Really, Lark."

"So you were all in love with the old guy."

"He was a dashing and well-seasoned fifty at the time, darling. Hardly an 'old guy.' And he read poetry like an angel."

I tried to imagine a bunch of early '50s college girls in pleated skirts and bobby socks languishing over the visiting poet. Not my style. "Is he good?"

"A good poet, you mean?" She was still amused. "He was a pioneer." That word again. "He made an impact on the young writers of the '30s and '40s—liberating them from the tyranny of the iamb and so on. He particularly hated rhyme, as I recall, and, yes, he was good."

"Not 'is good.' 'Was.'"

Mother's turn to sigh. "Did I say that? I always thought Dai's wealth was a handicap. He didn't have to scramble after prizes and fellowships, so there's a whiff of the dilettante in most of his work, but he has a surprisingly good ear for an imagist and, of course, his visual observations are exquisite. Yes, he's important . . ."

"But his importance is historical?" I finished the thought for her.

"That makes me uncomfortable." She paused. I could hear her thinking. "But it's true, unless he's been writing and not publishing. For all practical purposes he was literary history twenty years ago. That's when he retired from Muir."

Muir College was an excellent private liberal-arts college in the heart of the wine country. If Llewellyn had taught at Muir he was good in more ways than one. Muir was famous for the quality of its teaching.

Another thought clicked in, something she had said. "You talked to him a couple of months ago. Why?"

"He's an old friend." Mother paused again. "He asked me to be one of his literary executors, Lark. I had to think it over."

"An honor?" I ventured.

"Of course, but one that could entail a lot of work. He always meant Hal Brauer to act for him—Hal was his lover—but Hal died in a car wreck several years ago. Dai went into seclusion for months. The fact that he's ready to think about his work again is a good sign. I didn't like to refuse him."

"But you did?"

"No," she said calmly. "When he told me the other executor was willing to do the shitwork, I agreed."

"Who's the lucky man—or woman?"

"Somebody named D'Angelo. One of Dai's students."

I groaned.

"I believe he teaches at your little junior college."

Monte J. C., a state community college, had 7,000 students. It wasn't little, except in Mother's mind. I declined to argue the question. "D'Angelo's head of the English department."

"Is he? He sounded pleasant enough when I spoke with him. All of this is in confidence, Lark."

I assured her I would be as soundless as a dot on a disk of snow, an excursion into Emily Dickinson that tickled Mother so much she was still chortling when we hung up. I finished my salad.

Out front I could hear Ginger murmuring something to a customer who rumbled back. I decided to let her deal with him. When the door bonged on his departure, I strolled out to see what was happening. A hairy person in shorts and a T-shirt was still drooping over the map file.

"What's doing?"

"I sold one of those Ansel Adams books and a guide to the lake." "The lake" was Lake Shasta, a hundred-odd miles south, though there were thousands of natural lakes nearer.

I commended Ginger's enterprising spirit. The Adams book was expensive. In fact, I laid on the soft soap.

Ginger preened.

"Uh, I probably ought to go to this place of Llewellyn's over the Fourth. Do you think you could handle the store yourself?"

Her eyes went wide and her mouth formed an O.

10

"Don't panic," I said hastily. "I haven't accepted yet. Maybe Jay won't be able to get away. Probably not. It's a holiday." Jay was a cop—acting head of the Monte County CID, in fact. Cops tend to do heavy business on holidays.

"You could go alone," Ginger ventured.

"Yes, but I don't want to. Could you handle it, Ginger? I'll drive in and spell you for a couple of hours Friday and Saturday."

"Well, maybe. If it gets real busy, though . . ." Her face brightened. "There's Annie. She could come in during peak time and help me."

Annie was Ginger's best friend and a part-time clerk in the liquor store. Annie needed money even more than Ginger did. I protested. "She doesn't know the stock."

"No, but she could ring up and I could answer questions and so on. That might work."

Two clerks would also cost an arm and a leg. Chalk it up to PR? "I'll think about it," I said decisively. "Here's Dennis."

The door did its bonging thing and Ginger's love interest barged in, beaming. I was fond of Dennis, but if ever there was a bull in a china shop, he was it. He brushed against the science-fiction rack and gave Ginger a hug, smiling shyly at me over the top of her perm as William Gibson's latest slipped to the floor. "Hi, Lark. How's business?"

"We may have to have a fire sale. How's business with you? If the heat keeps up, *you'll* be having a fire sale." I picked up the paperback. Fortunately, books aren't fragile.

Dennis looked blank, then frowned. Forest fires were Serious. "They wanted to do a controlled burn at Castle Crags. Lots of underbrush. But it got hot too soon. There's already a big fire up across the border. We may have a bad fire season."

"Again?" I had only been in Monte a year, but both summers had been dry. Dryer than normal, everyone said. I had the sneaking suspicion dry *was* normal and they just didn't like to admit it.

As Ginger and Dennis made for the door I said, "Think about the Fourth, Ginge," and she nodded.

I closed at nine. I had sold a climber's map of Black Butte and a paperback guide to local flora. Not much for two hours' work.

My bookstore is in a mall near the interstate that also contains a dry cleaner/laundromat, a liquor store, two small bad restaurants, and a supermarket. Off by itself in weedy isolation lies the health club I belong to. I drove there, ran half a dozen halfhearted laps of the gym, swam, showered, and drove home.

Jay's Blazer was parked two slots down from the front-entry stair by the Calfirst Bank's big door. So he was home from Los Angeles. He might have given me a ring. I drove around back and parked in my specially reserved tenant slot next to the bank vice president's BMW, grumbling to myself. My pulse quickened—naturally it did, who can suppress hormonal surges?—but Jay's presence in my apartment sans ceremony suggested he was taking his welcome for granted, and we had been bickering when he left. He'd been gone a week.

I took my time on the back stairs.

Jay was on the sofa, blinking himself awake, when I entered. I gave him a quick kiss and moved out of range.

"Hey!" He levered himself up to a sitting position.

"Time for a talk."

"Uh-oh."

I slid a disk into the CD player and turned the volume low. Instrumental jazz. Jay thinks to jazz and makes love to classical, at least sometimes. "How was LA?"

"Peachy keen."

"I suppose you watched a lot of old movies on the motel cable."

"I stayed with Ma in Beverly Hills and watched a lot of old movies on cable."

"A week's worth?"

"Freddy's on a 1940s kick." Freddy was his fifteen-year-old half brother. "He says hi."

I had met Freddy the previous summer, a nice shy kid. "How's your stepfather?" Jay had escorted a prisoner to Los

Angeles and testified at the arraignment. It was unusual for him to stay with his family.

Jay made a face. "Alf won't last a year, according to the doctors."

"Heart?"

"Yeah. Ma's pretty depressed."

I commiserated.

He stood and stretched enormously, yawning. "On top of everything else, the flight from LAX to San Francisco was delayed half an hour and bounced around like a Ping-Pong ball on a geyser when it did take off. I missed dinner."

"No foil-wrapped packets of delicious dry-roasted almonds on the turbo prop?" Monte is served by a commuter line through the tiny airport at Weed.

"I eschewed the cheese-flavored peanuts," he said gravely.

"Ugh. Eschewed?"

"Must be the opposite of chewed."

"I'd better feed you." I made for the kitchen, nuked a frozen dinner, and poured two beers.

He ate with exasperating slowness. I sipped my beer and stood at the front window, which overlooks Main Street.

The streetlights were just coming on. They turned the geraniums in front of City Hall punk purple. A police car slid to a stop in the loading zone, and two uniformed cops got out and walked down the stairs that led to the police station. One of them was gesticulating and the other was shaking his head. A Winnebago with bicycles on the roof made its sluggish way past City Hall and turned down a bystreet. A kid on a skateboard whooshed by on the sidewalk below me. I like a cityscape, even if the city tops out at 17,347 counting dogs and bicycles.

"You wanted to talk?" Jay joined me at the window.

I wanted a Meaningful Discussion of our Relationship. I groped for an opening.

Jay gave me his best negotiating-with-terrorists smile and smoothed his mustache.

I chickened out. "I want us to spend the Fourth of July at Dai Llewellyn's lodge."

"Die?" The mustache whiffled. Jay's eyebrows shot up.

I spelled it, adding, "E. David Llewellyn. He has a lodge up past Murietta."

Jay frowned. "Llewellyn . . . hey, 'Siskiyou Summit'! I'm damned. I didn't know the old guy was still alive."

"My mother assures me he's history," I said when I overcame my chagrin. What was I, illiterate, that I'd never heard of the damned poem? I told Jay what I knew about the weekend festivities and watched his face as he processed the data. I expected him to cite a backlog of work and plead off, as he usually did when I suggested some kind of sustained social interaction. Jay was inclined to be reclusive, and he had a snug house out in the wilds for us to be reclusive in. I was half hoping he'd refuse to go. When I described the guest list, however, he just looked thoughtful and sipped at his beer.

I finished outlining the horrors of four days of literary small talk. "And the head of the English department will be there. He knows my mother, too." The culminating horror.

Jay missed the point—or ignored it. "Four days, huh? Okay. I'll see if Kevin can hold the fort. He owes me."

I must have been gaping.

Jay gave me another grin and finished his beer, looking bland.

I rallied. "I'll say Kevin owes you. Memorial Day, Easter, Christmas . . ."

"Thanksgiving, Veterans Day, Yom Kippur . . . I don't like holidays."

"So I gathered when you refused to fly back home with me at Christmas." That was a sore point. However, it wasn't a new sore point and I refused to let myself be distracted. "Why change your habits now? Think of all the DWI arrests you'll miss out on."

"And the Domestic Assaults," he said nostalgically, "and the Reckless Endangerments and the Vehicular Manslaughters."

"How can you give all that up?"

He kissed me on the mouth, breaking my concentration. I slopped beer on the rug.

. . . .

We mopped together and sat on the carpet for a while smelling like hops and roses. We made it to the bedroom eventually. However, the night was but young. Somewhere around midnight we drifted back out to the kitchen. I made tea and we sat at my nice gate-legged table, sipping, and flirting with our eyes. A week without Jay was a long time.

"Tell me the truth." I took a swallow of herb tea. "Why did you agree to go with me over the Fourth? I mean really," I added, rather cross, when he leered over his cup.

"I was overcome by the irresistible attraction of the biggest pot farm north of Fort Bragg."

I set my cup down and gaped. "What?"

"This guy Peltz . . ."

I was completely at sea. "Angharad's husband?"

"Name of Ted. A poet and a naturalist, so he says. They live in a cabin at the lake, and there's no visible means of support except the woman's job as a part-time English instructor. Her family's wealthy, of course, so that could explain the fancy van and the TV dish and the general air of laid-back posthippy prosperity. Their movements in and out are suspicious, and we know he's a user."

"Wow." I was revising my mental image of Ms. Peltz.

"Of course, we leave the big pot busts to the feds these days. But it's interesting. The place is interesting. Half the developers in northern California are lusting after that lake. I thought the title was in dispute or something, but if Llewellyn is still alive, *he* may be the snag."

"He doesn't like power boats, according to Lydia Huff."

"He's not the only one." Jay's house overlooked a tiny lake that was technically on Forest Service territory, but he was apt to feel proprietary about it. Motorbikes and snowmobiles infuriated him, too. "Some outfit from Sacramento was nosing around the county commissioner's office last winter, talking about putting in condos. The Sierra Club called out its troops."

I was feeling a lot more cheerful. Ecological protests. Pot busts. "Should be a great weekend."

15

"Yeah. There's Denise, too. I'd like to meet her." He was eyeing me. "Are you sure Dennis Fromm is her son?"

"Incongruous but true."

He rose and carried his cup to the sink. "I saw her dance once. She must have been fifty, but she was graceful as all get out. She came out of retirement for a benefit."

"Pardon me," I said politely, joining him at the sink, "if I have trouble imagining you at a modern-dance concert."

"My wife dragged me to it."

"Your what?"

He edged out of the kitchen. "My wife. I was married for about eight months to a psych major who was determined to improve my taste and my sanity."

This was news to me. We'd been together nearly a year and he'd said nothing of a wife. I was dumbfounded. I followed him out of the kitchen like a basset on the scent. "You were married?"

"About ten or, Jesus, twelve years ago. I was a senior at Northridge, and Linda was working on her masters. She thought I needed a shrink and I thought she needed a husband. We were both wrong."

"Why have you never mentioned this interesting fact?"

"It never came up," he said mildly. "Don't you have skeletons in your closet, Lark? I seem to remember a pro football player."

"Yeah, but I told you about him. And, anyway, I didn't *marry* the jerk. You're so damned secretive," I grumbled at him, but I was more stunned than angry. We had *some* communications gap.

The next morning I sent Llewellyn a note accepting the invitation for myself and Jay, and then my bookstore started drawing a respectable number of customers and I got too busy to brood. Lydia Huff came by again just to make sure we were going. That set my teeth on edge, but the Huffs didn't know Mother, so it wasn't collusion. I also ordered a copy of *The Collected Poems of E. David Llewellyn*. I figured I'd better read "Siskiyou Summit."

"**I** begin to see what the old boy meant by summit." I peered over the shoulder of the county road and about 200 feet straight down.

Jay shifted into second and the Blazer rumbled. "We're only twenty-two miles from downtown Monte."

"As the crow flies." I am not fond of heights. "Let me know when both edges of the road go up," I shut my eyes.

"Did you bring firecrackers?"

"Dennis would not approve." The fire danger was "Extreme"—red on the Forest Service's little pie-wedge scales. They had closed down logging and were discouraging people from camping in the mountains. Five weeks of ninety-degree heat and no rain in sight. It was six-thirty and stinko hot even at that altitude. Jay had the air conditioner on for a change. He rarely used it.

"You can look now."

I opened one eye. We were tooling along a high, wooded plateau, but a bend ahead promised more winding.

"So," he said, as if picking up the thread of an argument, "do we tell everybody I'm a cop or do we play it cool?"

"For heaven's sake, Jay." I swallowed and my ears popped. "Bill Huff knows what you do. He's a journalist."

Jay grimaced. He was not fond of journalists, but was usually prepared to tolerate them. "You have to admit, my job tends to create awkward pauses in the conversation."

That was depressing but true. Otherwise mild and law-abiding citizens edge off muttering about traffic tickets when they find themselves in social contact with a policeman. My brother, who is a lawyer, says people at parties pump him for free advice, and I've heard doctors say the same thing, but the only professionals besides cops who evoke the guilt reaction are English teachers. Or so I've noticed. "Guess I'll have to watch my grammar"—it's the same reaction cops get. There's a big difference, though, between cops and English teachers. Cops tend to associate only with cops, whereas English teachers have no shame.

I explained English-teacher avoidance and told Jay he could hang out with Winton D'Angelo when we got to the lodge. Still, I wasn't surprised to hear Jay say he worked for the county, as Dai Llewellyn, cocktail in hand, began introducing us to the others.

We were the last set of guests to arrive. That afternoon Jay had been buried in paperwork and I got nervous about my bookstore, so we weren't on the road until five-thirty. Everyone else was well lubricated and anticipating dinner by the time we showed up at the lodge. We gave our bags over to the chauffeur-houseboy, Miguel, who was indeed young and pretty, as Ginger had promised.

Llewellyn himself was a handsome, white-haired old gentleman with marvelous waxed mustachios and a warm voice. I had seen his photo on the dust jacket of *Collected Poems*, so I expected the mustache. I didn't expect him to be short.

I am six feet tall. A little over, in fact. My mother, who is five feet two, didn't mention her mentor's stature. Maybe it didn't occur to her that he was short. To be accurate, he was probably five six—not tiny. Still, he had to look up at me, and I could see him blink as we shook hands. He was too suave or too kind to ask how the weather was up there, and he accepted Jay with every sign of pleasure. I liked him.

I was surprised to find everyone indoors, because the natural setting was spectacular even for that spectacular country. We had taken a good look before knocking at the vast wooden door.

A rolled lawn starred with daisies embraced the narrow arm of a lake so deep the water was blue-black. The lowering sun cast a lazy gold light over madrones and Douglas fir, yellow pines and incense cedars. Low, shiny-leaved clumps of manzanita were pruned back from a path that led to a gleaming beach and a long, narrow wooden boat dock. Two red canoes reposed upside down on the dock, and I saw a couple of rowboats bobbing on the water. By that time the lawn was in half shadow and a dim porch light across the water already showed at the Peltzes' cabin, the only other sign of habitation.

"We dine tonight," Llewellyn said, reaching up to guide me across the shadowy lounge by the elbow. "Tomorrow we picnic." I was, alas, dressed for a picnic and I somehow didn't think he'd delay the banquet while I changed. I blinked my vision clear and felt the welcome brush of refrigerated air on my bare arms.

A woman a couple of years younger than I and Angharad Pot, sorry, Peltz, raised languid wine glasses to greet me. Angharad was wearing one of those dresses that look like Victorian underwear. Bill Huff's daughter Janey was a librarian home on vacation, Llewellyn explained. Janey gave me a tentative smile. I said something polite. Lydia was leading Jay clockwise around the huge room.

I stumbled on a throw rug that had to be handwoven Navajo and nearly fell on Denise. She extended a graceful hand as if she expected me to kiss it. I didn't. Dennis was off fighting a fire. I wondered if he'd been invited. Ginger hadn't been.

"Let Miguel pour the poor child a drink, Dai darling. She looks hot."

I do not enjoy being referred to in my presence in the third person. Lark was not hot. She was embarrassed.

Denise patted the leathery couch she was sitting on, and I had to sink down beside her. Darn it, basketball players are coordinated, even if they're not graceful. The couch was very, very deep. I peered out at the others between my jeans-clad knees as my host drifted off to find me a glass of white wine.

Jay was standing by D'Angelo and a surly bear in bib overalls I took to be Ted Peltz, Angharad's husband. D'Angelo was saying something earnest. I met Jay's eyes and he crossed them. Briefly. I grinned and decided I'd better listen to what Denise was saying.

". . . dancing for my oldest friends to your mother's little tone poem. One of my fondest memories."

"Uh, how nice."

"Poor Hal did the score."

Hal? Poor Hal—Llewellyn's friend who had been killed in a wreck. "I didn't realize he was a composer."

Denise's dramatic eyes flashed. "Superb. Of course that dreadful bank kept him busy most of the time. If he'd been able to devote himself to his music, he would have rivaled Schoenberg."

Schoenberg. Atonality. I felt as if I were trying to follow the dialog in a foreign movie with bad titles.

Denise raised her glass in melancholy salute to the departed Hal and sipped. "My dear, as you grow older you will find memory a bittersweet gift. All your golden days shadowed by the fell hand of death."

"Now, Denise." Llewellyn had returned. He handed me a delicate fluteful of good stuff.

"I know, Dai. I promised." Her voice throbbed. "No more repining."

"Isn't Denise's diction wonderful?" He sat on a straight-backed chair that looked as if it had come from someone's dining room. "Right out of Swinburne."

La belle Denise was not amused. She had very little sense of humor.

"I don't see Bill Huff," I murmured.

The silence continued a beat too long, then Llewellyn said lightly, "Bill's putting his paper to bed. A special for the Fourth." He brushed imaginary lint from the sleeve of his natty blue blazer. "He'll be along after dinner. Tell me about your bookstore, my dear. Lydia says it's splendid."

"Did I hear my name?" Lydia swarmed up, lacy shawl awhirl. I contrived to rise from my leathern pit. We shook hands.

"Have you met my stepdaughter? Of course you have. You and Janey have so much in common. She wind-surfs."

I must have looked blank.

"So athletic," Lydia murmured. "I'm sure you'll get along famously."

I had never tried wind surfing. I smiled and let Lydia sink into my spot on the couch. I perched on the arm, between Lydia and Llewellyn, and we talked bookstore for a while, Llewellyn listening with cocked head, like a white-plumed egret. He made several surprisingly practical suggestions, seconded by Lydia, who was, after all, in the business of selling books, too. Denise sipped at her drink, probably something poisonous like absinthe, and brooded. I was grateful to Lydia for coming over to us, and to Llewellyn for existing. I began to relax and settle into a discussion of computerized inventory systems.

"A cop? Jesus H. Christ!"

I craned around. Across the room, the bear in bib overalls had turned purple and swollen several sizes.

D'Angelo made anxious, soothing noises. Jay was looking into his beer.

"I don't give a shit," the bear roared. He stalked toward us. If the floor had been wood instead of flagstones, it would have shuddered. "By God, Dai, it's harassment. If you think you'll get me off the fucking place by . . ."

"Ted!" Angharad had risen at his first roar, white as her dress.

He shook his head at the sound of her voice like a bear shaking off a fly. "I'm goddamned if I'll . . ."

Llewellyn had risen, too. He said coldly, "I have no idea what you're bellowing about, Ted, or what you've snorted, smoked, or ingested, but if you can't behave like a civilized human being to my guests—all my guests—you can get out. Now."

The bear raised its paw.

Llewellyn didn't bat an eyelash. "Now." His waxed mustachios bristled.

I had jumped up at the first roar. Now I started to move between Llewellyn and Attila the Hun. I thought Peltz was going to strike a man fifty years older and a hundred pounds lighter. I didn't stop to wonder what I could do to prevent him.

Then, out of the corner of my eye, I saw the white flash of a uniform jacket. Miguel had come up. Reinforcements.

"*Señor* . . ." He touched the sleeve of Peltz's blue-clad arm.

Peltz jerked away. "Get your fucking hands off me, you greasy little queer."

"Now," Llewellyn said very quietly.

There was a moment of pure stillness. Then Peltz gave an inarticulate, muted roar and rushed out a pair of French doors that led onto the veranda. They must have been ajar because I don't think he would have stopped to unlatch them. One of them slammed against a white metal table. Glass tinkled on the flagstone porch.

"Such a . . . stirring young man," Denise breathed.

Dai Llewellyn was icily outraged. "I beg your pardon, my dear."

I gave a sickly smile.

He made his way across the flagstones to Jay and D'Angelo. "And yours, Dodge. What set him off?"

Jay took a swallow of his beer.

"I happened to mention that Dodge worked for the sheriff's office," D'Angelo said in the injured tones of someone who has made a social gaffe and is trying to evade responsibility. "And Ted just blew."

I looked over at Angharad. Her color had come back—in fact, she was flushed—but she made no attempt to defend her

23

husband or apologize for him. Beside her Janey Huff sat straight up, looking indignant.

"Please, *patrón* . . ."

Llewellyn turned. "What is it, Miguel?"

"Domingo says the dinner is ready."

"Ah. Well, we can't keep Domingo waiting. Let's not allow this little contretemps to delay our meal. Domingo makes a superb gazpacho." Llewellyn began describing the menu, drawing it out like a *Gourmet* columnist, and, with Lydia's and Miguel's help, herding us in the direction of the dining room. The tension in the air eased but didn't disappear.

As we seated ourselves around the huge mission-style table, I noticed two things. Someone—Miguel?—had already removed Ted Peltz's place setting; there was an empty space on the host's left. And Dai Llewellyn was trembling. It was very slight, but I was close enough, sitting at his right hand, to spot it. When he had tasted and approved the wine, I saw him fumble something from an old-fashioned silver pillbox. He took the pill with a sip of wine.

Miguel served the wine, a pleasant Chardonnay, with silent efficiency, Lydia chattered about the upcoming Frankfurt bookfair she was about to fly to, D'Angelo responded, and Janey began telling Jay, across the table, about wind surfing. Thank God for Miguel and the female Huffs. As the spoons clinked in the soupbowls and the conversation grew general, I could almost feel Llewellyn relax beside me.

Jay was telling Denise that he'd seen her dance. When she had ransacked her memory and recalled the entire program of dances in order, she wrung him dry of flattery. Jay is not without aplomb, but I could see he was groping after synonyms for "graceful." The woman was insatiably vain—or insecure.

An unhappy accident had placed Angharad Peltz at Jay's left. She turned her shoulder to him and listened to Lydia, who sat on her left in the hostess's chair, with desperate attention. I felt sorry for Angharad. A little. On the other hand, she probably agreed with her boorish husband.

Llewellyn was telling me a gently self-mocking story about word processors. As Miguel began to clear the soup, the old man interrupted himself, frowning. "Mr. Dodge."

"Sir?" Jay looked up from the roll he was crumbling.

"I hope you haven't let this unpleasantness take away your appetite."

Jay said mildly, "No, sir. I'm fine."

"You don't like gazpacho?" A certain sharpness indicated that Llewellyn was one of those hosts whose pride is involved in their choice of menu.

Jay laid the butter knife neatly on the bread plate. "I was shot in the stomach a couple of years ago in LA. I'm supposed to avoid spicy food."

I stared at him. Ordinarily he hates to admit his little problem to strangers. In fact, he mortally insulted his part-ner's wife his first month in Monte. Joelle Carey is a notable Creole cook (her mother runs a restaurant in Oakland that draws aficionados from San Francisco and Berkeley) and she had gone all out to impress Jay. He ate rice and bread, and refused everything else politely. No explanation. When she finally discovered his reason for avoiding her filé gumbo, Joelle took six months to forgive him. I didn't blame her. So what was this—had he turned over a new leaf?

Everyone was staring.

Jay took a bland sip of water, his face expressionless.

Llewellyn cleared his throat. "I trust you'll be able to accommodate the poached trout."

"Sure," Jay said amiably. "As long as it's not full of peppers."

"A little *beurre blanc*." Llewellyn sounded depressed. He was probably going over four days' menus in his mind and editing out the jalapeños.

Jay got his comeuppance. All through the fish course Denise exclaimed and cross-examined and moralized, and he was hard put to avoid telling her the more gruesome details of his ordeal. I watched him while I made conversation with Llewellyn, who was off on my mother's latest book, and felt only the mildest sympathy. He could just have said he didn't like the soup.

The medallions of veal were so tender, and the new potatoes and carrots so meltingly luscious, we survived the main course with no further dramatic scenes—and not much conversation. Everybody, including Jay, was too busy eating. When the whole party retired to the veranda for dessert and coffee, I dashed upstairs to use the bathroom and check out the accommodations.

The stair was dark wood, steep, and highly polished. The hall was paneled in a wood that glowed like honey in the light from half a dozen pink-shaded sconces. Jay and I had been given adjoining rooms with a communicating door. That tickled me—preserving the proprieties for Ma's sake. I hoped nobody was sleeping in a closet because of the arrangement. I laid out our nightclothes on the bed with the firmer mattress, gave my hair a quick brush, and dashed back down. I left the communicating door open.

By then it was fully dark. We sat on lawn chairs facing the lake. When he had served sorbet and coffee, Miguel slipped down to the boat dock and set off some fireworks over the lake. A small preview, Llewellyn said, of coming attractions. The sorbet was homemade, and the coffee tasted like java nectar. I squished my chair closer to Jay's and we held hands and gawked at the Roman candles. Between bangs and booms, I could hear the crickets chink-chinking.

Bill Huff drove up after Llewellyn had seduced us back into the lodge with an offer of brandy. We heard the car on the gravel. Lydia slipped out to greet her husband as Miguel brought us brandy or a choice of liqueurs. At Llewellyn's suggestion I joined him in a tiny glass of Chartreuse. It was okay. Jay passed, as he had on the coffee. He is not supposed to use caffeine, hard liquor, or tobacco, and doesn't, though I once saw him smoke a cigarette.

"Miss Dailey . . ."

I met Winton D'Angelo's dark, rather soulful eyes. "You'd better call me Lark. We're colleagues."

He blinked. "Oh, the basketball."

I waited. We were standing by the French doors, now definitely open to admit the night breeze and an occasional mosquito. I noticed that the broken pane had been replaced with a neat square of cardboard. The glass shards were gone. Efficient Miguel.

"I don't keep up with sports, I'm afraid. Your team did well, didn't it?"

"Second in the regional tournament."

"That's nice. I meant to compliment you on your bookstore."

As far as I knew, he had never crossed my threshold and bonged the bonger. Perhaps he sensed my skepticism.

"The mere presence of a bookstore that stocks something besides popular paperbacks is a service to the community."

"Actually, I hope to turn a profit. And I have two racks of popular paperbacks." I sipped and watched Jay and Janey Huff. Janey had kicked off her high-heeled sandals and was demonstrating the proper stance for balancing on a sailboard. Jay used to surf. I could tell he was getting interested—in wind surfing, I hoped. Janey had honey-blonde hair and a curvy figure, maybe a little bottom-heavy, and she was two inches shorter than he is. I am an inch taller.

D'Angelo was telling me about students who had never seen a bookstore in their lives before they enrolled at Monte J.C. I believed him.

"Bill, you promised me . . ." Lydia's voice, sharp, cut through the chatter. Everyone turned toward the door to the foyer, but her voice lowered. I heard Bill Huff's basso rumble as he made some response. When nothing immediately awful happened everyone started talking again, but there was an edge to the muted murmuring. Llewellyn, who was sitting with Denise, kept glancing up from his conversation toward the hallway.

Lydia reentered alone. She looked, as usual, cool and very much in charge of things. She gave a general smile round the room. "Bill had a few celebratory rounds with his staff. I

sent him to bed like the bad boy he is." She laughed, flipping
the edge of her lace shawl over one arm, and pranced over to
the silent Miguel at his station behind the bar. "My turn."

Beside me, Winton D'Angelo heaved a sigh. Of relief? I
glanced toward Jay and caught a glimpse of Janey Huff's face.
A lock of hair had fallen across one flushed cheek and her
mouth was set in a thin line.

Jay and I took our time testing out the beds.

He was up before I woke at six. I splashed water on my
face in the little bathroom tucked between our rooms and
decided I didn't really have a Chartreuse hangover. I pulled
on running shorts and a T-shirt, scuffed into my sneakers,
dragged a comb through my hair, and went downstairs.

Everything was very quiet. Outside, the day was at its
pleasantest. One thing about high-altitude living—the air
cools off at night. The morning, though sunny, had a crisp
edge. I spotted Jay down by the wooden boat dock and headed
toward him. He saw me coming and met me halfway.

"Want a run?" He was also dressed *pour le sport*.

"Sure. Where?"

He gave me a large, invigorating hug. "You smell good."

"Eau de Jay. I haven't showered yet. Where, you animal?"

"Well away from Mountain Man's territory. I don't need a
blast of buckshot before breakfast."

"Up the road?" I started jogging across the rolled lawn.
Despite its smooth appearance, it was full of little hummocks.

We puffed up the paved highway a mile or so and trotted
back down, neither of us pushing it. The thin air tested our
lung capacity enough without trying for speed. We didn't
meet with traffic either way—or shotgun blasts.

Afterward we sneaked upstairs and showered. The stall
was bitty. I could hear mild sounds of stirring from the other
bedrooms, but no serious getting-up noises. A toilet flushed
somewhere. When we tiptoed back downstairs, we found
Miguel drifting sleepily through the lounge.

His eyes widened at the sight of us. "*Señorita, señor*, the coffee, it is no . . . not . . ."

Jay said something to him in rapid Spanish and his face cleared. He gave us a big, happy smile and rattled off a reply.

Outside I poked Jay in the ribs. "What was that?"

"I complimented him on his efficiency and told him we were going to take a long hike before breakfast."

"Are we?"

"Might as well. The old man set breakfast at nine."

I groaned.

"Coffee at eight."

"That's better." I can wait for breakfast, but I do like my coffee. "Which way?"

"Let's see if we can sneak up on Godzilla's cabin. I'm awake now." A path led off toward the east through the trees and brush along the lakeshore. Jay headed for it.

"Geez, awake and spoiling for a fight."

"I was hoping for a truce."

"You want to talk to the jerk?"

"No, but I don't want another scene like last night's either. Not fair to Llewellyn."

"You like him, too, don't you?"

"Yeah, he's a feisty old geezer. Also, I was rude at the dinner table."

I grinned. "I wondered what was going on. Trying to spoil everybody's appetite?"

"Something like that. I was embarrassed and I thought I might as well spread the joy."

"It didn't work. Denise ate it up."

"The lady is a vampire."

"But graceful."

We strolled along side by side until the path narrowed at a clump of manzanitas. I took the lead.

"Walking point," Jay said wryly.

"You have a diseased imagination."

"Not entirely. Take it slow."

I did, but I thought rattlesnakes were more likely than

land mines—or shotgun traps. The huge trunks of the pines and Douglas firs were dappled pink and gold in the early sun. Gold motes danced in the air. The ground was springy from layers of fallen needles. We made no noise walking along.

When I saw the gable and chimney of the cabin through the trees, I came to a halt. The white curve of the satellite dish showed in the clearing, and a thin plume of smoke curled on the still air.

We moved cautiously forward. As we came within sight of the front door, Angharad Peltz drifted around the side of the cabin. She was carrying a gardening fork and gloves, and when she saw us she dropped them.

We stood staring at each other for several breaths, then she picked up her belongings and strode over to us. "What the hell . . . ?" She kept her voice low. The bear was apparently in hibernation.

"Out for a morning stroll," I said brightly. "Nice place." It was a solid, rather large 1930s cabin made of squared, dark-stained logs. The silvery shakes on the roof looked as if they might have been hand-split. Nasturtiums grew along the walkway by the side of the house. In that setting the satellite dish looked like something from outer space.

Ms. Peltz was frowning, more at Jay than at me. She wore jeans and a print camp shirt, and her long apricot-colored hair, by far her most striking feature, was piled atop her head. "What do you want?" She directed the question at Jay.

"Peace."

She gave a short laugh. "Don't we all? Look, I'm sorry Ted blew up yesterday, but he's been under a lot of pressure from the narcs."

"That was a federal bust," Jay said mildly.

"But you knew about it."

"Public information. I'll bet Huff and D'Angelo do, too, and I'm damned sure your uncle heard about it, because he called the sheriff and asked us to start patrolling the road more often."

"Did Dai . . ." She bit her lip. "He didn't say anything to us about patrols." She sounded aggrieved.

"He's a big property owner, Ms. Peltz. It *is* his land."

"And when he says jump, you jump."

Jay ignored the jibe. "I imagine he doesn't want to be hauled into court as an accessory."

Her mouth tightened. "He won't be. We're clean. The feds tore out the plants, and, anyway, they were on Forest Service land." She jerked her head in the direction of the National Forest. "Dai has no beef with Ted. Really."

She didn't sound sure of herself, which wasn't surprising. I suspected they had the cabin rent-free. Embroiling Llewellyn in a federal narcotics case might look a little like ingratitude.

"It'll be my land," she said sullenly. "Someday."

Nice lady.

"So you're the designated heir." Jay sounded as if he were settling in for a nice, cozy chat. He was trained to negotiate with hostage-takers.

Angharad Peltz was not up to his weight. She tossed her apricot curls. "Who else does he have to leave it to? My mother? They quarreled years ago."

Dumb lady.

"He could leave it to a dog and cat hospital." Jay smiled a negotiator smile to show there was no offence meant.

Angharad gave a small snort. "Not likely. Llewellyns keep their property in the family—always have, always will."

"That must be comforting."

Abruptly her suspicions kicked in again. "You'd better go. I'll calm Ted down before we come tonight, but I don't want you hanging around here. He's apt to be grouchy when he wakes up."

And when he goes to sleep and in between, I added to myself. "See you later." I pulled Jay along the path. He didn't resist, and neither of us looked back. Let sleeping bears lie.

We were well out of earshot of the cabin before I stopped and stuck my face into his. "What federal bust?"

31

"Ted Peltz was arrested as a grower in March. He's out on bail while some very expensive lawyers dicker for him. The feds set an October trial date. They're still trying to turn Peltz into a witness, so it's been kept pretty quiet."

"Oh. Then he's . . ."

"Supposed to be on his best behavior," Jay interposed, wry.

"I'd hate to see his worst."

"He's a bad actor. I don't envy the wife."

I was horrified. "You don't mean he abuses her?"

"I don't know that he does, but you saw him yesterday."

I shook my head, speechless. I certainly wouldn't risk my body in the same cabin with that maniac.

When we got back to the grounds of the lodge it was still only half-past seven. We experimented with one of the canoes. I grew up near the Finger Lakes in upstate New York, so I'd done a lot of canoeing at summer camp. I instructed the great negotiator, and we paddled along the western shore. The water was so clear we could see bottom—rocks and little speckled fish and an occasional strand of waterweed in sharp focus. I had no idea how deep the water was.

We headed for the dock when we saw Janey Huff standing on it, waving at us.

"Hi! Miguel says the coffee's ready," she called as we slid across the last glassy yards. "You two are up early."

"Normal business hours."

She helped pull the canoe alongside the dock and tied up for us as we clambered out. "Want to go wind surfing?"

"There's no wind." Jay retrieved the paddles.

"You could get the feel of it, though." Her smile included me, too. "I'm a fanatic. It's fun around six at night when the sea breeze comes up. Otherwise this isn't the place."

"We'll try it," I decided. Why not?

We had coffee and a wind surfing lecture in the lounge. Jay finagled a cup of herb tea. About eight-thirty the others started to come down, Denise first in a flowered pajama outfit and twenty pounds of assorted rings. She looked heavy-eyed and drank two cups of black coffee before she was capable of articulate speech.

"Somebody was playing a radio this morning. At dawn."

"Not guilty," I replied. "We didn't bring a radio. Against our religion."

She pouted as if she weren't sure whether I was teasing or not. I decided not to tease.

"I listened to the weather report about half an hour ago," Janey confessed.

Not dawn.

Denise touched her forehead in an infinitely graceful gesture that indicated . . . what? Pain? Anguish? Weltschmerz? "I'm a martyr to insomnia, darling. Could you use one of those little earplugs tomorrow?"

Janey flushed. "Okay. Sorry."

It was clear that Denise was about to treat us to a detailed account of her nocturnal thrashings. Fortunately Lydia bounced in, full of sparkle, and forestalled her.

Lydia was wearing a droopy skirt of mauve homespun and an off-white hand-crocheted top that showed her firm arms. A chunky art-major necklace hung over the crochet work, and her earrings looked like medicine bundles. There were feathers in them. Surprisingly enough she did not look ridiculous.

"Happy Fourth!" She beamed at all of us impartially. "Janey darling, was that your radio at dawn? So inconsiderate, my dear. You know Dai likes to sleep in."

"It was not. Dawn." Janey spoke through clenched teeth.

Lydia poured herself a cup of coffee from the gleaming urn, fiddled with the sugar, and looked at the cream. "Too rich for my blood," she murmured and trotted off toward the kitchens in search of milk.

I sipped at my own brew, luxuriating in the cream. The real thing, full of calories and cholesterol. Lovely.

Janey drank hers black, and she was scowling into it.

Jay seated himself on the raised hearth. "Where do you keep your board?"

"It's still on the roof of my car." She sipped again. "I could use some help unloading it."

"Sure."

"Now?"

"Okay." He set down his cup of stewed weeds. "Coming, Lark?"

"Not before breakfast."

Janey bounced to her feet, restored to good cheer. "See you later!" Jay trailed her out.

I peered into my creamy coffee. Was I perhaps losing my marbles? Prudence suggested that I go out and wrestle with bungie cords.

"Such a pleasant young man," said Denise. "For a policeman."

I gritted my teeth. "I saw Dennis yesterday. It's a big fire. He thought he'd be gone through the weekend."

"Dear Dennis," she said vaguely.

"Morning," Bill Huff growled from the doorway. "Coffee?"

I pointed.

Denise and I watched as Bill made his way to the urn. He managed to fill a cup, but his hands were shaking. He drank where he stood, wincing, and poured another cup.

"Where's Lydia?"

"Here I am, darling." Magical Lydia, just in time.

"I need juice."

"They're setting up the buffet."

"Go swipe me a glass of tomato juice. And see if Domingo has any Worcestershire sauce. Gawd." He sank into the leathery couch and spilled coffee on his bright-yellow golf slacks. "Gawd. I'm too old for this business."

Lydia had disappeared. She returned almost at once with a juice glass garnished with parsley and a slice of lemon. "Here you are, darling. Just what the doctor ordered. No, don't rub the coffee in." He was dabbing at his knee. "There, there, Lyddy will take care of it."

Oh, ick, I thought. I hoped Jay and Janey would have no problems with the sailboard.

34

Bill regarded his wife with pitiful gratitude and drank his tomato juice. After that he seemed to feel better—well enough, at any rate, to acknowledge my existence and Denise's. We talked for a while of the fire burning fifty miles east in the huge National Forest. Bill was up on the latest details. It was, he reported, a crown fire—that is, the huge old-growth timber was "crowning," burning up crown and all. Ordinarily a quick brushfire was good for a conifer forest, because it cleared out the underbrush and killed off some of the insects that preyed on the big trees, but a crown fire benefited nothing and left only devastation behind.

Llewellyn, dapper and neatly outfitted in cream slacks and a matching polo shirt, entered as Bill was describing the fire. They were soon off on reminiscences of the Big One, a fire both had witnessed years before. There was something constrained in Bill's response to Llewellyn, though. It puzzled me.

Jay and Janey came in before I could decide what was going on, and I forgot about it in the general bonhomie inspired by an inspiring breakfast. Domingo had produced a delicious frittata.

We had finished breakfast except for our last cups of coffee when Angharad appeared with an invitation to view her garden. Ladies only.

At first I thought she was making a joke, but Lydia's immediate enthusiasm and Win D'Angelo's protests at being excluded persuaded me otherwise. It seemed they were all passionate gardeners, innocent of irony.

I knew Denise was an herbalist. Dennis was always bringing her cuttings and always making excuses not to drink the teas and tisanes she brewed for him. I'd seen the Huffs' heroic landscaping at a cocktail party they hosted in May, but I'd assumed they owed the profusion of spring greenery to Greenthumb, the local firm of landscape gardeners. Not so. Lydia, it seemed, propagated irises and had once manufactured her own line of herbal cosmetics. Winton D'Angelo, though Angharad was firm in refusing to let him come, grew prize-winning roses.

Janey Huff looked as if she'd rather be out on the lake, but she got up obediently when the older ladies rose to go. I had to follow suit. I like to look at people's gardens and, since I moved west, I've begun to learn how to identify the native plants. They're so different from the deciduous growth of upstate New York I find them fascinating. Even back home, though, I never tried to grow anything more complicated than a potted fern, and I hoped I wouldn't have to display my ignorance. All the same, I went with the ladies like a meek sheep.

We strode briskly along the path to the cabin, retracing our steps of the morning. Grisly Ted was standing on the porch as we came up and grunted something that was probably meant as a greeting. We did not dally to chat with him. The garden lay behind the house in a clearing protected by a deer fence.

I had to admit the Peltzes' display was impressive. Almost entirely annuals and biennials, the flower garden was then in the first riot of summer color. Petunias, pinks, cosmos, daisies of all heights and colors, including Shastas, brilliant mission bell and California poppies, sweet peas, larkspur, hollyhocks, and giant sunflowers—I recognized those. There were other plants I didn't know. I decided to trust they were licit.

Angharad insisted that her husband was a trained botanist. She was merely his handmaiden. I thought she protested too much. There was no further sign of Ted. Perhaps he was brooding over seed catalogs.

Denise and Lydia spent a lot of time exclaiming over the herb garden. It did smell good and all that basil would be nice for pesto, but the herbs themselves were rather ugly. The bees seemed to like them, though.

I found the vegetables more satisfying than the herbs and flowers. So, according to Angharad, did the rabbits. She was stern about bunnies. The Peltzes ate a lot of rabbit stew. The lettuces and other salad veggies in Mrs. McGregor's garden were interplanted in raised beds, with marigolds to keep down the insects. They seemed to be flourishing, though the green corn wasn't very tall. I sneaked a pea pod.

It was almost eleven by the time we escaped. On the way back to the lodge, Janey and I led the pack.

Janey talked books. I think she was being polite, or sounding me out. I said something about best-sellers, and she began telling me about Martha Grimes's latest with all the gusto of a true mystery buff.

I sold a lot of mysteries in hardcover, so I knew of the book, though I hadn't read it. Listening to Janey rehearsing the intricate plot, I wondered why I didn't warm to her. I had made no friendships with women my own age in Monte, which was unusual for me. I missed having someone to confide in. Of course there was Jay, but right then I needed to confide about Jay, not to him.

I decided, reluctantly, that Janey was not going to be my confidante. Neither, obviously, was Angharad Peltz. Ginger, alas, looked on me as a mentor. I felt very lonely. "Do you run?"

Janey turned, head cocked like a wren. "Sure. Three days a week. Do you?"

We agreed to go running together when we got back to town.

Jay and Win D'Angelo had gone rowing on the lake. Janey and I put on our swimsuits and piled into a canoe.

An ancient swimming platform floated well out into the lake, and the four of us spent an hour or so swimming and sunning. The water was so frigid three feet below the surface it was necessary to climb out every ten minutes to thaw. We splashed a lot and laughed a lot, and I got a sunburn.

After lunch I called Ginger. She and Annie had everything under control. No, she didn't need me, but if I didn't show up in the bookstore by three Saturday I was dead meat. She had sold a *Collected Shakespeare* to somebody heading north to Ashland. Dennis had sorted out his fire crews, the blaze was trailed, the crisis over, and he was taking her down to Lake Siskiyou for the fireworks. I applauded and made promises. Then I went upstairs to anoint my rapidly freckling shoulders.

I wound up napping.

Jay woke me when it was time to take the sailboard out for a spin. He caught on to the trick of keeping the mast erect right away. Janey had a wet suit and bobbed in the water giving directions. She said we were her star pupils. When the breeze picked up around six we had several flutters across the waves, but my shoulders burned through the long-sleeved cotton shirt I wore for protection, and by the time we came ashore my legs were half-frozen from the knees down. Winton D'Angelo, who was forty-five if he was a day, had pooped out early.

Miguel and a small cross-looking man I took to be Domingo, the cook, were already setting up a buffet table on the veranda when we came back to the lodge. Jay and I showered and changed very fast.

With my height I look like a walking Christmas tree in frilly dresses, but I'm not dumb enough to buy frilly dresses. I slipped into a turquoise linen sheath that enhanced the color of my eyes and contrasted nicely with my black hair. I wore straw sandals (for no poet in creation would I swelter in panty hose with the temperature above ninety), heavy silver earrings, and a wide Navajo bracelet, silver with a turquoise setting, that Jay had given me at Christmas as a guilt offering. I even touched up my eyelids with turquoise shadow.

Jay pursed his lips and whistled when I presented myself for his inspection. "Classy."

"You look good enough to eat yourself, James B."

He grinned. "Who needs dinner?"

Being civilized guests, we wended our way downstairs. Everybody but Janey was also tricked out like a fashion ad. The food was, as promised, Lucullan. Jay could even eat some of it.

We ate early, around six-thirty, and drank and talked and milled around the lawn, waiting for darkness and fireworks. Ted Peltz was there, dressed almost like a human being and very subdued. Someone had trimmed his whiskers. He had eaten everything in sight, but I think someone was also rationing his drinks. Maybe *he* was. Maybe he was not entirely stupid.

At any rate he caused no direct crises, though he sulked in a lawn chair on the edge of the gathering. Angharad fetched things for him like a well-trained gun dog.

Miguel set up the bar as the sun sank behind the hills to

the west. Twilight lingered. I wished for fireflies. Jay and I took our beers down to the boat dock and looked at the fireworks setup, then drifted back across the lawn.

Llewellyn was sitting with Lydia and Bill in a nest of lawn chairs. He smiled at me, so I pulled an extra chair up beside him. Bill sat on my right.

"Pleasant day?" Llewellyn was drinking Campari and soda. He toyed with the stem of his glass.

"Fantastic. This place is paradise."

"I thought all you young people liked fast boats and hot music." Bill, in a grumbling tease.

"Your daughter supplied the entertainment."

"Dear Janey," Lydia murmured from the other side of Llewellyn's chair. "She looked like a seal in that wet suit."

That was unkind. Janey was only a little bottom-heavy. I took a sip of beer and didn't comment.

Bill gave a snort of laughter. "Barks like a seal when you jaw at her, too, Lydia. Better lay off." He sipped at his scotch. "She's a good kid."

Lydia sighed and rose. "I know, darling. I wish she didn't live so far away. We don't see enough of her." Janey worked in a small town up north on the Columbia Gorge, the better to wind-surf. And, I suspected, avoid her stepmother.

Lydia strolled over to the others and sat by Denise. I could see Janey edging away from her.

"Tell me something, Lark."

I looked at Bill over the rim of my schooner.

"Your mother's name, Mary Wandworth Dailey . . ."

"I know." I resigned myself to answering the inevitable question. "It's too good to be true, but it's her real name. She was Mary Wandworth and she'd published a couple of poems by the time she and Dad married, so she kept both names. It's just a coincidence that they make her sound like Wordsworth and Henry Wadsworth Longfellow."

Llewellyn said drowsily, "Nothing would compel Mary to sound like Longfellow."

I grinned at him. "True. She was well taught. No bumpity-bump meters for Ma."

He took a swallow of the bitter red wine. "You have a way with words."

"No, sir, I do not. The Wandworth eloquence skipped a generation. Ma always says she should have named me Audrey."

Both men looked at me.

"You know, in *As You Like It*—Jaques's shepherdess."

"'I would the gods had made thee poetical'?" Dai Llewellyn gave a crack of laughter.

I was pleased with my little joke, though Bill had the uneasy look of one who doesn't quite get it.

Llewellyn was still choking. It took me a second to realize he was not choking with laughter.

I jumped up. "What's the matter?"

"Wine . . ." He gave a convulsive shudder and leaned forward. The wineglass tipped over on the little metal table between us. Red liquid puddled the white enamel.

I set the glass upright. As I reached out with the vague idea of helping him to his feet, he began to vomit.

Bill shot up, overturning his chair. I took Llewellyn's shoulders. "Help me. He's sick."

Jay was at Llewellyn's other side before the words were out. He must have seen we were in trouble.

The poet's frail body shuddered under my hands as he retched up his elegant meal. Bill was making bleating noises.

I tried to pat Llewellyn's shoulders. "Can we take him into the house?"

Jay met my eyes briefly. He was frowning. "In a minute. Bill, go for the phone—911. Tell them to send the life-flight helicopter."

"Good God, he's just sick, ate a bad egg or something."

"Do it, man."

After a moment of hesitation Bill shambled off toward the house. The others had come closer, Lydia and Denise clinging to each other, all staring. I noticed they stood out of splattering range in their finery. Miguel, crying out in Spanish, ran up with a bar towel.

Jay took it from him and rapped out an order in the same language. Llewellyn grabbed at the damp towel and tried to wipe his face, but a second wave of nausea racked him and the towel fell to the grass.

Miguel picked up the Campari glass, all the while wailing in high-pitched Spanish. As he took the glass away, he called something over his shoulder.

"Your pills, sir . . ." Jay bent over. "No, it's too soon. Janey, bring blankets. And check with your dad. I want that chopper."

Janey dashed off, with Lydia trotting after her. Winton D'Angelo was holding Denise, who was weeping on his polo shirt. The Peltzes gaped. They were holding hands.

Llewellyn vomited until he was heaving dryly. When Janey came back with a pillow and an armload of blankets, Jay had her spread them on the grass. She said Lydia was with Bill. The helicopter was hauling victims of a car wreck to the county hospital. They were sending an ambulance in case it took too long. She made her report in a high, breathless voice while she spread the blankets a few yards away and Jay and I held Llewellyn.

Slowly Llewellyn's spasms eased and he sank back onto the chair, shuddering under our hands.

"Now, sir," Jay said, "we're going to help you over to those clean blankets. Miguel said you take heart pills."

"Digitalis. Chest hurts." He stumbled as we half carried him to Janey's pallet. She handed Jay a damp towel and he wiped Llewellyn's face and shirt clean when he had eased the old man down. Llewellyn lay on his side, half-curled in a fetal crouch. Jay swaddled him with extra blankets, and I slipped the small pillow Janey had brought beneath his head. He seemed to be drowsing.

"Should you give him the digitalis?" I had seen the outline of the little silver pillbox against the damp shirt. I eased the box out. "Do these look right?"

Jay was taking Llewellyn's pulse. "Jesus."

"Digitalis," I repeated.

"Uh, yeah . . . no." He took the box and looked at the pills. "I wish I knew whether he'd taken one in the last couple of days."

"Last night. I saw him."

Jay frowned at me. "Are you sure?"

"Same pillbox."

He slipped the box into his pants pocket and began checking the pulse rate again. Llewellyn stirred. "Sir, Dai, can you hear me?"

"Mmn."

"Can you tell me how you feel?"

"Mouth burns."

No wonder—all that stomach acid.

"Tingles," he mumbled after a moment, blinking. "Hands feel funny." He closed his eyes. His jaunty waxed mustachios had wilted.

Jay was muttering under his breath. Abruptly he stood up and looked around. "D'Angelo, Peltz, clear the chairs and tables off the lawn. I want you to mark off a place for the chopper to land. That flat area by the boat dock. Let's hope the damned thing gets here before dark. If not, you'll have to drive cars down here to light up the grass."

I was still kneeling beside Llewellyn. I smoothed his hair. His breathing came shallow and quick. It was dusk, still fairly light out, but hard to distinguish colors. I was looking at his lips. If he had trouble getting enough oxygen, they were supposed to turn blue.

"Oh, God, don't let him die!" Denise moaned. She made to kneel by me.

"Take her into the house," Jay snarled. Janey and Angharad Peltz almost had to drag Denise off Llewellyn's body, but they eventually persuaded her to go into the house with them. She moaned all the way.

D'Angelo and a very subdued Ted Peltz began dragging the lawn chairs and little tables to the veranda. Miguel was back, wringing his hands. I had never seen anyone actually do that, not even Denise. His beautiful dark eyes were wide with anxiety, and he seemed to have forgotten the English language. Jay said something to him in rapid Spanish and he nodded and began helping with the chairs.

Jay knelt down again and took a pulse.

When he finished, I cleared my throat. "What do you think?"

"I think the chopper will come and they'll transport him to the hospital." He looked over at me and touched my face briefly. "Take it easy. Do you know CPR?"

I nodded. I had learned it in college and relearned it the previous November as part of my certification to coach at Monte J.C. They had wanted me to teach a hygiene class, too, but I had to draw the line somewhere.

Jay didn't say anything else. Llewellyn's light, quick breathing shook the mounded blankets. I wondered if our words had registered with him and hoped not.

Bill made his way back to us and gave the same report Janey had made. He sounded aggrieved. Lydia was helping Janey and Angharad cope with Denise, he said. "Is it a heart attack?"

"Probably." Jay spoke quietly.

Bill shuffled his feet in the grass. "Domingo wants to know should he make something."

"Not for Llewellyn. Tell him to brew coffee for the rest of you."

"Okay." Bill wandered off.

Llewellyn's breathing had quickened and Jay was frowning at his watch, trying to time the heartbeat. Suddenly the old man's body jerked. His back arched and his face contorted horribly, eyes rolling back in his head.

"Back off!" Jay shouted.

I scrambled out of the way, but the convulsions didn't last long. All too quickly Llewellyn lay still on the crumpled blanket, and Jay was feeling his throat for a carotid pulse. "Cardiac arrest."

"Want me to do the chest?"

"Breathe for him." Jay straightened the still form, clearing the old man's tongue and wiping his face clean.

46

I knelt, removed the pillow, and slid my left hand under his neck to tilt his head back. I put the heel of my right hand on his forehead and reached down to pinch his nostrils shut. Then I took a lungful of air and puffed four sharp breaths into his mouth. His chest rose. I could taste bile.

Jay was kneeling opposite me and down a bit. He had found the breastbone and measured up from it with his thumb the requisite inch and a half. He pressed straight down with the heel of his hand—not too hard—and relaxed and pressed again, once every second. He was counting so I could hear the time—one thousand and one, one thousand and two . . . Every five seconds I breathed for Dai Llewellyn. Every second Jay pressed his chest. We found our rhythm almost at once.

I was vaguely aware of D'Angelo and Ted Peltz running up with questions. Miguel was sobbing. After fifteen minutes Jay tried for a pulse again. We kept rhythm. Eventually we changed over, still keeping time. It was like a bizarre squatting dance—or a strange poetic meter. Boom, boom, boom, boom, puff. Llewellyn didn't like meter.

Bill Huff and Janey came down, and Jay told Bill to phone again, that we had an infarction. Bill ran off.

Sometime in the afterglow one of the others had the wit to turn on all the yard lights. They didn't quite reach the flat area by the boat dock, and D'Angelo and Janey eventually moved four of the cars down, shining their headlights so the landing spot was lit. Jay and I kept to our rhythm. It was all-absorbing, and it went on and on.

Finally we heard the wail of an ambulance in the distance. We kept our rhythm even as the emergency vehicle jounced down onto the lawn and the doors were thrown open.

Then the pros took over with their fibrillators and oxygen tanks and injections. Dai Llewellyn, still not breathing on his own, still without an independent heartbeat, was bundled onto the gurney and into the ambulance. The life-flight helicopter was dealing with the massive chain-reaction accident on I-5.

Jay had called for Miguel as soon as the paramedics relieved us. Now the chauffeur came running with a paper sack. Jay took it from him, peered into it, and handed the sack to one of the attendants.

"He was drinking wine, Campari, when the attack started. Some of the symptoms—prolonged nausea, tingling, hands feeling peculiar—made me think he might have ingested a poison. I saved the glass. Better check it out. I'm Dodge, county CID. It may be a police matter." The two men spoke quietly and I don't think anyone else heard them, though the others were standing on the veranda, watching. They had seen Miguel run up with the sack.

Poison. Surely not. Food poisoning, maybe, except nobody else had turned sick. If it was poison, that meant attempted murder. My thoughts raced.

One of the paramedics was in the ambulance with Llewellyn. The other slammed the doors and got in on the passenger side, paper sack in hand, and the ambulance jounced off. Its light revolved. The siren yelped once as the ambulance pulled onto the county road.

Jay put his arm around my shoulders. "All right?"

I took a deep breath. "Yes, I'm fine. How about you?"

"I'd be happier if the damned chopper had showed up. That's a long drive."

"Do you really think he was . . ."

"Hush."

I bit my lip and tasted bile, at least I hoped it was bile. "I want to brush my teeth and rinse out my mouth."

"Me, too."

We walked over to the porch, tails dragging, and were instantly surrounded. Everybody gabbled questions at us at once, Bill in a journalistic roar.

Jay held up a hand. "Give us a break. We need to clean up. Have a cup of coffee or move the cars or something. We'll be back down in ten minutes."

We trudged upstairs and took turns gargling. My dress had grass stains at knee level.

Jay was standing by the open window staring through the screen at the lake. He had pulled on a pair of sweatpants, but he was barefoot and shirtless.

I blinked the sleep from my eyes. "Jay . . ."

He started and turned.

"S'matter?" I stretched.

"Nothing. Go back to sleep." He yanked a T-shirt over his head.

I thought about dozing off again, but our CPR marathon was coming back to me—and with it all kinds of questions.

Jay sat on the foot of the bed and began to put on his sneakers. I poked his backside with my toe. "Can't sleep?"

He bent over, mumbling something as he laced his shoes.

I rose on one elbow. "You're going for a run? At four in the morning? It's pitch-black out."

He sat up and turned. "I had a nightmare." He kept his voice low. We did have neighbors. "When that happens I go for a run. Don't let it bother you."

I reached out and touched his face. It was cold with drying sweat. "Okay. Hang on a minute and I'll come with you."

I slid out and rummaged for the shorts and top I'd changed into after the ambulance left. As I scuffed into my sneakers I could hear his low-voiced protests. I ignored them. I tied the sleeves of a sweatshirt around my waist. Maybe Jay wanted to be alone. I didn't. Also, I was wide awake. A stroll by the lake might calm me down enough to sleep again. I didn't think he was serious about running in the dark.

I was wrong. When we had bumbled our way outside, Jay headed for the long stretch of county highway behind the lodge. It wasn't pitch-black out. The stars were shining and an outdoor light still burned by the graveled driveway, but it was dark enough. Jay was trotting by the time he reached the gravel, and running flat out and uphill when he stepped onto the asphalt road.

I followed at a discreet jog, mindful of the uneven surface, though I could see better than I'd expected to. Jay ran on the white mid-stripe, half out of my sight and lengthening his lead. I picked up my pace a little but slowed down again when I twisted my ankle on a piece of gravel. Jay had rounded a corner. Bemused, I jogged after him.

I wondered how Llewellyn was doing. It was Jay's single-minded intensity that had kept me to the exhausting and rather disgusting CPR process. If I had been alone, I would have given up after the first half hour. Llewellyn had not responded.

The road twisted upward, and I was starting to puff a little. I couldn't see Jay. A nightmare? His skin had felt clammy, almost like a person in shock. I'd had that kind of nightmare a few times myself. This wasn't the first violent death I'd seen—if this *was* a death—and what else could it be? Often enough those weeks after the others Jay had been there at night, holding me and talking to me until I remembered who and where I was, and that I was going to be all right. My response to my nightmares had been to cling to Jay. Obviously his response differed from mine. That was an oddly desolating thought.

I turned my ankle again, harder, slowed to a stop, and stood on the graveled shoulder of the road, panting and flexing my knees. Dumb thing to do, running at night.

I walked on, feeling the sweat dry on my body and shivering, though the air was still fairly warm. Was Jay running a marathon? I untied my sweatshirt and pulled it on. Well, I had wanted a stroll. I would take a stroll. The heck with running races.

There was no wind at all. On either side of the road, enormous conifers towered in black silence. What if the old man died? I didn't want our efforts to go to waste. More than that, I had liked Llewellyn in spite of my prejudice against poets. He'd enjoyed playing the host and after the picnic he'd even seemed relaxed. I knew too little of medical matters to say a heart attack was impossible, and I liked that thought better than poison in the Campari.

I skirted a dead chipmunk. More evidence of mortality. Ugh. I walked on.

After the ambulance had raced off, my mind had widened its focus to include the other guests once more. They had all seemed human in their shock. Now I wondered whether any of them besides Angharad stood to gain from Llewellyn's death. He was a very wealthy man.

Our holiday was over. I thought of the lake with regret, and of my need to have a peaceful time with Jay. We were going to have to talk, have it out, clear the air, put up or shut up—stale phrases slid in and out of my awareness. That was one of my motives for coming to the lake, a little crisis counseling. But the crisis was over. I stopped dead in the dark road.

It was true. Maybe the fact that we had spent an hour and twelve minutes breathing together in perfect unison had told me something. The tangled resentments had vanished. Jay and I, for better or worse, were a team and we would work things out.

Where was the man? I cocked my head. Silence. Maybe he *was* running a marathon. I walked slowly onward, taking in the spangled arch of the Milky Way and savoring the new insight into our relationship.

If Jay and I had been out of synch the past six months, the fault was at least half mine. The sheriff had shoved a load of work at Jay about the time I began drilling my basketball team. If either of us had been less busy, we could have adjusted our schedules. As it was, we had seen each other perhaps twice a week. Not nearly often enough. But it hadn't been his fault any more than mine.

As I came to this safe conclusion Jay hove into sight, up the twisting stretch of asphalt a good quarter mile and still running steadily. Downhill now, toward me.

I began jogging in place as I watched him approach. When he heard me I turned, lengthening my stride until it matched his. "You can pass the baton now."

He gave a short choke of laughter, breathing hard, and put an arm around my shoulders, pulling me toward him. We did not stumble and fall on our faces. We jogged, striding along, even-paced, until we were in sight of the lodge, then Jay broke step and slowed, panting. I was a little out of breath myself.

We crunched across the graveled drive, but as we approached the veranda steps I touched his arm. "The dock?" I wasn't ready to go in.

He nodded and swerved aside, and we skirted the porch at a slow jog. Jay stumbled on something, a grass-clod probably, and fell to one knee. He got up again, but we both slowed to a walk. Jay's breathing was almost back to normal. I had no excuse to huff and puff, and I'm happy to say I didn't. It pays to stay in shape. I was wide awake and in the mood to talk.

When we reached the dock I went clear to the end. I sat down by Miguel's sad, unlit fireworks display, pulling off my sneakers. The water felt good on my bare feet. After a moment Jay hunkered down beside me and splashed his face. The dock bobbed.

"Hello."

He sat and pulled off his sneakers, dangling his feet in the lake, too. "What's up?"

"Us."

"Smartass."

"I love you a lot," I said seriously.

He put his arm around my shoulders and I hugged his middle with my right hand. "I love you, too."

53

"Why?"

"Because I'm nuts about women who run in the middle of the night."

"I was just following your lead. Why, Jay?"

"Let me count the ways."

"Cut it out. I mean, why the nightmare? Did something happen . . . he's dead, isn't he?"

He sighed and pulled away slightly. "Yes. I phoned the hospital from the kitchen extension while everybody was going upstairs to bed."

I shivered and withdrew my arm. "You should've told me. It's not fair. We did our best."

He didn't answer. Something plopped in the lake. We both stared out across the black water. On the other shore the roof of the Peltz cabin gleamed a dull gray against the black evergreens. My ankles were aching with cold, so I drew my feet out and swiveled sideways, leaning against Jay and staring at my pale toes. "What a stinking, rotten thing to happen on the Fourth of July."

"Yeah."

"I liked him. I didn't expect to, but he was funny and sharp as a tack—and obviously in charge of his life."

Jay said nothing.

"We did our best," I repeated.

He swore under his breath.

"Didn't we?"

I felt him take a deep lungful of air. "You did your best. I did mine. Our best just wasn't good enough. It's an old story. I'm sorry, Lark."

I sat up and turned, trying to see him. His head was bent and his feet still dangled in the icy water. I reached out and touched his cheek. "Me, too. Don't go too far from me, Jay. I need you."

"Jesus." He pulled me to him and hugged me almost desperately. He was trembling.

A light came on in the lodge.

Jay groaned.

"What is it?"

He gave me a last squeeze and scrambled up, feet dripping. "Shit. Telephone—can't you hear it?"

I was squishing my damp feet into my shoes. "Dimly. Is it for you?"

"Bound to be. Miguel will be wandering around looking for me . . ."

"And waking everybody up."

"You got it."

It wasn't that bad. We found Miguel as he drifted back downstairs looking sleepy and gorgeous in white pajamas bottoms and nothing else.

As usual his conversation with Jay was conducted in rapid Spanish. Jay went off to use the phone in the hall. Miguel and I looked at each other.

"You want me to make the coffee, *señorita?*"

"I'll make a pot. Show me where, Miguel, and go back to bed. We're sorry to wake you."

He shrugged philosophically and led me into the gleaming, state-of-the-art kitchen. A coffee maker stood on the tiled counter. He pulled out a jar of coffee and a box of filters for me and wandered off, yawning. I found herb tea for Jay.

Janey stumbled downstairs about six-thirty. By that time we'd showered and dressed, and I'd drunk about a gallon of what tasted like fresh-ground Colombian. With cream.

"Is there any news?" Janey rubbed her eyes and took the cup of coffee I poured for her. We were standing in the kitchen.

I looked at Jay.

He said, reluctantly, "Mr. Llewellyn died last night."

"Oh, no!" Janey's face crumpled and her nose turned pink. "That's so sad." She set the cup on the counter. "And worse for you two. You worked so hard."

She was a sweet kid. I felt my eyes fill.

Jay said, "Did you know him very well, Janey?"

She picked her cup up again and took a distracted sip. "I've known him for years, since I was in high school, actually.

Mom and Dad got divorced when I was a freshman. Lydia knew Dai, and when she married Dad they started coming out here in the summer. I spent my summers with them, so I came, too. I didn't talk with him much. I don't think he found me very interesting." She flushed and looked into her cup. "You know about his . . . about Hal Brauer?"

"Yes."

"Well, that was two years ago. I'd just started my job, so I didn't come that summer. Lydia said Dai was really down, and I can see why. Hal was fun, and they'd been together a long time. When Hal was alive the joint really jumped." Her melting brown eyes lifted to Jay's. "It was like they were married, really."

Jay nodded. "Did Mr. Llewellyn come to the lodge last summer?"

"Yes, but he only stayed a week or so." She blushed again. "Then there was that business about Ted Peltz and the pot farm this spring. Lydia said Dai came up for a few days then."

"How long have the Peltzes lived in their cabin?"

"It's not *their* cabin. Dai let them stay there. To keep an eye on the lodge." She glanced at me and back to Jay. "Lydia says he did it to spite his niece, Angharad's mother. She didn't approve of Angharad's marriage to Ted." Janey frowned. "I don't see it, though."

"Why not?"

"That's just Lydia. Dai wasn't spiteful." She teared up. "Gosh, I can't believe he's gone."

"It was sudden," Jay said gently, "but he was an elderly man and he had a long, productive life."

He wasn't ready to talk murder, I supposed. I felt uncomfortable listening in on their conversation, because Jay was interrogating Janey and she didn't know it. I wished he'd warn her or something.

On the other hand, he didn't know for sure that the drink was poisoned. He was just doing a little fishing while he waited for the hospital toxicologist to phone.

The earlier call had been Kevin Carey, Jay's second in

command, reporting that the medical examiner had already begun the autopsy. The fact that it was Saturday and the Fourth of July weekend made everything awkward. The state forensics lab in Sacramento was in a holding pattern during the holiday.

Maybe Jay decided he shouldn't push too hard, because he turned the conversation to wind surfing and Janey cheered up. She was heading north again in another week and could hardly wait to get out on the river.

At that point we were interrupted by the cook, who burst into a speech I knew was hostile without understanding a word. We had invaded his territory. Janey and I refilled our cups and we slunk out to the lounge. Jay claimed the man was speaking Tagalog—he hadn't understood a word either.

Bill Huff came down at seven. When he heard the news of Llewellyn's death he said a few conventional phrases and went off to the hall.

We heard him rummaging around for a while, swearing. He returned with a pile of creamy stationery and a plebeian-looking ballpoint. Reportorial instincts. He began roughing out a news story for the San Francisco *Chronicle* and an obit for his own weekly. I thought that was cold-blooded, but he was just doing what came naturally—like Jay with Janey. I reflected cynically that if Llewellyn's death from natural causes was a story, his murder was going to be hot stuff. When Bill found out about it.

Miguel came in with a big coffee urn on a wheeled cart and announced that Domingo was setting up a breakfast buffet. There would be food in half an hour. Not a minute too soon. I was starving.

"*Señor* . . ." He was addressing Jay.

"What is it?"

"Is it true *el patrón* is *muerto?*"

Jay drew a breath. "I'm afraid so, Miguel. I'm sorry."

"*Ay, Jesús!*" His hand flew to his mouth.

Jay said something in soft Spanish. After a moment Miguel nodded and trailed out looking like a whipped dog.

"You speak really well," Janey said admiringly. "I had two years in college and I can barely say *huevos rancheros*."

"I grew up in one of the barrios."

That was not quite true. Jay had grown up at the edge of one of the barrios with bilingual classmates in the days before bilingual education became respectable. He grew up speaking street Spanish, but he also studied it for three years in high school and four in college. For the second time in two days, I wondered why Jay was being so loquacious about his background. Maybe he wanted to distance himself from the privileged.

He succeeded in making Janey uncomfortable. Conversation languished. Bill was on a second draft when Lydia walked in wearing white slacks and her lilac tunic.

Bill glanced up from his scribbling. "You'd better wake Denise. Llewellyn died last night. Somebody will have to break the news to her."

Lydia's hands flew to her throat in a curiously theatrical gesture, but there was nothing fake about her pallor. She sat down slowly on the nearest chair. "That's terrible."

"Yes." Bill crossed out a line. "Poor old duffer. Heart gave out for good."

I cleared my throat. "Had he suffered an earlier heart attack? I know he took digitalis."

"Angina, my dear," Lydia said sadly. "For his age he was remarkably healthy. Poor, poor Dai. Someone will have to tell Ann."

"Mrs. Peltz?" Jay had been standing silently by the big fireplace.

"I was thinking of her mother," Lydia murmured, "but Angharad, too, of course."

At that point the telephone rang and Jay went off to answer it looking thoughtful.

Bill scribbled, Lydia poured herself a cup of coffee, Janey and I sipped and looked at each other. When Jay came back I could tell from the taut, on-the-scent look that his suspicions had been confirmed. It was murder.

He waited until he had caught everyone's eyes, then said, without preamble or explanation, "I want to talk to all of you—that is, everybody who was here last night—before you leave for home. Mrs. Huff, if you'll wake Denise, maybe Lark can walk over and let the Peltzes know. At nine, say. That'll give you all time for breakfast and packing."

Janey and Lydia gaped at him. Bill frowned. "What the hell, Dodge? Aren't you taking a lot on yourself?"

Jay said flatly, "Police business. I have some questions to ask you, and I might as well do it while you're still here in one spot. Lark?"

I stood up. "What do you want me to tell them?"

"That Llewellyn is dead and I want to question them."

That was going to go down really well with Ted Peltz. "All right. Will you come with me, Janey?"

Janey nodded, eyes wide.

Janey was very quiet. About halfway along the path she stopped and addressed a manzanita bush. "There's something fishy, isn't there—about Dai's death?"

I wondered what to say.

"Was it the Campari?"

I sighed. There are limits to discretion, which, in any case, isn't my middle name. "Jay thinks he was poisoned."

She looked at me. "Murdered?"

I nodded.

She closed her eyes. "And the Peltzes are prime suspects."

"They do have a motive."

"No wonder you didn't want to come over here alone."

I bristled, then wilted. "I needed a bodyguard and you're it—she."

Janey covered her mouth with her hand and giggled. "Oops. God, I'm sorry. It's not funny, just crazy. The whole thing's crazy. Dai wasn't murdered. He was an old man who took digitalis for angina and had a heart attack on a hot day."

"Maybe." I was pretty sure not.

"Well, let's get going." She set herself in motion.

Nobody was up *chez* Peltz. I knocked at the front door, a varnished slab of timber. No answer. I knocked again. And again. Finally Angharad undid the latch and the door creaked open.

"Whaa . . . ?" She slept in a long T-shirt that said "Property of the 49ers."

I delivered Jay's message.

Angharad blinked. Her hair hung down in apricot witchlocks. "You mean Uncle Dai is dead?"

"That's right."

She was wide awake now. She bit her lower lip and her eyes narrowed. "Ted!" she yelled over her shoulder, "Ted, wake up . . ." and shut the door in my face.

"Nine o'clock," I yelled back at the unresponsive door. "Be there."

Janey and I looked at each other.

When we got back to the grounds of the lodge, Jay and Miguel were making a barricade of lawn chairs and rope around the patch of grass we'd been sitting on the night before.

I don't think I tasted breakfast, though I ate a lot. I'm sure it was as exquisitely prepared as our other meals at the lodge, though. Domingo, impassive, seemed determined not to admit that anything had changed.

Miguel kept sighing and watching us all with dark, reproachful eyes, as if he knew whom to blame. His grief rang true, but I didn't know exactly what it meant. He was a very handsome young man. Pretty, even. But he had called Llewellyn *"patrón"* and, unlike Ginger, I had seen no sign of flirtation between them. Miguel was good at his job, too—quick, thorough, mostly unobtrusive. It was possible he was exactly what he purported to be—chauffeur and houseboy.

Or he could have been Dai Llewellyn's Abishag.

Denise did not come down to breakfast. Lydia had administered a Valium for which, she assured Jay, the dancer had a prescription. Jay made no comment, but he looked wry. The evidence crew had not yet come.

Bill Huff was still pretending he was a cub reporter with a scoop. Lydia had found his notebook for him. She was probably too occupied dealing with Denise's theatrics to take in the personal significance of Jay's suspicions. She said she had packed her things and Bill's.

Of the houseguests, only Winton D'Angelo seemed to have grasped the likelihood that he would be considered a murder suspect. He picked at his food and drank a lot of coffee, and when we began to assemble in the lounge, he paced the floor. I thought he was very much afraid. Janey looked bewildered, or maybe it was just the big brown eyes. She blinked a lot. She had very long lashes. Occasionally she gave a small nervous giggle, stifled at once.

The Peltzes strode up at three minutes past nine. Apparently Angharad had been appointed spokesperson. She went directly to Jay, who was again standing in front of the stone fireplace.

"We called our attorney. We have nothing to say."

"Fine. Go have nothing to say over there." He jabbed a finger at the vacant leather couch.

Everyone watched the exchange. When the Peltzes had sunk into their pit Jay stepped up onto the raised hearth. Winton D'Angelo stopped pacing and gawked.

"If you'll all take seats, I'd like to get this over with."

Rustles and shufflings. I sat on a hassock next to Janey. The elder Huffs occupied a wooden settee, and D'Angelo sat on the straight-backed chair Llewellyn had used the first evening.

"Thanks." Jay was frowning. "As you know, Mr. Llewellyn died last night. That is, the doctors at County Hospital took him off life-support when they got a flat EEG."

"Brain death," Bill Huff rumbled. He began writing.

Jay ignored him and went on, eyes roaming impersonally over the room. "I directed the medical examiner to perform an autopsy. That's standard procedure in any case of sudden, unexplained death. I also asked the hospital toxicologist to analyze the stomach contents and traces of Campari in Mr. Llewellyn's wineglass."

Bill Huff's hand paused on the paper and he stared at Jay.

"The police lab analysis will take a couple of days, but the toxicology report gave the department enough to act on. The death has been ruled a homicide."

By that time most of the guests must have anticipated the verdict, but the word *homicide* provoked gasps. D'Angelo groaned. He was very pale, and his eyes glistened.

"You are all too intelligent not to realize that your presence here last night makes you suspects. At this point I don't know whether the poison was administered in Llewellyn's drink or in the bottle of Campari. The food is unlikely, since everyone ate it. I secured the bottle last night and the contents will be analyzed. The soda was used in Mr. Huff's scotch without effect, so it can be ruled out."

"What was the poison?" Bill interjected.

Jay avoided my eyes. "Aconitine and . . ."

"Aconite?"

"No, aconitine." Jay drew a breath. "It's the active ingredient in aconite. The poison was a mixture of aconitine and delphinine in liquid form. A homemade decoction of the annual delphinium."

Winton D'Angelo sat up straight.

"Hey, wait a minute." Ted Peltz gave a sudden, huge guffaw.

"But that's just larkspur," Janey said in a puzzled voice. "What's the big deal?"

Larkspur. My turn to sit up. I went cold, then hot.

"Miss Dailey's bookstore is called Larkspur Books," Jay was saying. He sounded cool and detached. "Llewellyn made a point of inviting her, well in advance, to this gathering, though she's an outsider in what seems to have been a tight little group of old friends. The related plant, monkshood, would have produced a quicker, more potent poison, so the choice of delphinium was plainly deliberate. I'd say offhand that the killer is either mentally unbalanced or a sociopath with a sadistic sense of humor. I'm not sure which." He let his gaze move leisurely from one guest to the next, taking them all in.

Ted Peltz gave another bark of laughter. Har-har.

Jay regarded him without expression. Angharad looked as if she might faint. "I *am* sure," Jay said softly, "that the murderer knows a lot about plants."

Peltz jumped to his feet. "Now wait a minute . . ."

"I thought you had nothing to say, Peltz."

"I . . ."

Angharad was tugging at her husband's sleeve. He sank down beside her, no longer grinning. "It's a frame."

"For Godsake, Ted, shut up."

"Listen, bitch . . ."

This delightful marital exchange was interrupted by the sound of cars on the graveled drive.

Jay looked relieved. "If you please . . ."

The Peltzes fell silent.

"I sent for the crime-scene investigators. They have warrants to search your belongings . . ."

Uproar.

". . . this house and grounds, and the cabin and grounds occupied by Mr. and Mrs. Peltz, for the poison container. I also intend to take statements from each of you."

"We'll be here all day!" D'Angelo protested.

"All of us? What about the servants?" Lydia, a little shrill.

"Yeah, what about the fag, little Miguelito? He ran the bar." Needless to say, that was Ted Peltz.

"None of you"—Jay looked round, unsmiling—"is in immediate danger of arrest, but you are all material witnesses, including the members of Mr. Llewellyn's household staff and Ms. Fromm."

Everyone had forgotten Denise.

"You can't question Denise," Lydia said firmly. "She's in a state of emotional collapse."

"I've sent for her son."

Dennis. Good God. I shifted on my hassock, still numb. "When he gets here, I fully intend to question her."

Lydia clucked her tongue. Janey swallowed another titter.

Jay went on, dispassionate. "I'll want to establish who drank what and with whom, and, in particular, Mr. Llewellyn's movements in the last hour or so before he was taken ill. It's your duty to answer my questions clearly and accurately. You are not to leave the county without notifying me. As friends of Mr. Llewellyn, I'm sure you'll want to assist the investigation in any way you can." He let that sink in. I thought D'Angelo was going to faint.

Dennis drove up in a Forest Service pickup just after Kevin Carey, formerly Jay's partner and now his chief assistant in the CID, had finished taking my statement. I think Jay was out on the lawn scraping up vomit, or maybe he was rooting through the garbage looking for the container the poison was brought in. The search of our effects had been thorough. So far no vial of suspicious liquid had appeared. So Jay was destined to grub. I was outside loading our junk into the Blazer.

Dennis parked the green truck with his usual deliberation and got out, shutting the door neatly. "Hi, Lark."

"Hi. You took your time."

"I finished breakfast. Ginger says to tell you she'll hold the fort."

"She won't have to. I'm going home in about fifteen minutes."

"Is it true old Llewellyn's dead?"

His air of calm annoyed me. "He was murdered, Dennis."

His jaw dropped. "Geez, no kidding?"

I stared into Dennis's eyes. They were as startled as a deer's. "Jay didn't tell you?"

"He said Llewellyn took sick last night, that you tried CPR and it didn't work." Dennis's Adam's apple bobbed. "He said my mother was pretty upset. That's all. Murder?"

I explained.

Dennis whistled. "Geez, that's awful. And there I was thinking it was a good thing he was dead."

I must have looked as if I'd swallowed a mosquito. Dennis never had bad thoughts about anybody.

He blushed. "Well, not really. But I'm glad he won't be coming up here every summer, reminding her of how it was before."

"Before what?"

"Before she had to stop dancing. See, she was always a part of that world, artsy, glamorous stuff, and she misses it. Every time he comes . . . came up here she'd get all sad and mournful, thinking about what she was missing living in the tules."

"Did she have to move up here, Dennis?"

"Not have to, exactly. The thing is"—his wide brow wrinkled—"she hasn't got anything or anyone else. My grandparents are dead. She used to have her dancing and me. Now it's just me."

Oh, Dennis, I thought, you poor schmuck.

"So she bought that little farmhouse on Beale Creek and moved in," he went on earnestly. "But she still gets real homesick for San Francisco."

Then why doesn't she go back? I left the question unasked. "Go in to her. They'll want to take Denise's statement, but they don't want to trigger a bout of hysteria."

He flushed. "She's not a hysterical person."

I sighed. "I'm sorry, Dennis. I'm a little hysterical myself. I keep thinking I'm calm and I keep saying dumb things."

He rubbed his forehead. He was wearing his Forest Service shirt and twill pants, and he looked as wholesome as a Boy Scout. "Yes, well, she's sensitive, you know, and she has strong feelings. It comes from being an artist. Sometimes people don't know how to take her."

My mother is an artist. I had time to be glad she didn't stage-manage her emotions at Denise's high pitch. "Go in to her. Lydia gave her a Valium and she slept a little, but I think she's probably awake now. Jay's going to want to take her statement."

"Why? What can she tell him? He was there."

"He was on the scene. So was I, but neither of us saw the murderer lace Llewellyn's Campari. Maybe Denise can fill in some of the blanks."

He didn't look convinced, but he knocked on the door and went in when Kevin Carey opened it for him. I finished loading the car.

I reached town about eleven-thirty, unloaded our belongings, and showered in the hope of waking up. When I had changed into something clerklike, I drove to the bookstore.

Ginger and Annie hung on my every word. Fortunately no customers showed up while I was telling them what had happened. Ginger was ready to rush to Dennis's side. I thought that was a bit excessive.

"Yeah, but murder," she said, big-eyed. "Whodunit?" She had lately begun to read mysteries instead of romances.

"It's not a game, Ginger. The old man died." A human being full of wit and fire was now a cold, decaying sack of chemicals. I thought of Llewellyn's frail shoulders shuddering with the force of the poison, and I wanted to throw up. I did start crying.

"Oh, hey, I didn't mean . . . oh, gee, Lark."

I fumbled a Kleenex from my purse. "It wasn't what you said." I blew my nose. "I guess it just hit me. Last night I was breathing for him." I mopped at my eyes and groped for another Kleenex. "And now he's d-dead."

Ginger patted my shoulders. The door bonged. "It's Annie!" There was a note of panic in her voice. She hustled me into the back room and sat me down in the new padded office chair with the adjustable back.

I could hear Annie making nervous conversation with somebody. I blew and swabbed and got myself under control, but I felt miserable. I hoped Jay didn't feel as rotten as I did. I thought of the nightmare. He probably felt worse. He probably felt responsible.

* * *

Annie left at one, just before we had a rush of customers. For about fifteen minutes I was so innocent I thought all those strangers were in town for the holiday and just happened to want a good book to read.

We sold out our hardcover and paperback mysteries, and the half-dozen copies of Llewellyn's *Collected Poems* before six, plus assorted maps, half the science fiction, and all the Stephen Kings. Ginger and I barely had time to go to the rest room. Customers kept asking if this was the store with the murder. I kept saying there had been no murder on the premises. Some thought that was funny. Some didn't. Some were very strange folks.

Around two-thirty the TV car from Channel 3 showed up. The reporter had herself taped making hard-hitting comments by the door while the cameraperson panned over the sign. LARKSPUR BOOKS. Step right up, name your poison. I refused to give them an interview. I also said no comment to the *Chronicle* stringer who drove his camper into the lot and was obviously set to lay siege.

"Tomorrow I close the store," I said grimly.

"We're making money hand over fist." We were both at the checkout counter. Ginger was enjoying herself.

"That's the point."

"Oh. Exploitation." Ginger is not dumb. She rang up the paperback edition of a low-cholesterol diet book for a teenage girl who tittered when I looked her in the eye.

"Did Dennis say how his mother was?" Dennis had called two hours earlier, but Ginger and I hadn't had a minute to discuss what he'd said.

"He took her to the hospital."

"Really?"

"Just nerves."

"No, we have no more copies in stock, madam." That to a plump woman in her fifties who looked like the stereotype of an English teacher. She wanted Llewellyn's poems. "Try the public library."

Ginger rang up a map of Portugal. Portugal? "You were going to leave at six."

"I won't desert you. No, sir, that's out of stock." I told the man, who looked like the stereotype of an accountant, that we might have copies of Llewellyn's poems by the end of the week. I recommended H.D. if he liked imagist poetry. He left without H.D. I wondered whether he'd have bought Ma's latest if he'd known she was one of Llewellyn's literary executors.

So it went. We didn't have time to eat. The TV camera and its auxiliaries left by three, the better to make the five o'clock news, but they were replaced by a dozen assorted children on bikes and skateboards. Two teenage girls rode up bareback on a roan horse, and sat and stared. The horse crapped on the asphalt. Dozens of cars drove by, some with bad mufflers, all with gawkers. The *Chronicle* man's camper stayed. The "customers" kept coming.

None of the intruders who entered the store had anything intelligent or even kind to say, but about half had enough shame to think they had to buy something. One nonbuyer handed me a tract about the wages of sin. I told her the Bible Life Bookstore's address on Main Street. She called me a jezebel, on what grounds I know not, and flounced out, having exercised her First Amendment rights.

Ginger stayed with me. At five minutes to nine I dimmed the lights and by nine-fifteen I had rung up the last sale, a school-year calendar boosting the Monte J.C. women's athletics program. I yanked the shades down and locked the front door.

Ginger and I looked at each other. "Phew," she said.

"Let's total out the register. Can you take the money to the night deposit?"

She nodded. "Dennis is picking me up."

"Thanks. Thanks for staying, too. I'm going to have to put in an emergency order with the supplier in Sacramento." And hope he could get me a dozen copies of Llewellyn's *Collected Poems* at $29.50 retail.

"Were you serious about closing the store tomorrow?"

"Absolutely. It's Sunday. All the religionists in the county would come in and lecture me and feel righteous about not buying anything. Besides, I think I ought to close. Staying open isn't respectful."

She raised her eyebrows. "How about Monday?"

"Monday will be business as usual. Well, not quite. You'd better count on a one-to-nine shift all of next week, though I'll close again for a half day if the funeral is held here. I don't imagine it will be. Llewellyn lived in San Francisco."

Ginger tried not to lick her chops. She was attending classes full-time, but she needed as much work as she could get. Her kids were in college, too. "I'll drop my one o'clock class."

"The art history class? I thought you liked it."

"Sure, but they teach it every semester, and besides, I need more time to study." She looked virtuous.

I had to laugh. "Don't do anything hasty. This flurry of business will probably peter out in a couple of days."

I let Ginger out the front door when I saw Dennis's pickup pull in. That was a ploy to distract the *Chronicle* reporter while I escaped out the back. I set a record shutting off the back-room lights and locking up, and zipped out the alley. I took the back way in to my apartment.

My telephone answering tape was full of urgent messages from members of the press looking for exclusive stories—and a somber request from my mother to call her whenever I got in, even if it was 2:00 A.M. in New York.

I dialed home and Mother answered on the fourth ring. My father had heard a news story at around 3:00 P.M. their time, and they'd been stewing with worry ever since. I should have called them from the lodge. I knew that, and my bad conscience made me defensive.

When I'm defensive, I wisecrack. Understandably in the circumstances, Mother didn't appreciate my flippancy and we almost quarreled. Then she found out I hadn't eaten since 8:00 A.M., forgave me, and told me to call again the next morning.

Jay let himself in the door as I was scrambling eggs. I added three to the bowl and grated some cheese. "You look beat," I said.

"You, too. Was it bad?"

"The store? A circus." I told him what had happened and that I wasn't opening Sunday, and he approved. We ate all the eggs and were still starving—he hadn't eaten either—so I made a stack of sourdough toast and broke out a couple of cold beers afterward. Haute cuisine.

We sat on the couch, sort of leaning on each other, and sipped our beers. After a while I said, "Are you going to shut me out of this one?"

He straightened and looked at me without smiling. Jay's eyes are the color of Glenlivet. When's he's feeling good, they have gold lights in the depths. They were dark as a peat bog. "You know I'm not supposed to discuss criminal cases with you."

I nodded, watchful.

He sighed. "But I'm going to, of course. It's inevitable. The thing is, Lark, you've got to promise not to blab."

"Thanks a lot."

"You told Dennis Fromm Llewellyn was murdered."

"Dennis is a friend."

"Dennis's mother is a suspect."

I made a rude noise.

"It's unlikely she's the murderer. She doesn't strike me as a planner, and this crime took elaborate planning. Still, she grows her own herbs and flowers, and she brews salves and teas all the time. She could have stewed the damned delphinium. And her relationship with Llewellyn struck me as very murky."

That was interesting. "Murky, how?"

"Murky as in puzzling. Are you going to promise me you'll keep your gorgeous mouth shut?"

"As far as is humanly possible," I said with dignity. "I

know the people involved, so I can't pretend absolute ignorance, but I won't say anything to them you don't want me to. And to the press I guarantee I will make No Comment. It will give me great pleasure."

"Do you include Bill Huff in there with the press?"

I took a sip of beer and didn't answer.

"Huff filed his story from the lodge—on the UPI wire." He was insistent.

"I'll read it and decide."

"Cut it out, Lark."

"You always say that." I relented. "I promise I will keep my lip zipped. You would have been proud of me at the bookstore. One of the Twinkie-brains even asked for my autograph."

That amused him, and the tension eased a little. "Who has a motive?" I asked casually. "Angharad Peltz, obviously."

"Not so obvious. Nobody's seen the will." He rolled his bottle of Henry Weinhardt's Private Reserve back and forth between his palms. "I don't even know the law firm he dealt with."

"Didn't you ask the Peltzes?"

"The Peltzes weren't giving me the time of day." His mouth quirked. "Especially after Dan Cowan confiscated a stalk of larkspur, roots and all, from the middle of their flower garden."

"Cowan," I said, awed. "You have this vindictive streak I never noticed before." Deputy Cowan was not exactly suave. Jay always insisted he was a good cop, but I wasn't so sure.

"I figured I owed Peltz." He took a swallow of beer. "When I've talked to the lawyers I'll have a better idea of motive, though greed isn't the only reason for murder."

"Miguel."

He frowned. "I don't think Miguel was Llewellyn's lover, if that's what you're suggesting. I talked with the kid, of course. Kevin wanted me to take him in. Maybe I should have. Miguel was at the bar, so he had a better opportunity to poison the drinks then anyone else."

. . . .

"Drinks?"

"Two."

"How about the Campari bottle?"

"It was okay. We found the poison container, by the way. In the garbage can. No prints."

"Did anybody see . . ."

"The murderer could have disposed of half a dozen bottles that size while you and I were administering CPR. Everybody was milling around."

I sighed. "I suppose it was an ordinary bottle, too."

"It was a flavoring bottle, the kind you buy vanilla or lemon extract in."

"Small."

"It would fit in a small woman's palm."

"Are you looking for a small woman?"

"No, dammit. I don't know who I'm looking for. That's the point. It had been rinsed out, probably run through a dishwasher or boiled before the poison was poured into it."

"Is the poison hard to extract?"

Jay snorted. "The toxicologist said you could puree a plant in your Cuisinart and strain the juices through cheesecloth."

"Easy."

"Yeah. He said the mess was boiled down to concentrate the poison. That could have been done on a kitchen stove. Probably was."

"Then it's going to be hard to prove . . ."

"Anybody at the party could have brewed the poison—maybe weeks in advance. There was no trace of a label or flavoring, though there was a bit of the poison left in the bottle."

"Easy to smuggle into the house."

"Dead easy."

We drank beer.

The flavoring bottle made me think of the cook. "Did you get old Domingo to talk?"

Jay sighed. "Yes. He knew nothing and saw nothing, and

was watching a videotape of *The Sting* when the crime occurred."

"I didn't see any TV sets at the lodge."

"He has a small color set, a large VCR, and a library of old flicks my brother Freddy would kill for. I believed him—provisionally. As far as I know he didn't stand to gain anything from Llewellyn's death, and he'll be losing an easy job."

"Easy!" I was thinking of the elegant meals Domingo had produced.

"Ordinarily he only had to cook for Llewellyn and give the other servants their orders. He was well paid, had posh quarters in the San Francisco town house, and Llewellyn dined out a lot. Of course Llewellyn may have insulted his *crème fraîche* or seduced his baby brother, but I don't think so. It's not going to be that easy. Domingo refused to discuss his employer's private life. He had nothing to say about Miguel either, though I gathered he was jealous of the kid."

"Aha!"

"Not necessarily sexually jealous. Miguel is a newcomer. Domingo started working for Llewellyn right after World War II. He said the kid was an okay worker."

"Where does Miguel come from?"

"Baja. I know the town—it's a scabby place outside Mazatlán. Miguel says he was parking cars at the Casa Miranda last year. Llewellyn hired him to drive around the resort, and offered him the chauffeur's job later. Miguel jumped at it."

"Naturally."

Jay didn't smile. "Naturally. According to him, he's supporting his grandmother, his mother, five brothers and sisters, and an ailing uncle. He showed me his green card and said he was going to apply for citizenship. I believed him. I wasn't so gullible when he denied having a sexual relationship with Llewellyn. He was bound to do that. The culture looks down on homosexuals."

"He was very demonstrative, sobbing and wailing a lot."

Jay shrugged. "That's culture, too. He was grateful to

Llewellyn, and he's afraid he'll have to go back to Baja. He thought *we* were cold fish."

I finished my beer and set it on the coffee table. "What about the others? Did you turn up anything interesting?"

"Janey Huff doesn't like her stepmother."

I hooted. "The great detective."

Jay grinned. "The Huffs were very cooperative, even if Bill was mentally writing leads for the *National Enquirer* the whole time I was questioning him."

"The *National Enquirer?* Be fair. The Huff Press is a class outfit."

"Yes, but that side of it's Lydia's doing, according to Janey. Bill goes along, but he's a no-holds-barred newspaper-man at heart. Worked for the *Chronicle* until his father died and left him the local rag."

I digested that. "Well, okay. What about Denise? Dennis took her to the hospital, according to Ginger. Did you use your rubber hose on her?"

Jay shuddered. "I'm the one who should've been sedated. That woman is an emotional shark."

"The kind that eats its young."

"I don't think sharks do that." He put his arm around me. "Just swimmers and surf bums and unwary prime ministers. Come to bed, Lark. We won't solve the case tonight." We didn't try to solve anything else either. We were both too tired.

At 7:00 A.M. my mother called. It was ten for her, so I may someday forgive her. She talked sadly about Llewellyn and what his influence had meant to her, and I eventually woke up. Jay did, too. He glowered at the ceiling for five minutes of uh-uh and unh-uh and apparently decided the phone call wasn't going to go away.

When he came back from the shower we were still on the line. I had given Ma a full account of our rescue attempt and talked to my dad, too, and cried on his shoulder, and gone back to Ma. She was speculating about what being a literary executor would mean when bells went off and lights flashed.

"Hey," I interrupted. "I bet you know the name of Llewellyn's lawyer."

"Well, yes."

"Jay needs to know. To ask about the terms of the will." I waved Jay to me. "Here he is."

"Hello." He listened. "Yeah. I wish I didn't have to meet Lark's family under inauspicious circumstances."

"You could have come home with me at Christmas. That was auspicious," I said, but quietly, because he was listening to Mother.

"Paper."

I rummaged in the bedside table and produced a pad and pencil.

"Okay. Davis and Wong." He scribbled. "Do you have a phone number? I know the area code. Thanks. I'll talk to D'Angelo again, probably today." Mother said something. "Yes. Me, too. Nice to talk to you." He handed me the phone.

Ma said, worried, "Do you think I ought to fly out? Maybe I have to be there for the reading of the will."

"I dunno, Ma. You should talk to the lawyer."

"Surely not, if D'Angelo will be there. I'm supposed to spend next week in West Virginia."

"The Mountain Poets' Workshop?"

Mother sighed. "I wish I could learn to say no. Keep us posted, darling. I'm sorry you never had a chance to know Dai."

I swallowed. "I'm sorry, too. I liked him."

Jay was dressing.

I set the receiver on its cradle. "I apologize for the wake-up call. Ma always overlooks the time difference. Are you going to cook breakfast?"

"Cream of wheat?"

"Aargh."

"I'll think of something."

He made not-bad omelets and even brewed me a pot of

coffee, which was pure altruism since he can't drink it himself.

I said pensively, "Can't we go out to your house and have a day to ourselves?"

"You're joking."

I sighed. "More like wishful thinking. I have to track down the book supplier and feed yesterday's sales into the inventory control. And I suppose you're going to grill suspects."

"I'm going to have another talk with D'Angelo."

"Didn't he tell you he was Llewellyn's literary executor? He and Ma."

Jay dolloped marmalade on a slice of bread. "The question didn't come up. What's a literary executor?"

"I think they try to see to it that unpublished material is brought out, and in a decent edition, and that nobody does anything rotten to the works already in print. If there's anything to sell, they're supposed to do that in the interest of the heirs. Ma said Llewellyn kept a journal, and there are bound to be letters. They might find a biographer who'd be interested in working on the personal stuff. Choosing a good one could take a lot of time. They're supposed to protect Llewellyn's literary reputation, basically."

"Doesn't sound very rewarding."

I finished off a bite of toast. "If you mean did D'Angelo—or Ma—have a motive for doing Llewellyn in, no. They don't profit." Not directly. I brooded over my coffee cup. "Of course, if D'Angelo does a good job, it will enhance his reputation in academic circles. He might even get hired by a good school."

"He's head of the English department at Monte, isn't he?"

I took a bite of omelet. "A dead end, believe me. Nobody's reputation is enhanced by teaching at a junior college."

"Sounds like snobbery."

"Sounds like? Is. My mother would never be rude enough to say so directly, but as far as she's concerned, junior colleges are a few millimeters above the kind of school you enroll in on matchbook covers."

"That's dumb," Jay said reasonably. "Long Beach J.C.

salvaged my brains. I slept through high school. If it hadn't been for junior college I'd be driving a pizza wagon."

"Believe me, that doesn't matter."

He blotted his mustache. "Your mother sounded down-right human."

"She is, on a personal level. But she scaled the heights of the prestige pyramid before I was twelve, and she doesn't question its validity."

"You're depressing me." He stood up. "I've got to go. Where are the keys to the Blazer?"

I pointed at my purse, which was lying where I'd left it on the kitchen counter. "You and Win D'Angelo got along like a house afire. That surprised me. What's the big attraction?"

"We'd met before. That job at the college," he said vaguely, slapping his pants pockets. "Left my wallet in the bedroom." He disappeared.

"Job?" I asked when he came back.

"I interviewed for the vacancy they had in police science. D'Angelo was on the selection committee."

"Oh, yeah, the director's job." The job had been adver-tised about the time of my big basketball tournament. Jay had told me he was applying. "Who did they give it to?"

"Me."

I think I gasped.

Jay grinned. "I have until the fifteenth to refuse it."

"Are you going to?"

He grabbed his keys, relented, and returned to give me a kiss. "When I screw up this investigation, they'll probably withdraw the offer. Go order books, Lark. Stay away from the press, and I'll see you tonight."

I decided to take advantage of the early hour and sneak off to the store to do my bookkeeping. It turned out that we had made more money that one day than in the month of June. At that rate the shelves would be empty by Friday.

I rearranged stock, putting the benefit calendars up front and moving every cheap paperback in the place onto the empty mystery rack. I rang the book distributor five times, and was finally promised a delivery on Wednesday. Then I scurried to a supermarket across town to lay in a supply of Jay-style bland groceries and went home.

Nothing much happened the rest of the day. Jay reported that he had interrogated D'Angelo and Miguel. The Peltzes had informed him that they were flying to San Francisco for the reading of the will. They had seemed taken aback when he said, "Ah, yes, Davis and Wong," but that was a minor triumph in a day of frustration.

I didn't open the store until ten on weekdays, so I had a leisurely hour after Jay left. I washed clothes. As I was about to go to the store, my mother called.

"They're holding a memorial service for Dai Thursday at the Episcopal cathedral in San Francisco. I'm flying out for it . . ."

"What about West Virginia?"

"I traded sessions with Jordis Pembroke." Pembroke was another poet who did the workshop circuit. "I want you to be there, Lark, and I'm going back to Monte with you."

That knocked the wind out. "Uh, what about the store? It's a one-bedroom apartment! I haven't cleaned the refrigerator!"

"If I were a sensitive person, I'd say you didn't want me to come."

"Now, Ma . . ."

"I'll take a room at that place your father stayed in last year—what's it called?"

"The Eagle Cap Lodge," I said gloomily. "Shall I make a reservation for you? You could sleep on my bed, I suppose, and Jay and I could sleep on the couch."

"I thought Jay had a house of his own."

"He does, but it's a fifty-minute drive from the courthouse. He'll be on this case all hours of the day and night, and I don't see why he should have to waste his time driving back and forth." Besides, I liked having him around.

"Eagle Cap for me," Ma said. "You might as well rent me a car, too. An automatic. I have to confer with this D'Angelo person."

We hung up. I leapt down the back stairs, into my nonautomatic Toyota and onto the street, gears grinding. I was ten minutes late opening the store, and the first "customer" was a tabloid reporter.

Ginger showed up, red-eyed, at twelve-fifteen.

"Are you okay?"

"Dennis took his mother to San Francisco for a whole week. He got leave and they caught the morning plane at Weed."

"That's too bad, Ginge. Awful for Dennis."

She gave me a watery grin. "You said it."

The place was aswarm with browsers. One or two of them looked at books instead of at the freak who had bumped off a poet with puree of larkspur to publicize her bookstore. Ginger and I worked. Hard.

At three Janey Huff burst in, pop-eyed with excitement. "Have you heard the news?"

Every browser in the place leaned in our direction.

I pointed to the back room. "I'll be with you in a minute, Janey."

She blushed and scooted around the counter and into my sanctum. It was ten minutes before I could join her.

"What news?"

She laid down my copy of *The Collected Poems of E. David Llewellyn*. "He was pretty good, wasn't he?"

"Janey . . ."

She gave an annoying giggle. "Miguel took off this morning in the Mercedes and hasn't returned to the lodge. Lydia heard it on the radio. That's pretty conclusive, isn't it?"

My impulse was to call Jay. "Are you sure?"

"Turn on the local station. It's almost time for a news break."

After a heartrending Loretta Lynn ballad and three ads, the DJ confirmed that "a major suspect in the murder of poet David Llewellyn has disappeared. An all-points bulletin has been issued for the arrest of Miguel Montez. Montez, Llewellyn's chauffeur, was last seen wearing jeans and a white short-sleeve shirt. He is Hispanic, of medium height, slender and twenty-three years old. The missing vehicle is a pearl-gray Mercedes 580 SL, California license number . . ." The DJ read the number and instructed his listeners to contact the sheriff's office if they had seen Miguel or the car. His voice modulated. "And now for Conway Twitty. . . ."

I turned the radio off, feeling sick. Jay had trusted Miguel against his better judgment. He had to be catching all kinds of flack from the sheriff and the press.

"That means the rest of us are off the hook," Janey was saying. "Doesn't it?"

"Not necessarily. Maybe Miguel thought they'd take away his green card and panicked."

Janey snorted. "I'll bet he panicked. He killed Dai and

84

decided he'd better head back to Mexico before he was arrested. It's as plain as the nose on your face."

"It's not plain. He didn't have a motive."

"Come on, Lark. Lover's quarrel?" She giggled again.

I wasn't liking Janey very much. "The Peltzes . . ."

"Pooh. Even Ted Peltz wouldn't be stupid enough to kill Dai while he was waiting trial on another charge. Dad says it's an open-and-shut case."

"But the larkspur—where's Miguel supposed to have got the poison?"

Janey shrugged. "It's a common plant. He could have swiped a stalk of it from the Peltzes' garden."

"And stewed it in Domingo's kitchen while Domingo was preparing a banquet? I don't buy it."

"If Miguel's not guilty, why did he run?"

"Maybe he saw the killer in the act and got scared."

"Lark, I'm swamped out here!" said Ginger, near tears.

"I've got to go back to work. Nice seeing you, Janey."

"I thought you'd be relieved." Janey got up and preceded me into chaos. She was pouting.

At some point in the melee I called Avis and the Eagle Cap Lodge. I also called Annie, who promised to come in half-time the next two days, full-time Thursday and Friday. Ginger and I got rid of the last customer at nine-fifteen and were out the back at nine-thirty. An enterprising reporter caught me as I was sneaking into my car and I gave him no comment until the engine turned over. Surprisingly, I made it into my apartment without being trapped a second time.

Jay showed up at ten looking frazzled but wired.

I eyed him curiously. "Beer or food?"

"Beer. I got in touch with the lawyer, Lark."

I poured. "Good. What's with the will?"

"You're not going to believe this." He took his glass into the living room and stood near the window, scowling into it. "Jesus, *I* still don't believe it."

I sat on the couch. "Believe what? He left it all to the symphony?"

85

"Llewellyn left the bulk of his estate to his natural son."

"Not to Angharad?" I started to laugh. "I'll bet Ted is fit to be tied."

"Aren't you curious about the son?"

"Who?"

"Dennis Fromm."

"What!" I slopped beer on my hand and set the glass down. "You've got to be kidding! Dennis?"

"That's what the man said."

"Oh, gosh, Ginger will wig out." I suppose I babbled for a while, repeating myself. I *was* shocked. Pleasantly at first. Dennis was a sweet guy. "He probably feels as if he's won the lottery."

"Do you think so?"

I tried to do a total recall for Jay of the conversation I'd had with Dennis at the lodge. I have a good memory for details, so I came close, and finished, "Surely he didn't know Llewellyn was his father."

Jay had set his beer down on the wide Victorian window-sill and was rubbing his forehead. "You think not? How sure are you?"

I considered. "Darned sure. He was worried about Denise, but I could swear all he felt about Llewellyn was a kind of mild annoyance."

"Write it down. Your impressions could be important," Jay said somberly.

"Why . . . oh, God, the will gives Dennis a motive for killing L . . . his father."

"About forty million bucks worth of motive. Llewellyn owned a block of downtown San Francisco."

"My God."

"If you think Dennis was in the dark about his paternity, that shoves the suspicion onto Denise."

"She did collapse when she heard Llewellyn was dead." I ran my hand through my hair. "But I thought you said she was an unlikely suspect."

"Unlikely but not impossible. And that was before I knew of the liaison."

"But the planning . . ."

"Denise is not stupid, just temperamental and self-absorbed. I knew she could have extracted the poison, and she had as good a chance of spiking Llewellyn's Campari glass as anyone. Now I know she had a motive, maybe half a dozen motives. He didn't marry her, or acknowledge Dennis while he was alive. He got her with child and left her for a male lover. Lots of room for vengeful feelings. And, of course, the money. If Miguel hadn't split with the damned Mercedes . . ." He grabbed his beer and took a hefty swig. "You heard about Miguel?"

I told him about Janey.

"I wish," he said savagely, "that the fourth estate was not so damned quick to make judgments. They've tried, condemned, and hanged the kid already."

"And strung you up by the thumbs."

"That, too."

"Was it bad?"

"My ass is grass. Even Kev gave me a hard time." His nose wrinkled. "And the sheriff trotted me out to make a statement to the press."

"The bastard! He's quick enough to take credit . . . all those press conferences he gave last year . . . you won the election for him!" I was spluttering.

Jay shrugged. "He's a politician. I goofed, Lark. I just hope I didn't goof as badly as I think I did."

"What do you mean?"

"Miguel was keeping something back, something that was eating at him . . ." He shrugged again. "Time will tell, as they say."

"You're awfully philosophical."

He took another large swallow. "Not philosophical. Confused. The will threw me for a loop. I was just trying to rearrange my thinking when Kev barged in with the news about Miguel. We sent out the APB and drove out to question Domingo. The Peltzes were gone by then."

"To hear the will read?"

He gave a brief grin. "Are *they* in for a surprise. The lawyer said he'd be reading it tomorrow in his office. Mrs. Peltz gets a small annuity and the cabin. Access road, no land."

"Good for Llewellyn."

Jay said somberly. "I'm sorry for her. Peltz will give her hell."

"I suppose so, though he probably spoiled her chances when he got himself arrested."

"No, the lawyer said the will is two years old. I wonder why the old guy didn't warn Dennis. It's crazy to leave that kind of money to a . . ."

". . . a woolly lamb?"

"Something like that. Dennis is not exactly a high-powered intellect."

"He's just naive and inexperienced."

"Naive, inexperienced, and thirty-eight years old," Jay said wryly.

"Wasn't Denise named in the will?"

"No."

"That says something."

"It says Llewellyn didn't trust her with money."

"But she's shrewd about money."

"According to Dennis?"

"Oh." The buzzer went off. "Food?"

He heaved a sigh. "I had a Danish sometime around eleven and I've been on the go since."

We were too hungry to talk. We polished off the fettucine (with a nice, mild Alfredo sauce), bread, salad, and pieces of thawed cheesecake, and then we talked.

There was more exclamation (me) and information (Jay) about the will. The lawyer had not read it to him, merely described it, but Jay had made him detail any provision that mentioned the guests and servants at the lodge. The Huff Press was down for $250,000 to use in seeking grants for its publication of new poets and another quarter of a million for new equipment. Llewellyn had also forgiven two major

88

business loans. Domingo would get a handsome pension, and a codicil added $25,000 for Miguel.

"Not a lot."

"He could support his family for ten years on that in Baja."

"I suppose so." A depressing thought.

The provision that made me sit up (we were in bed by then) was the establishment of a nonprofit foundation to run a writers' colony. Llewellyn had left the lodge, the lake, and the land around it, plus a generous cash endowment, to Siskiyou Summit—that was the name he had chosen for his foundation—and he had specified that Winton D'Angelo was to serve a five-year term as its first director.

The foundation board was to include Llewellyn's accountant, his lawyer, and three poets "of national stature." I wondered whether Ma had got word of the foundation from D'Angelo? from the lawyer? It was right up her alley.

I mentioned my suspicions to Jay, along with an account of Ma's phone call. "I'll bet ten bucks she's lobbying to be named to the board."

He pulled me back down beside him. "Why not? She's a logical choice."

"Yes, but she'd be out here every summer! Maternal surveillance."

He laughed.

"Maybe *Ma* hired Miguel to poison Llewellyn." I pinched his bare arm. "Have you looked into that?"

"No, and I'm not going to. Miguel didn't poison his boss."

"Then why did he run?"

"I'm more worried about how he managed to slip a pearl-gray Mercedes out of town. It's not exactly inconspicuous."

"Out of town?"

"He told Domingo he was going into town to gas up and have the oil changed. Cowan was on duty near the Peltzes' access road, and Miguel even waved at him. The kid drove the car to the Chevron station on Grand, did what he said he was going to do, and took off. The station attendant thought he headed west on Grand but wasn't sure. That's as far as we can trace Miguel. We did a helicopter search, and the county cars have been poking down every back lane and log skid. The highway patrol didn't come up with anything either. Maybe some citizen will call tomorrow with more information. Until then, we're completely at sea."

"He probably got on I-5 and headed south."

"No." Jay was stroking my back with happy results. I purred. "Somebody would have spotted him at that patch of construction north of Weed."

"Where it's down to one lane both ways?" I rubbed against him.

"That's the spot."

"Mmm-mmh," I murmured, distracted. "*That's* the spot," and we forgot about Miguel.

Jay was gone before I woke up the next morning. I dimly remembered the telephone ringing. I got up, showered, and ate breakfast to the country-and-western twang of the local radio station. The news break revealed no further developments in the disappearance of Miguel Montez. Jay's phone call must have been about something else.

I opened the store at ten, reminding myself that Ginger did not know Dennis was the heir to millions of dollars and to keep my mouth shut. I did that so well she thought I was mad at her. I explained that I was worried about Miguel.

"Worried about him?"

"About his disappearance. It made Jay look bad with the sheriff."

"Oh." She accepted that. We were too busy to carry on a discussion. Around three the phone rang. I was waiting on a customer who seemed to be a customer. She wanted a copy of *The Secret Garden* for her granddaughter. Ginger answered the phone.

I had waited on three more people before I noticed Ginger was missing. I rang up the last sale and ducked into the back room.

She was sitting at the desk, staring at the telephone.

"Hey, snap out of it."

She lifted her dazed brown eyes to me. "That was Dennis. He said old Llewellyn was his father and that he just inherited a fortune."

I tried to project astonishment. I am not a good liar.

"You knew!"

"Well, Jay talked to the attorney yesterday. But he said I couldn't tell anybody. Congratulations, I think."

"I'm scared."

"How was Dennis?"

"He sounded . . ." She screwed up her face. "He sounded lost." She started to cry. "It's not fair. The filthy old bastard. Why did he have to do that to Dennis? He could have told him." She was really howling.

I handed her the box of Kleenex on the desk. "It is strange."

Ginger hiccuped. "Dennis is going to be rich, and he won't want me anymore."

I assured her Dennis had good taste and was as faithful as a collie.

"But Denise hates me."

"Denise is a vampire. Drive a stake through her heart."

She hiccuped again. "I'm being silly, aren't I? Gosh, Lark, what am I going to do?"

"Wipe your eyes, check your makeup, and come out front. It sounds like a riot out there. I need you." I dashed back to the cash register.

Ginger finally gathered herself together. Around five, things slacked off. I sent her out for hamburgers, waited on a lone hiker who wanted a map of the Rogue Valley, and was tidying the paperback racks when the phone rang again. I answered, dragging the phone around to the front counter.

It was Lydia. She gossiped a bit about the will. Apparently the lawyer had called the Huffs and explained their legacy. Lydia was deeply touched. She had also heard about the writers' colony; D'Angelo had called her from San Francisco.

"Did he say anything about the Peltzes?" I asked in the first pause.

Lydia chuckled. "I feel sorry for Angharad, God knows, but it is funny. They're planning to sue. But, my dear, only think—Denise and Dai. How strange." My own word bouncing back at me.

"I don't think Dennis knew he was Llewellyn's son."

"Really? That's hard to believe. Denise is not exactly closemouthed." There was a thoughtful pause. "Of course things were different forty years ago—about gays, I mean. Dai never did proclaim his sexual preference. But everybody knew. Maybe Denise didn't want Dennis to know his father was, er, queer."

That was an interesting thought. Jay had been assuming it was Llewellyn who had refused to acknowledge Dennis. Maybe Denise would not allow him to claim her son. I could imagine Denise being that melodramatic—and that egotistical. If she hadn't known to begin with, it would have offended her sense of womanliness to realize that her lover preferred men. Perhaps Dennis was her revenge.

". . . a quiet little family dinner," Lydia was saying. "Tomorrow, sixish. We're flying south next morning for the memorial service. Can you come?"

"Who did you say would be there?" A middle-aged couple in matching T-shirts and slacks had entered the store.

"Win, Bill and I, and Janey. And yourself." She did not mention Jay.

"I'd have to hire a replacement at the store. Uh, thanks, Lydia. I have a customer. Can I get back to you?"

"Surely, my dear."

Between customers I toyed with the invitation. I also remembered I was supposed to reserve plane tickets for myself for Thursday, so I called the commuter line. Ginger came back with my burger, having eaten hers in peace. I ate and fed some data into the inventory program and brooded some more. Finally I called Lydia and said yes. She sounded ecstatic.

Jay came in a little earlier that night. I told him I was having dinner with the Huffs the next evening and he said he'd probably survive without my cooking. I kicked him under the table and said I would keep my ears open for dramatic revelations. He said fat chance. We ate.

The early phone call had been a false lead on Miguel. A gray Mercedes 300 had surfaced in Medford, Oregon—stolen. Mercedes appeared to be the vehicle of choice for car thieves. I reminded myself not to buy one.

Jay had spent the day in the courthouse digging for background on the suspects while Kevin supervised the on going search for Miguel. Jay wasn't very forthcoming about his discoveries. It was just gossip, he said rather irritably when I pressed him for more detail.

The long-term relationship between Llewellyn and his friend Hal had begun shortly after Dennis's birth and had had ups and downs. Both men had had flings outside the "marriage," but they had always come back together. Jay was trying to track down the flingees.

Denise had never married, nor had she taken another lover after Dennis's birth, though she had been seen in fashionable places with a variety of leading men. Jay thought he would find evidence that Llewellyn supported her. She had not danced professionally in fifteen years, though she taught master classes at the prestigious Wayne Studio until she was fifty-five.

Dennis had attended public schools in San Francisco and Humboldt State. He had worked summers for the Forest Service while he was still in school and permanently after that. Single-minded, our Dennis. He had spent two years in Alaska and the rest of the time in northern California. He had had girlfriends but had never married. (Poor Ginger.) Everybody thought he was a nice guy. Nobody thought he would amount to much.

The Huffs were slightly more colorful than Dennis. Bill's

father had inherited the paper from *his* father and built a reputation as a crusty eccentric. Bill attended Muir, majored in journalism, and landed a job as a reporter for the *Chronicle* after three years with *Stars and Stripes* in Germany. He covered the police beat for a while and did sports, married Janey's mother, and sired a daughter. When his father died of a heart attack, Bill moved his wife and child to Monte and took over the paper. They had seemed a model family. The divorce came as a big surprise to everybody, including, apparently, Bill's wife and daughter. Bill and Lydia had gotten acquainted at meetings of the county-wide arts council.

When they met, Lydia was already widowed. She had no children. She had grown up in the Midwest, the daughter of a hardware store owner with a fondness for hot cars. She went to college in Iowa and was still famous at her sorority for daredevil pranks and speeding tickets, but her marriage to an insurance broker had seemed sedate enough.

When he died in a car wreck she moved west and tried her hand at several small, craftsy businesses. That was during the '60s when craftsy businesses sprang up all over California like magic mushrooms. Lydia had managed to avoid bankruptcy, no mean feat, but had never made a killing. Her interest in papermaking and bookbinding was the key to her connection with Bill Huff, and from then on it was love's middle-aged dream. Both Huffs were popular locally, and Lydia had a reputation for public spiritedness. She was on the library board.

The Huff Press had been expanded ten years earlier. It enjoyed a growing reputation for excellence, both in the quality of the writers represented and in the workmanship of the books. It was not particularly profitable, but it broke even. The paper, by contrast, produced solid profit margins every year, probably because it was the only newspaper in the county. It carried the book-publishing end.

As far as Jay could find out, Janey Huff was squeaky clean. Her mother had taken her north to Portland after the divorce. The mother had eventually remarried and now ran three successful newsletters out of her home. Janey had spent her summers with Bill and Lydia, and had attended the University of Washington's school of library science. She dated a journalist for a while, but nothing had come of it. Dull stuff.

Jay was closemouthed about Winton D' Angelo. D'Angelo had a Ph.D. from Stanford and had begun his academic career on the tenure track at Presteign, a small, very exclusive liberal-arts college near Santa Barbara. He had married at twenty-five, the year he took the job at Presteign, and divorced at thirty, the year he came to Monte. Two sons. Was known as a man-about-town. Skied. That was as much as Jay was going to give me. I accused him of holding back.

He sighed. "*D'Angelo*'s holding back. I don't know what. Why don't we watch *It Happened One Night* on cable and forget about the damned case? I don't want to think about it anymore. How's Ginger?"

I told him about that and we watched half the film and went to bed.

"**P**oor darlings." Lydia gave the tall stalk of delphinium a delicate pat. "They don't like the heat."

I had not wanted another garden tour, but the charcoal briquettes had proved balky and the steaks weren't yet done. We had already endured a tour of Bill's gun room—lots of hunting rifles. A deer head had stared down at us from above Bill's desk. I do not like guns. In a spirit of contrariness I asked to see larkspur when Lydia offered to show me her flower garden. She didn't bat an eye, though Janey made a small, strangled noise and D'Angelo winced.

We were waist-deep in *Delphinium elatum*, and they were a trifle droopy. All of Lydia's larkspur were blue perennials. Lydia gave me a matey wink. "So pretty. They're good in bouquets. Delphinium and white glads with a puff of white or yellow mums at the base make a striking formal arrangement."

"I'd get bored with blue." D'Angelo had carried his scotch with him from the patio. He took a swallow. "They're a bit leggy, Lydia. What do you use on them, steer manure?"

"I try not to overfeed them." Lydia picked her way back to the flagstone path. We all followed. "They need a lot of water in this dry heat. I hope the boy remembers to soak them Friday morning." She bent and broke a dead blossom from something I couldn't identify. "Maybe I'll try the annuals next year, with daisies and cosmos. What do you think, Win?"

"Too tall." D'Angelo swatted at a bee and the ice clinked in his glass. We had interrupted the bees. "Get Denise to give you cuttings of her grandiflora."

"I do like that color." She turned back to me. "It's a Chinese variety, very deep blue. Also a perennial."

"There's a native California annual," D'Angelo said. "It has scarlet blossoms, though. Grows wild around here. Larkspur likes high altitude."

Janey said flatly. "I think you're all horrid."

A ginger-colored cat nosed onto the path, tail erect.

"Well, you *are* horrid," Janey insisted when nobody responded to her.

D'Angelo took another gulp of scotch. "People tend to be horrid. Especially when they're relieved they won't be hauled off to the pokey and charged with murder."

We looked at him, Janey red-faced.

"When I heard that kid had run off with the Mercedes," he went on, dispassionate, "I felt the purest relief and gratitude."

"Gratitude! He killed Dai!"

Lydia said. "Don't be obtuse, Janey. All Win means is that he's glad we can get on with our lives. Mourn Dai properly," she added, lest Janey imagine she meant business as usual. "A police investigation is apt to be unpleasant, darling. None of us was looking forward to the intrusion into our private lives."

"Or to being pilloried in the press," I said sweetly.

"Hey, there's old Ethelred!" D'Angelo snapped his fingers. The ginger cat gave him a bored look from cold, amber eyes, turned, and leapt into the air. Hunting dragonflies. Balked of his prey, Ethelred stalked past D'Angelo and looked up at Lydia and me.

"Win named the cats," Lydia explained. "Ethelred because . . ."

"Because he was unready?" I touched Ethelred's flank with the toe of my sandal. He rubbed against my bare ankle, purring.

Janey sneezed.

Lydia laughed. "Because he's red."

"God, there's the other one." Janey turned on Lydia. "You promised to lock them in the garage!" She sneezed again.

"It was too hot." Lydia made a face at me. "Janey's allergic to cats."

A white cat with green eyes ambled onto the path and made an interrogative sound. Ethelred cocked his head. The white cat teased him, swatting once, and then they were off, chasing each other across the shade-dappled lawn.

"What did you call the other one?" I asked idly as we strolled on. "Ethel White?"

"Got it in one!" Lydia laughed and patted my arm to show how clever she thought I was. "Win! Lark guessed Ethel's name."

"Either she's a genius or we're obvious." D'Angelo's diction was the slightest bit blurred.

Janey blew her nose, muttering.

"Lydia!" Bill was flipping the steaks.

"Coming," Lydia called. "Mind that patch of mud, Lark. No point in ruining your sandals."

I trod carefully.

We reached the round, wrought-iron patio table. Its striped umbrella fluttered in the evening sea breeze.

"Ready?" Bill roared. "T-bones coming up." He flopped three steaks onto a platter and handed it to Lydia. "Ladies first, eh, Win?" He moved the other two steaks to the center of the grill. The fat sizzled and smoked.

D'Angelo finished his scotch.

"Do have another drink, Win." Lydia pried the top steak off the heap onto my dinner plate, helped herself, and passed the platter to Janey, who was still sniffing and muttering.

"I was about to." He made for the wet bar.

The steaks were large. I wondered whether Lydia gave out doggie bags.

"Make me another, Win. Splash of soda." Bill looked around. "Dammit, Lydia, where's the platter?"

Lydia rose and took the platter to him.

"That's the ticket. Where are those drinks? Ah, good. Put

on the feedbag, Win. Chow down." He laughed heartily. Bill was in high good humor, somewhat exaggerated by alcohol. He patted Lydia's handwoven skirt as she turned to come back to the table.

I took a sip of wine, red this time—Pinot Noir, nice with the steak. Lydia sat.

Bill trundled over with the platter, forked the steaks onto the plates, laid the platter on the serving cart, and sat down. The table wobbled. I steadied my wine.

"Where the hell's the Worcestershire sauce?"

D'Angelo turned back to the bar and retrieved a bottle of Lea & Perrins. He let Bill pluck it and one of the scotches from his right hand, then sat with his own drink.

"My kind of meal," Bill said unnecessarily. He shook Worcestershire sauce over his steak and slathered butter on his baked potato. "Sour cream anybody?"

We ate. As Bill beat his steak into submission and defeated the potato, he told us his sensations when he saw his byline on the lead story in the Sunday *Chronicle*. The acme of journalistic achievement.

I listened to Bill, wondering at the existence of the Huff Press, given his clear predilection for news. Not just news, news with punch and screamer headlines. How frustrated he must have been all those years writing editorials about sewer bond elections and publishing slim volumes of confessional poetry.

The steak was tender. I ate about half of mine and some salad Niçoise, and sipped wine. Janey was listening to her father and picking olives out of the salad. Win D'Angelo pulled steadily on his scotch. Lydia chewed.

Finally, Bill wound down.

"I'm sure you read Bill's story, Lark." Lydia smiled at me. "What did you think?"

About halfway between *USA Today* and the *National Enquirer*. "It was fine," I lied.

Bill beamed. "Doing another follow-up on the Montez boy for the Sacramento *Bee*. Something has to be done about all these Mexicans flooding the state."

"Miguel has a green card," I said coldly.

D'Angelo was watching me over his scotch. He had matched Bill drink for drink, but he seemed cold sober. "Dodge talked to Miguel a lot that evening. What did they say?"

"I don't speak Spanish."

"Dodge had the kid save the wineglass." D'Angelo cut a bite of steak and looked at it. "He must've suspected poisoning all along."

That was obvious. I didn't respond.

Lydia said briskly, "Let's not keep hashing over the past, Win. Do you want a ride to the airport?"

"No, thanks. I'll drive down myself."

"We'll have a couple of hours to kill afterward, Lydia." Bill speared a forkful of salad. "I'm going to drop by the paper."

"All right." Lydia glanced at me. "Your mother is coming, isn't she, Lark?"

I nodded. "She'll fly back with me afterward. She wants to meet Win."

"She wants to go through Dai's journal and letters," D'Angelo muttered. He swallowed scotch.

Janey was mushing her baked potato.

Lydia said brightly, "How exciting. Will you be doing a book together?"

"No!" D'Angelo bit his lip. "Sorry, Lydia, but that's silly. We're both going to be too busy."

"Ah, of course, the foundation . . ."

"Congratulations," I interposed. "It sounds exciting, a West Coast Bread Loaf."

"What bread loaf?" Bill blinked over his scotch glass.

"Oh, Daddy, the writers' colony," Janey muttered.

"Will you resign your job at the college?" I asked.

D'Angelo drew a deep breath. "I already have."

That was news. All three Huffs looked at him.

"It'll take at least a year for the will to be probated." Lydia leaned forward, eyes keen. "That's what the lawyer told me."

"That's right."

"What are you going to live on?"

"My wife." D'Angelo began to laugh. "God, that's funny."

"Wife?"

"I'm getting married." He laughed on a cough and wiped his face with his napkin. "Sorry."

"Good heavens, congratulations!" Lydia beamed at him. "Who's the lucky girl?"

"Martha Finn."

Everybody looked as blank as I felt.

Janey drew a breath. "Oh, the actress?"

"That's right."

"Well, well, this is a surprise." Lydia raised her wine glass in a half toast. "Martha Finn."

Bill looked from D'Angelo to his wife with an expression of glazed bewilderment. "Who's Martha Finn?"

"She runs that repertory company out on the coast." Lydia set her glass down and began stacking plates. "Wasn't she with the Shakespeare Festival for a while?"

"Five years." D'Angelo set his salad bowl on his mostly uneaten steak. "That's where we met."

"You've been very secretive."

"Yes." He smiled at her like the shark in *The Threepenny Opera*. "That's one thing I've learned as a result of my long association with Dai Llewellyn—circumspection. Martha and I are going to spend the winter in Italy. We leave as soon after Labor Day as she can wind up her accounts. When we come back, I'll start setting up the writers' colony and she'll go into production at San Patricio. You can print that, Bill."

"Huh?" Bill was half-asleep.

I got up to help Lydia clear the table.

"I envy you," Lydia said lightly. "Italy in winter. "

"When all the tourists have gone home. I have been looking forward to it," D'Angelo finished his scotch, "all my life."

"Where are you staying, Florence?" I liked the thought of Italy myself.

"We'll gypsy around." He got to his feet. "And now, friends, I am going to ask the delightful and steel-nerved Miss

Dailey to follow me home. I have imbibed more scotch than is strictly legal, but I don't see any other way to get my car to my apartment."

"I'll drive your car over," Janey muttered. "I can run back. I need the exercise."

D'Angelo blinked. "Ah. Well, if you don't mind. I do have to leave for the airport by five-thirty in the morning."

"It'll be there."

He gave her a wide, sweet smile. He was a good-looking man in a grizzled, middle-aged way.

Janey blushed.

"Thanks." He fished in his pocket. "Here are the keys. No, I'll need the key to the apartment." He detached the car key from the ring and handed it to Janey. "There."

"Can I interest anyone in coffee?" Lydia was losing control of the situation and looked as if she didn't like the idea. She probably had black bottom pie waiting in the pantry.

"No, thanks," I murmured. "I ought to try for an early night, too, Lydia. And you'll be wanting to pack. It was a nice dinner. Thanks." I grabbed my handbag.

Lydia gave in gracefully and followed us out to my car.

We had turned the first corner and were just out of sight of the house when D'Angelo said without preamble, "I want to talk to Dodge. Is he at the courthouse?"

I had strayed over the center line in my surprise. I pulled back into the right lane. "What is it, eight-thirty?" The clock on my dashboard didn't work. Never had.

"Ten to nine."

"He may be, or he may be at my apartment. Won't it keep?" I negotiated the bridge across Beale Creek, a dry, boulder-strewn streak of gravel at that season.

"'It' will keep, but my resolution won't. I'm going to make a confession. They say it's good for the soul."

I clutched the wheel and drove very, very carefully. I did my best to beat back my imagination, but I had never believed Miguel guilty of Llewellyn's death and there *was* a murderer at large. If the murderer was Winton D'Angelo, I wasn't going to do or say anything to trigger him off.

Fortunately there wasn't much traffic on the road. D'Angelo appeared to be drowsing. His eyes were closed. I entered Monte on the old highway, which turns into Main Street at the first set of traffic lights. My apartment was closer than the courthouse, so I drove slowly around back. Jay's Blazer was in the bank vice president's slot, and there were lights above.

"He's home." Oh, the relief.

D'Angelo gave a slight start and straightened up. "Yet once more into the breach . . ."

I parked. "I'm going to take you up the back way. The press has been camping on my doorstep."

"Circumspection called for." He giggled. "I'm a doctor of circumspection." He sounded more drunk than he had at the Huffs. However, he followed me up the back stairs quietly.

Jay was sitting on the couch reading a sheaf of papers. He was wearing his favorite off-duty outfit—cutoffs and a T-shirt—and looked freshly showered to me. I don't know how he looked to D'Angelo. Unkempt, probably. D'Angelo was a natty dresser. "You're home early . . ." His voice trailed when he looked up and saw D'Angelo. He set the papers on the coffee table and got to his feet.

"Win has a confession to make," I said in what I hoped was a neutral voice.

Jay met D'Angelo's eyes for a long, unsmiling moment. "I think it's more likely Professor D'Angelo has something to add to his statement." He looked at me. "Coffee?"

"Good idea." I tossed my handbag at the couch and went into the kitchen. As I loaded up the automatic brewer, I could hear Jay and D'Angelo exchanging courtesies. The little light came on, the machine burped, and coffee began to trickle into the pot. I went back into the living room.

". . . if you have a tape recorder," D'Angelo was saying.

"Is it going to be necessary?"

Jay had seated D'Angelo on my grandma's platform rocker, the most comfortable chair I own.

D'Angelo ran a hand through his hair. "Well, I thought . . ."

"Why don't you just give me your explanation? We can worry about the formalities later." Jay sat on the couch. I slid in beside him.

"If that's all right . . ."

"Sure."

D'Angelo cleared his throat, then looked away, giving a tight little laugh. "Jesus, this is not easy." He drew a breath. "I wouldn't tell you at all if I thought I had a chance of getting away with it, but Mary Dailey is coming. She'll bring Dai's papers with her—*we* will, because we'll meet the lawyers and get the stuff from the town house together. That was her suggestion."

Jay said nothing. He looked casual, relaxed even, but I could feel his coiled-spring tension.

"Dai kept a personal journal, you see." D'Angelo drew another breath. At that rate he was going to hyperventilate.

Jay said mildly, "Take it easy, Professor D'Angelo."

"Oh hell, don't be so formal. Did the three of us freeze our asses together in Dai's lake or did we not?" A brave attempt at jauntiness.

"We did."

The chair rocked. "The thing is, I had an affair with Dai one summer at the lodge.

Jay nodded. I kept very still.

D'Angelo closed his eyes, opened them. "It was fourteen years ago. I was married by then, and my wife and kids came up with me. Hal, that was Dai's lover, got jealous. He told Paula what was happening. She took the kids and . . ." His voice broke.

Jay stirred beside me but said nothing.

D'Angelo cleared his throat. "The upshot was she divorced me and kept the boys. She also threatened to expose my . . . conduct to my colleagues at Presteign. It's a good school, but private and church-related. So she had me over a barrel."

I must say my sympathies at that point were with the former Mrs. D'Angelo. I tried to keep a blank face.

D'Angelo was gripping the wooden armrests, very hard. Every time he moved the chair creaked and rocked a little. "That school year was hell," he went on in a low, tight voice. "I was up for tenure. My publications were okay and I'm a pretty good teacher, so I suppose they would have awarded me a permanent contract, but I couldn't take the strain of waiting."

I heard the coffee maker giving its last grumbles and slipped out to the kitchen, but I kept my ears tuned. I poured two cups.

"Paula got the boys, half my salary, and the house we were buying." The chair creaked. "She stayed there, licking her wounds and biding her time. Sooner or later, the lid was going to blow off. The Monte position was the first thing that came along, and I grabbed at it. I said I wanted a change of scene because of the divorce." He gave another tight laugh. "Some of my friends even believed me, though Monte was a long step down the academic ladder."

I brought him his mug. "Cream?"

"What? Oh, no thanks." His hands shook when he raised the cup to his lips, but he drank a little.

I went back to the couch.

Jay said quietly, "Did the relationship with Llewellyn continue?"

"No!" He bit his lip. "It's damned hard to explain this. You see, Dai . . . I guess the word would be seduced . . . he seduced me when I was an undergraduate at Muir. I don't mean to suggest it was rape. I was . . . willing."

Beside me, Jay stirred again, but he said nothing.

D'Angelo took a hasty sip, burned his tongue, and swore. "I was an awful kid, what my students would call a nerd, and Dai was a suave sophisticate. I enrolled in his seminar on modern poetry. Dai liked my writing. His attention was enormously flattering, and he was . . . charming."

"I met him," Jay said. "Remember?"

"Yeah, but when he was younger . . ." He set his cup down, leaving the thought unfinished. "So he persuaded me into his bed a couple of times. Then he went on to better things." His mouth twisted. "I was devastated and confused. I thought I hated him, but I still needed his approval—of my work, I mean. Surprisingly enough, I continued to get it."

"Then you left Muir and went to graduate school," Jay murmured.

"Yeah. I met Paula in a Spenser seminar and we fell in love." He was frowning now, as though puzzled. "You probably don't believe that, but it was true. I loved Paula, and I found her desirable. All this stuff about gay rights and coming out of the closet and so on, it's a good thing. It's good if you're not, well, ambivalent. I'm ambivalent."

"Bisexual?" Jay suggested, cautious.

D'Angelo heaved a sigh. "If you have to have a label. Believe me, I've tried to understand my . . . peculiar orientation. But Dai was my only experience of a male lover. And I'd always been a nerd, so my experience with women was limited, too. I was susceptible to being loved."

"Who isn't?" Jay said mildly.

D'Angelo picked up his mug, drank a good swallow of cooling coffee, and set his cup on the end table. "In any case, I kept on needing Dai's academic approval, and I got it. I'm a critic, not a poet, but he liked my approach to poetry, wrote me glowing recommendations, even offered me advice on my dissertation—good advice. I owe . . . owed him my academic career."

Jay rubbed his nose. "You must have had considerable talent and energy to finish out a Ph.D. program. I doubt that you owe your career to Llewellyn or anyone else."

D'Angelo flushed, but he looked less as if he were going to fall to bits on my carpet. The rocking chair creaked. "Well, I worked hard, but connections matter. I *felt* as if I owed it all to Dai. I was flattered to be invited to the lodge when the invitation came. Hell, so was Paula." He paused, brooding.

I swallowed coffee.

"Strangely enough," he went on, "I no longer found him sexually exciting. I went along . . ."

"For old times' sake?" Jay's measured sarcasm made D'Angelo sit up straight.

The rocking chair gave a large creak. "You don't believe me."

"I'm trying to understand what you're saying, D'Angelo. Your heart wasn't in the summer fling, but you went along."

"Yeah. Afterward I could see Dai had been using me to provoke Hal. By then it was too late. Paula and the boys were gone. He ruined my life . . ."

"Isn't that a little melodramatic?"

"Christ, who's supposed to be the literary critic?"

Jay smiled.

D'Angelo heaved a big sigh. "I'll try to more precise. It felt at the time as if he had ruined my life. I hated him and hated myself for needing his . . . love or approval or whatever you want to call it. The worse part was losing my sons. That was a kind of death." He looked at his hands. "I was a good father. I'd started Mikey in Little League, and I was looking forward to all that . . . that *Leave It to Beaver* stuff. I missed my kids horribly."

"Didn't you have visitation rights?" I asked, incredulous.

"I didn't ask for fear Paula would tell the judge why not. She would have, too. I saw them, supervised, one afternoon a month until I moved to Monte. Then we had to make do with phone calls and letters. I wrote great letters."

I felt my eyes sting with sympathetic tears. I'm a sucker for good fathers.

"Five years ago Paula and I came to an arrangement. The boys spend a month with my parents in Sonoma County every summer. I go down and we spend August together. She's still suspicious, though. She never told the boys why we got divorced, but Mike's a college student now, plenty old enough to wonder, and I'm having a hell of a time reestablishing any kind of father-son rapport with him. He's a bright kid, but he's rebellious. Fortunately, both boys like their stepfather."

"So your life didn't come to an end after all, and you kept on visiting Llewellyn's lodge until he died and left you in charge of his foundation."

D'Angelo started at the sudden harshness. So did I. Jay's hand closed briefly on mine. I subsided.

"He felt guilty." D'Angelo's eyes pleaded. "He knew what had happened, how I felt about losing my family and my place at Presteign. He was remorseful. Maybe I played on that. I wanted him to know how rotten it was for me."

"You knew about the directorship?"

"Yes. After Hal's death Dai put his estate in order. Last year he told me how he wanted the foundation administered. And he promised me the directorship."

Jay was silent for maybe a minute. I could tell he was turning D'Angelo's story over in his mind.

D'Angelo bit his lip. "I'm getting married."

Jay's eyebrows shot up.

"To a woman who knows as much as I know about my peculiarities and wants to marry me anyway. She's had her own experiments and failures. We decided we've both had enough solitude. And enough charades. The directorship will free me of the need to masquerade as good old Win, man-about-town and universal escort. I'm forty-five years old. I don't kid myself. I love Martha, partly because she loves me and mostly because she's a damned attractive human being. I'm also looking forward to having someone to talk to at breakfast."

Jay leaned forward and picked a sheaf of papers up from the coffee table. "Why did you decide to tell me all this now, sir?"

"Mary Dailey . . ."

"Yes, I can see that would be awkward, but names in the journal are in a private code . . ."

"You've seen it?"

Jay gestured with the sheaf. "The current volume was in

Llewellyn's room at the lodge. I had it photocopied and asked the San Francisco police to secure the rest of his private papers. There were a lot of them. I got a bale of photocopies yesterday afternoon, and I've been sifting through them since."

D'Angelo leaned back in the chair, eyes closed. Creak, creak went the rocker.

"The journal is kind of like a painter's sketchbook. Pictures in words, phrases. Like notes for poems."

D'Angelo's eyes opened wide. "My God, what a bonanza that would be for a critical biography. You could see the stages of a poem from its inception."

Jay nodded. "I guess so. There isn't a lot of stuff about people, except for his relationship with Hal Brauer. He kept a running account of their emotional ups and downs."

"I wonder whether I was an up or a down?" D'Angelo mused.

I could see Jay swallow a grin.

D'Angelo must have, too. He smiled wryly. "You said the names were in code."

"Yes. He wrote enough about other people so you can tell when he was having an affair, or a family feud, or any other emotional upheaval, but he didn't go into detail. The relationship with Denise Fromm, for instance. I picked up on most of those references."

D'Angelo shook his head, disbelieving. "Denise . . ."

"Anyway, I might not have been sure about your connection with him just from reading the journal."

"I didn't know that."

"Maybe not, but why hand me a motive for murder?" Jay laid the papers down again. "Reinforce a motive for murder. The directorship was a motive in itself, and I was puzzled . . ."

"That he'd name an undistinguished jerk from a jerkwater school to head his big foundation?"

"I knew you'd been his student."

"So was Mary Dailey. So were a lot of people." D'Angelo got up. "Shit, it's ten-thirty already. I have to get up at five."

He walked to my window and looked out. "I told you because it was safe."

Jay stood up, too. "Safe?"

"You have the murderer, or you will have when you catch up with the Mercedes. I'm trying to clear my desk, Dodge. Metaphorically speaking. Dai gave me a chance to start over professionally."

"And you'll be starting a new marriage, too."

"That's right. This time around I want everything out in the open."

A short silence fell. Jay said mildly, "I ought to warn you not to leap to conclusions. The case isn't closed."

D'Angelo turned from the window and stared. "Even so."

"Even if Miguel isn't the poisoner?"

"Why do you say that? He ran."

"I'm hypothesizing, Professor D'Angelo."

D'Angelo nodded. He understood that kind of thinking. "Even if Miguel isn't the murderer, I think my motive would come way down the list. There are the Peltzes, who thought they were going to inherit, and Fromm, who did."

"It *is* a big estate."

"And Denise, who would love to do the woman scorned. Even the Huffs with their seed money." He drew a breath. "No, if I'd wanted to murder Dai, I would have done it fourteen years ago. I didn't want him dead. I just wanted to see him squirm."

There was more talk, of course. Jay needed a formal statement. He was willing to wait for it, though. He had corroboration of D'Angelo's story in the coded journal and a witness to the story (me) in case D'Angelo decided to recant. I didn't think he would. He seemed relieved to have the story off his chest. At eleven Jay drove D'Angelo to his apartment.

I sneaked a look at the famous journal. Llewellyn's handwriting was cramped and, as Jay had said, most of the entries were word pictures. Images. After all, he had been an imagist.

I love my mother.

I thought I'd better say that at the outset. What's more, she's a good poet.

She's also five two. When I'm with her I feel huge and inarticulate. I'm aware that the problem is mostly in my mind, but that doesn't make the feeling go away. With 3,000 miles between us, we get along well.

I reached San Francisco around 8:00 A.M., and the St. Francis Hotel in time for breakfast. Ma had already asked room service to send up eggs Benedict, assorted fruits, and lots of coffee. The cart arrived as we disentangled ourselves from the flurry of greeting. She was wearing a neat little gray faille suit, gloves, no hat. I was wearing a dark cotton print and flats. I felt like a dark cotton giraffe. Ma told me I looked just right. She checked out of the hotel at ten. I stowed her bag with the bell captain and hailed a taxi.

The memorial service had been scheduled for ten-thirty, but it started fifteen minutes late. By then half the academic poets in North America and a sprinkling of the rest, a segment of the gay community, a segment of the financial community, assorted representatives of the publishing industry, including the Huffs, a dozen lawyers, and Angharad Peltz's parents had assembled in the vast interior of the cathedral. Neither Ted nor Angharad showed up.

The organist was playing a Bach prelude. Llewellyn had

been cremated, so there was no casket. I could see through the floral arrangements in front of the altar rail that the priest was set to enter. As the organ swooped, a rustle, like wind on a wheat field, ran through the assembled mourners. I turned and looked back down the long aisle. Denise was making an Entrance.

She wore a black dress, chiffon with flowing sleeves, and a black summer hat with the hint of a veil. The outfit was vaguely nunnish. It suggested a great deal but stated nothing. Her face was composed, stark. Her hands clasped a black Prayerbook. Escorted by an usher and Dennis, she moved slowly up the center aisle.

Denise's looks were dramatic rather than beautiful and when she opened her mouth she invariably betrayed herself, but could that woman move.

I discovered I had been holding my breath. I let it out in a long sigh. Every step Denise took expressed grief, loyalty, pain reined in by dignity, yet it wasn't possible to analyze how she created the effect. Watching her, I understood at last that she was a consummate artist.

At her left hand, Dennis, in a dark suit, was red with embarrassment. The usher looked apprehensive. Denise moved serenely on.

When they reached the front of the church I thought she was going to demand to be seated in the family pew. I could even imagine her huge eyes flashing. However, she did nothing so vulgar. Head bowed, she made an infinitely graceful gesture of resignation and allowed herself to be seated in the second row. The occupants, lawyers by the look of them, moved aside for her as if they had been cued. She took her seat. Dennis, ears scarlet, sat beside her on the aisle.

A low murmur from the congregation—audience?— indicated that I was not the only one who was impressed. My mother stirred and I bent to hear.

"Magnificent," Mother murmured. She was, as usual, right on target.

I believe the Joneses, Angharad's mother and father, had

chosen the service. The conventional Episcopal funeral rite had dignity and a certain elegance, but it was also impersonal. The priest gave a sermon rather than a eulogy. He referred to untimely and violent death in a sensible way. He offered comfortable ideas about resurrection. He did not allude to Llewellyn's sexual preference, said nothing of children born out of wedlock, and mentioned poetic pioneering in only the most general way. I suppose it was a wise decision. Bill Huff must surely have been disappointed. I think the poets were, too.

Afterward—when we had watched the Joneses leave, heads high, and seen Denise droop past on Dennis's arm—we all adjourned to a large reception area. The Joneses received condolences at one end of the room. At the other, Denise stood receiving the unplanned homage of anyone with a speck of human curiosity, including several members of the press. Dennis was there, too, large and embarrassed. I wondered if the mourners were congratulating him. *I* gave him a kiss.

When Mother had paid her respects we went looking for poets. Since many of them were looking for her, we did not seek in vain. Soon she was deep in a discussion of the problems of editing a writer who had revised even his most successful works repeatedly. That had been a consideration in the definitive editions of other poets—Yeats, Auden, Ransom—so the subject drew the scholars, too.

Everyone seemed to know that Ma would be looking for an editor. That added urgency to the debate. Most of the poets favored following the artist's changes. The scholarly solution was a variorum edition. Some literary historians argued for the best-known versions of the poems.

I stood at the edge of this swirling controversy and looked for Winton D'Angelo. Finally I spotted him by the coffee urn in the company of a handsome, squarish woman I took to be Martha Finn. I had seen her play Gertrude so I knew she could exude a ripe sexuality when she wanted to, but she looked anything but flamboyant in person. She and D'Angelo seemed to be marking time. I detached myself and drifted toward them.

Halfway across the large room I was waylaid by Bill Huff.

"Morning." His eyes looked like poached eggs.

"Hullo, Bill. Where's Lydia?"

He gestured toward the Joneses. Lydia was standing next to Ann Jones, head bent, listening to something the woman was saying. Mrs. Jones was small, with Llewellyn's elegant bone structure, and she was dressed with understated elegance. Her husband looked as if he wished he were playing golf. Lydia cocked her head and said something, patting Ann Jones's arm.

I returned my attention to Bill. "Nice service."

"Yes." He looked disappointed. Maybe he had expected a newsworthy scene at the funeral, Ted Peltz rampaging through the sanctuary or something.

"Janey didn't come with you?"

He grunted. "She's house-sitting."

"Cat-sitting?"

He snorted. "The kid can't stand those cats. They make her sneeze. She and Lydia had a fight after you left last night. Cat fight."

I smiled politely at his witticism, wondering why Janey, an adult woman with a decent job, spent her vacation in the house of a stepmother she obviously disliked. Lydia's feelings were less clear, though I had detected a note of amused contempt in some of her remarks about Janey. I was glad I had been spared parental divorce and remarriage. Mother-daughter relations were difficult enough, let alone step-mother-stepdaughter.

Bill interrupted my train of thought. "Uh, Lydia said to tell you she'd like to meet your mother."

"Sure. I'll work it in when the debate cools."

He gave me the poached-egg stare.

"A little dispute over the definitive edition of Llewellyn's poems. They're going at it hot and heavy."

"Oh."

117

I concluded that Huff Press poets were entirely Lydia's province. Otherwise he would have known what I was talking about. "Never mind, Bill. I'll see to it when I've said hello to D'Angelo and Martha Finn." I oozed off, leaving him looking as forlorn as an abandoned child.

D'Angelo introduced me to his future wife in neutral tones.

We shook hands. "Awful, wasn't it? Llewellyn may have had his faults, but he was a first-rate poet. He deserved better."

"The service was not without its dramatic moments."

She threw back her head and laughed. "My God, what a wonderful woman. Has she ever considered theater? I mean acting in plays, as opposed to what we saw today. I suppose her voice is untrained."

"You could ask." If Denise took up acting, maybe she'd ease off Dennis and Ginger.

We talked for a while about voices that didn't fit the speakers' personalities. With Denise the problem wasn't so much her voice as what she said. D'Angelo listened and sipped coffee. Finally he murmured, "I'm supposed to join your mother at the town house in about an hour. It would be less harrowing if I'd met her."

I looked at the eddying poets. "Let's go get it over with, then. She's predisposed to like you, you know."

"Oh?"

"Llewellyn told her you were willing to do the shitwork."

After a startled pause, Martha Finn laughed her throaty laugh. D'Angelo's tension seemed to ease.

As we made our way through the thronged lawyers, I saw that Lydia had crashed the party. She was standing at Ma's right hand and saying something so hearty it shook the fringes of her hand-loomed shawl. Ma wore the blank look she puts on when she's about to say something awful like, "Do I know you?"

I picked up my pace. "Mother . . ."

She raised an eyebrow at me.

"I see you've met Lydia. Huff Press," I added with a warning grimace.

Ma's blankness gave way to comprehension. She said a flattering word about a chapbook the press had printed that spring.

Lydia's gray eyes lit and she was off on a technical discussion of the problem of woodcuts in computerized publishing. I let her talk for a while, then interrupted her as ruthlessly as she had apparently interrupted Ma's conversation with the poets, who were now drifting in Denise's direction. Someone had found Denise a chair. She was surrounded by admirers.

"Ma, this is your partner in crime."

"Really, Lark."

"Winton D'Angelo."

Mother brightened and shook hands with D'Angelo and Martha. Lydia watched the introductions with a proprietary air, shawl adroop, but she made no further attempt to monopolize the conversation. By the time we went out to hail a taxi, I could see that Mother had warmed to her. It's hard to resist eager admiration.

We were running late. I would have liked to have had time to savor Llewellyn's town house—decor and view. Llewellyn's taste had been cheerfully eclectic—a jade horse here, a French seascape there—but the whole had a lived-in charm that expressed the happier side of the poet's personality. I waited in a little brick-walled garden, a glass of wine in my hand, while the lawyers gave my mother and D'Angelo Llewellyn's papers. There were legal formalities. Finally we called another cab, whipped by the St. Francis for Mother's bag, and made it to the airport in time to board the small propjet.

D'Angelo and Martha had left before we did with the papers, nor had either of the Joneses come to the town house. I supposed it would belong to Dennis. It was hard to imagine him in a setting so essentially urban. Denise, however, would be in her element.

* * *

The flight north was bumpy and noisy. Ma dozed. I stared down at the dun-colored valleys and earthquake-scarred hills below. North of Red Bluff the air turned calmer. We flew by the west face of Mt. Shasta. It was short of snow, thanks to the drought, but Ma was impressed. We landed at Weed at five-thirty. Jay didn't meet us.

That was not a problem, though Ma seemed disappointed. *I* was disappointed. I wondered if there had been some development in the investigation. Had Miguel surfaced? We declined rides with D'Angelo and the Huffs, climbed into Ma's rented car, and headed north.

The drive to Monte takes about an hour. I was at the wheel. At first we talked family. Then Mother commented on the service and the reception. She seemed fascinated with Denise, whom she had seen dance thirty years earlier. She talked about her friends among the poets. She didn't mention D'Angelo. Of Lydia she said merely, "That is an ambitious woman."

We wound slowly up the wooded slope of the Siskiyous, where almost every turn produces a spectacular view. Ma was drinking in the scenery. After a while she said, "Tell me about the investigation. I gather the young chauffeur did it."

I hesitated. There had been little talk of the murder at the reception, probably because everyone was making the assumption Mother had made. "He's still missing," I said neutrally.

She sighed. "I suppose Dai used him. Dai was a good poet, but being a good poet doesn't necessarily translate into being a good person. Sometimes the opposite. Frost was a difficult man, Thomas an alcoholic."

"I liked Llewellyn."

"Yes, darling, but you didn't have to put up with him day in and day out. He had the arrogance of wealth as well as an artistic ego, a double load. I've seen him deliver crushing snubs."

"Are you saying he was asking for it?"

"Heavens. No, I'm just trying to understand. If Hal had killed Dai, I wouldn't have been surprised. They provoked each other deliberately sometimes."

I supposed Llewellyn's affair with D'Angelo could be classified as provocation. I didn't say anything to Ma about it. She'd find out sooner or later. "There's the money, too."

"But surely Dai didn't leave the boy much." She was still thinking of Miguel as the murderer.

When I didn't reply she went on, "Doesn't your . . . Jay tell you what's happening?"

"In a general way. He's been digging for motives, since everyone at the lodge had means and opportunity. Miguel will get $25,000 when the estate's settled."

Ma snorted.

"Junkies have killed people for a couple of dollars. Twenty-five thousand would go a long way in Baja."

We contemplated the impact of Yankee dollars on a depressed peasant economy. I took the first Monte exit, drove to the mall, and showed Mother the bookstore. I think she found the setting disappointing. She patronized Ginger, but not grossly. We left. I was hungry, and the Eagle Cap Lodge lay fifteen miles out of town.

I drove to my apartment and handed Ma the keys to the rental. "I'll lead you out there in the Toyota. Do you want to see my apartment now or tomorrow?"

"I need a shower and dinner. Let's go on to the lodge."

There was no sign of Jay's Blazer in the lot, so I hopped into my car and led the way. Dad had rented a separate cabin the year before, so Ma's suite upstairs in the main lodge was interesting to me. Different. The manager bowed us in the door and promised to reserve us a table in the dining room.

"Oh, Lark, look!"

I shut the door and turned. Ma was standing at a low table by the French door that led to a little balcony. "Nice view?"

"I mean the flowers! I wonder who sent them?"

My eyes adjusted to the indoor light. An exuberant

bouquet of daisies in a tall vase graced the table—white daisies, lilac daisies, black-eyed Susans, the Shasta daisy.

"Maybe Dad . . ."

Ma found a card, read it, and began to laugh.

"What is it?"

She handed me the card, still chortling.

"Welcome to Monte! Goats and monkeys! Sorry I couldn't make it." It was signed "Jay."

I was pleased but a bit jealous. He had sent me a bouquet of roses when he couldn't make the play-off game and a formal arrangement for the opening of the bookstore, to which he did come, but this bouquet showed imagination. "Uh, goats and monkeys?"

"Othello welcoming the doges to Cyprus." Ma plumped onto the couch and tossed her funereal gloves at the table. "Is Jay in the throes of jealousy?"

"More likely in the throes of investigation. You wanted a shower?" I was hungry.

Ma went off to get ready. I leaned back and stared out the window. The room overlooked a formal garden and a croquet lawn. Handsome people in fashionable resort wear were strolling among the flowers.

While Ma was dressing Martha Finn called to invite us to D'Angelo's apartment for cocktails on Sunday. I offered a tentative yes.

Dinner was worth waiting for. It was nearly ten before I reached Monte. A light showed in my living room.

I trudged upstairs and unlocked the door. "Ma liked the flowers."

"Good."

"And she got the joke." I set my handbag on the coffee table. Then I took a good look at Jay. I suppose I shrieked. "What happened?"

"I had an encounter," he said around a split lip, "with a bear."

"Oh, shit. Ted Peltz." I wanted to touch him and was afraid to, so I stood in the middle of my heirloom Turkish carpet and gaped. Besides the split lip, he had a purpling contusion on his right cheekbone and he was sitting in that careful way that indicates taped ribs. His right hand was swollen.

He eased his shoulders against the sofa back. "I went out to interrogate the Peltzes and stepped . . . excuse me, dived . . . into a little domestic disturbance. Fortunately I had . . . backup." His speech was the slightest bit slurred.

I sat very gingerly on the edge of the couch and touched his face—the unbruised part. "They must have given you something."

"Pain pill. How was the trip?"

I let my hand drop to my lap. "Of all the irrelevant questions . . ."

"Hey, don't cry. He looks worse."

At that moment I hoped Ted Peltz was dead. Being a civilized person I repressed the thought, but it was there. I sniffed. "Tell me."

He meditated. "Well, I pulled up and I could see there was trouble. Peltz and his wife were on the porch. The door was open, as if she'd run out to get away from him. She was screaming, and he was smashing at her with his fists."

"Jesus."

"I called for the patrol car. Then I got out and drew my gun. I yelled at him to freeze, but he didn't stop. It was like he didn't hear me."

I shivered.

"He was whaling away at her, and she was screaming and twisting around trying to escape. He threw her against one of the posts that hold the porch up. I couldn't get a clear shot."

"So you dived in."

He was silent.

"Didn't you?"

He closed his eyes.

"Why didn't you wait for Cowan—it was Cowan?"

"Dan, yeah."

"She should have left him," I gritted. "I can't understand

123

that kind of passivity. It doesn't make sense. She must have known what he was like."

Jay said carefully, "My stepfather—my first stepfather, not Alf—was an abusive drunk. I don't mean he was always drunk or always violent. Ma married him when I was four and I guess he didn't get out of control until the second baby, Karen, came. He was almost human when he was sober." Jay had two half sisters, Judy and Karen, as well as his fifteen-year-old half brother, Freddy, Alf's son. Jay's father had been killed in Korea when he was a couple of months old.

I waited.

"Richardson didn't want another kid. After Karen was born the . . . episodes got closer together. He was getting plowed every weekend, and when he got plowed he'd go after Karen. Ma would step in, and Richardson would beat on her. That went on almost three years."

"For Godsake, why didn't your mother leave him?"

"She was a high-school graduate with no job experience. Richardson made a decent living as a farm-machinery sales-man. She was afraid to stay with him and afraid to leave him."

I couldn't say anything to that. My own life had been so far removed from the threat of poverty as to make the dilemma incomprehensible. Almost.

He went on, eyes closed, "One Saturday he got himself wasted and started in on Karen. He threw her across the room. He broke her collarbone and knocked her cold, con-cussed her. Then he sobered up and started crying. Ma took Karen to the hospital. When they released her, Ma piled us kids into the Volkswagen and left Richardson."

"How old were you?"

"Ten. It was grim for a while." He drew a breath, wincing. "But not as grim as waiting around for my stepfather to murder my mother."

I was silent.

After a long moment he said, "I think I was trying to explain to you why I didn't wait for Dan to show up."

"I understand."

He looked at me. "No, you don't." He shut his eyes again. "I had this theory I would wade in and administer a choke hold. Mind you, that's a no-no, but I was well taught and I thought I could do it. Theory bumped up against fact."

"It didn't work?" A choke hold is supposed to render a perpetrator unconscious by cutting off the supply of blood to the brain. It sometimes does that permanently.

Jay said wryly. "It made him mad. Madder."

"Then what?"

"Then we rolled down the steps and across the yard. Tearing into it. He threw me against the satellite dish. That's when my ribs got it."

My hands were clenched in my lap. I flexed the fingers. "And?"

"He may be heavier, but I'm quicker. Also he was carrying a lot of blubber. I was bashing his head against the edge of the satellite dish when Dan pulled me off him."

I waited.

"I think Dan must have used the choke hold, but I'll deny it under oath. That fucker was on something, maybe angel dust, maybe crack. Feeling no pain."

"An animal."

"Whatever. When Dan got the cuffs on Peltz he radioed for the chopper. This time it came. They flew Mrs. Peltz to County Hospital, and they think they'll be able to prevent permanent brain damage. He fractured her skull."

"My God."

"The ambulance came, too. The medics strapped me up and hauled Peltz to the hospital, with Dan riding shotgun."

"Remind me to buy Cowan a six-pack."

"Goddamn, Lark, don't patronize Dan," Jay said through clenched teeth. "He's a good cop."

This was a bone of contention between us. After a moment I said, "*Two* six-packs?"

I can count on Jay's sense of humor. His mouth relaxed. "A case of Coors. Don't be cheap."

I leaned back against the couch. "When did all this happen?"

"Around eleven. The idea of sending flowers out to the hotel came to me around three. Must've been the hospital ambience."

When I didn't say anything, he went on. "I knew I'd be stuck at the hospital or the courthouse until nine at least. I was frustrated. I'd also prefer not to meet your mother looking like the wrong end of an Ali fight, but it was probably in the stars."

"Ma was flattered by the flowers."

"Good."

"Did you eat anything?"

"Please. Don't mention food."

I sat up. The couch jounced and Jay groaned. "I'm sorry. Did he hit you in the *stomach*?"

"He tried. In defense of my midsection I'm a regular tiger, though. I don't think he jarred anything loose. Except my ribs. And my professional judgment."

Quit, I started to say. Resign. Take the college job. I was ready to throw myself on the floor and beg and grovel, but it did occur to me that was not the right moment to raise the issue. I managed to bite back the words. "Tell me what I can do for you."

He sighed. "Help me out of this shirt."

"What?"

"I've been sitting here trying to figure out how to get myself undressed and into bed. It got to be a very large problem. Like the national debt."

I stood up and grasped his left hand. "Come on, tiger."

"Do I have to move?"

"If you wait, it'll get worse."

I put him to bed with another pain pill. Then I went back into the living room and thought.

I thought about Jay and about my own reaction to the Peltz story. Was I going to be able to handle that side of Jay's job? Jay was an investigator, at least temporarily a supervisor, and most of the time he pushed papers. He didn't particularly like pushing papers. I wondered if he *had* to have action, and thought miserable Freudian thoughts about the nature of accidents. Did he just happen to find himself in dangerous situations or did he seek them out subconsciously? I got a very bad headache.

My thoughts strayed, as they had been since Friday, to the murder of Dai Llewellyn. Ted Peltz would surely have been at the top of the list of suspects if Miguel had not disappeared. I wished Miguel would turn up. Sightings of the Mercedes from as far away as Arizona and Montana had consumed a lot of Jay's time during the past week.

Ted Peltz. I had been assuming a man out on bail on a serious charge would not be stupid enough to commit another crime, but my assumption was clearly wrong. He must have known he was under surveillance, yet he had assaulted his wife with deadly effect under the influence, if Jay was right, of an illegal drug. Whether stupid or not, Peltz had to be crazy. The murder of Llewellyn was a crazy act. Nothing straightforward about stewed larkspur.

Then there was Denise. If Peltz thought he had a motive for murdering Llewellyn, Denise must have known she had one. Jay believed Llewellyn had supported her—and Dennis. If that were true, then she must have expected Llewellyn to leave his son something, perhaps not as much as he had, but something. Denise had a straightforward motive for killing the old man, but she was not a straightforward woman and if she had made up her mind to commit murder, she would surely have chosen a melodramatic, even bizarre method.

If I had been inclined to regard Denise as a silly woman, my opinion had altered since the funeral. Denise was as clever as paint, and *capable de tout*.

That was a depressing thought, too. I was fond of Dennis. I wanted him to benefit from his father's death. The headache tightened around my temples. Well, there was always D'Angelo.

I could not imagine D'Angelo shooting Llewellyn or

stabbing him, face-to-face. Poison was well within his scope, though, and he had supplied us with the motive. That he had done so freely was not necessarily a sign of innocence. A clever murderer might well show such disarming frankness, so long as he believed others to be under heavier suspicion. I had no strong feelings about D'Angelo but I did like Martha Finn, so I hoped he wasn't guilty.

As for the Huffs, they had a motive of sorts. My brief experience of running a small business made me understand the importance of the canceled loans and the seed money—not a trivial motive but surely not as strong as Denise's. I had sensed that Bill was uncomfortable in Llewellyn's company. It was a mere impression, however, hardly evidence. Lydia seemed the more balanced of the two, but her interest in Llewellyn's work was clearly stronger than Bill's.

What about Janey? What about Domingo? At that point my headache reached the aspirin stage and I went into the bathroom and took two.

Jay slept heavily for about three hours. Then he started to toss and turn. I got him a pill, too.

"**Y**eow!"

"Sorry. Turn."

Jay rotated gingerly and water from the shower splattered out on the bathroom tiles. Also on me.

"Halt!" I had agreed to help remove the tidy Velcro corset from Jay's cracked ribs so he could shower, on the condition that he stand very still while I did the scrubbing. I am not into s-m. The sight of bruises, scrapes, and contusions, far from provoking ecstasy, kicks in my athletic-trainer persona and I get bossy. I was also getting very wet.

I lathered. Jay groaned—and yelped and muttered rude words. I was glad he wasn't the kind to suffer in silence, but I wished he'd censor his speech a little. I was just trying to help.

The phone rang.

"Shit. I'll get it. Stand still."

Mutter, mutter.

I squished into the bedroom.

"Lark, darling."

"Hello, Ma. Up early?" It was seven.

"Feels like the middle of the morning," she burbled. "Are you busy?"

"I was, er, in the shower."

"I'll make it quick then. I want to see Dai's lodge before I meet D'Angelo this afternoon. He gave me directions, but I'd rather you drove me. You did say your clerks were covering the store today."

"Uh, sure." I *had* said that. Incautious me. "What time?"

"Nine?"

"Okay." I could check on Ginger after lunch. I was worried about Ginger. I wondered if Denise had eaten her yet. Dennis had brought his mother home on the same flight we had taken.

When I got back to the shower Jay had turned the water off, strictly against orders, and was standing on the bath mat, dripping.

I grabbed a towel.

"If you don't mind, Lark, I'll just stand here until the water evaporates."

"I'll pat. Gently."

Eventually we got him into the Velcro contraption and some clothes. I showered, dressed, and made him drink a glass of ucky instant breakfast drink when he refused cream of wheat, eggs, and everything else I suggested. His mouth hurt, he said. I believed him. He looked as if everything hurt.

By the time Jay left for the courthouse, I was feeling downright cranky. I don't think I'm cut out to be a nurse.

I drove out to Eagle Cap Lodge rather too fast and pried my poetic parent away from her view of a mountain stream she swore purled.

"I could work here, Lark. It's beautiful."

"Tell D'Angelo to bring the papers out to you."

"No, I mean real work—poetry." She was genuinely elated. "And your father would love it. He could fish the stream . . ."

"Crick."

"I beg your pardon?"

"It's called Pumpkin Creek, and pronounced Punkin Crick, according to my sources."

She made a face. "A sadly large number of our pioneer forebears had prosaic souls."

131

"Maybe it was a very large punkin."

I'll lay odds Ma's next book contains a piece called "Punkin Crick." And it will deal poetically with prosy pioneers.

Ma ignored my comment, picked up her handbag, checked for her room key, and we were off.

On the way to the lodge I gave her a summary of Jay's encounter with Ted Peltz, and the consequences.

"The poor woman has a fractured skull?"

"That's right."

"It's fortunate Jay happened along in time to stop him."

"You wouldn't say that if you'd seen Jay's ribs."

"Was he badly injured?"

"Just bunged up. He's sore." But very clean.

I gripped the wheel tighter as the road twisted along a steep ravine. Driving was less acrophobic for me than riding as a passenger. Mother seemed unaffected. She kept making appreciative noises as vista after vista of blue fir-clad foothills unrolled below her.

As we entered a kind of tree tunnel, she said. "You'll have to visit her."

A logging truck laden with three thick cedar boles careened past. "Who, Angharad?"

"Yes, of course."

"I barely know her—and what I do know, I don't much like." Another truck. Making up for time lost to the forest fire.

"That doesn't matter."

"It does to me."

"There are occasions," said my mother, "when it's a woman's duty to stand by another woman. This is one of them, Lark."

"She's probably still in intensive care."

"Then visit the hospital and leave your name. And take a nice plant."

"Intensive-care patients can't have plants."

Ma gave an exasperated sigh. "A symbolic gesture, Lark."

We were climbing along the last stretch of forest before the lake. "I could take a slip of larkspur."

She clucked her tongue.

"Or a bouquet of *Cannabis sativa*."

"I hope your association with a policeman has not coars-ened your taste."

"Jay wallows in gross stuff. Like *Othello*," I said sullenly.
We bristled in silence the rest of the way.

At the lodge, we stood on the veranda for a while just looking at the glittering expanse of lake, then I made myself knock. According to Jay, Domingo had driven off the press by the simple expedient of yelling at them in Tagalog whenever one of them drove up.

I knocked a second time. As I prepared to knock again, the doorlatch clicked and the door opened a crack.

"Hi, Domingo," I said awkwardly. "I've brought my mother."

The door swung wide. "Mrs. Dailey."

"Oh, Domingo, it's so sad!"

I kept forgetting Mother had been a longtime friend of the household. She and Domingo fell on each other's necks, both weeping a little.

Domingo served us fresh-baked brioches in the gleaming kitchen, preserves that tasted as if he had plucked each berry himself, and his marvelous coffee. It was plain he had distracted himself from his grief by baking.

Owing to my efforts to poke protein down Jay's throat, I hadn't eaten much breakfast, so I devoured a brioche and a cup of coffee before I tuned in on the conversation.

Ma and Domingo were discussing the Philippines—then on the verge of the revolt that brought Corazon Aquino to power. Domingo had a grandniece who had had to leave the country because of persecution by the Marcos regime. She was living in San Francisco.

". . . and I'm going to help Letty set up a little restau-rant."

Ma beamed at him. "How exciting, Domingo. It must be hard to find a lease in San Francisco, though."

"Mr. Llewellyn promised me a spot on Chestnut. This

son, this Dennis, d'you think he's going to honor the boss's promise?"

"Haven't you talked with Dennis?" I licked a drop of jam from one finger.

"Not since Saturday morning. Of course I didn't know then he was the boss's son." He shook his head. "Surprised me. That Denise was always hanging around the lodge in the summer, and calling the town house, too. I should've guessed."

"Dennis is a very nice man," I said firmly. "If you like, I'll tell him you need to talk to him."

Domingo refilled my cup and Mother's, and poured himself about half a cup. "I drink too much of this stuff. Then I worry and get funny heartbeats." He sighed. Jay had been right about his English. It was fluent and virtually unaccented.

"The coffee tastes so good it's worth a few jumpy heartbeats." I took an appreciative sip.

He gave me a distracted smile that faded almost at once. "If you don't mind, Miss Lark, ask Mr. Fromm what he wants me to do. He could call me. I didn't like to leave the place vacant with that riffraff in the cabin and Miguel gone. And now Peltz is gone, too, I worry about crazies looking for souvenirs. But it's time I got back to San Francisco."

Mother said, "You know about the foundation, don't you?"

"Some outfit going to set up a summer camp for poets . . ."

I hid a grin. Camp Gitche Gumee by the shining big sea water. Poets romping through the woods and canoeing on the lake. Community sings around a campfire. Marshmallows toasting over Domingo's Jenn-Air range. Win D'Angelo blowing a whistle to bring them to order.

Mother was explaining about writers' colonies.

Domingo listened with grave attention. "Then Mr. D'Angelo's the one to talk to about the lodge?"

"D'Angelo and Dennis Fromm," Ma said. "They'll need a

caretaker. You wouldn't want to do that, but it's a pity the young chauffeur . . ."

Domingo growled.

"Do you think Miguel killed Mr. Llewellyn?" I had to ask.

His face darkened. "I think he stole the Mercedes. Maybe he killed the boss, too. Maybe not. That scum, Ted Peltz . . ." I thought Domingo was going to spit on his spotless floor, but he restrained himself.

"Jay says Ted will be out on bail by Monday if Angharad doesn't charge him with assault."

Domingo took a gulp of coffee. "I been here close to forty years, and I still don't understand your laws. They're crazy. A guy who'd marry a girl against her Papa's wishes, he's no good." He gestured with his cup. "I told the boss so, but he says little Ana has a right to her tastes. So he gives her the cabin rent-free and now look at her. She going to die, too, Miss Lark?"

"I don't think so."

He shook his head. "Letting Peltz out on bail. Crazy. I ran over to the cabin when I heard the sirens yesterday and I saw Ana, and Mr. Dodge, too, all bloodied up. Back home, if you beat up a cop . . ." He slashed his free hand across his throat. "They throw away the key. Here? Crazy."

I had to agree with that, emotionally if not politically.

Mother finished her last bit of brioche. "Will you show me around the lodge, Domingo? I want to see what will have to be done before the foundation can start inviting guests."

"Sure thing." He got up and took our cups to the sink.

I carried the plates and the jam pot to the counter. "Thanks for the brioches, Domingo. Doesn't it bother you, being all alone way out here in the wilds with a murderer running loose?"

"Ah, no." He winked. "I got protection." He pulled open a drawer by the sink. There, beneath a neatly ironed dish towel, lay a mean-looking handgun and a box of shells. "I was a guerrilla in the war, see? So I know guns. I always keep one

135

in my kitchen—here, in San Francisco, wherever we go. I can take care of myself."

I swallowed. "Uh, good. What about supplies? Do you need anything from town?"

He snorted. "There's enough stuff in the freezers to feed an army. Besides, if I need to go to town I got the Volvo."

It was a relief to know he had a car. I didn't like the idea of Domingo marooned at the lodge with Ted Peltz for company, gun or no gun, but I also didn't see turning the Toyota into a delivery wagon. Not on that road.

"Coming?" Ma called from the doorway. She had gone into the hall ahead of us. I think she missed the byplay with the gun. "Lark, darling, you must see Domingo's linen closets."

Mother's inspection of the facilities was almost embarrassing. She didn't quite count the sheets, but I could see she was thinking in practical, prosaic? terms. There would be room in the lodge for ten or twelve poets and a live-in staff of three, a rather small writers' colony, but of course there were acres and acres available for expansion.

I was impressed by the private study on the main floor. We hadn't been shown that. It was spacious enough to function as a library for a modest-sized group of writers, and contained most of the basic references. Mother made purring sounds as she inspected the shelves.

Llewellyn had used an electric typewriter. It sat on the workmanlike desk in its neat dust cover with a stack of unused typing paper beside it. The paper was already turning yellow.

I excused myself from the tour of the bedrooms, went outside, and sat on the boat dock. The sight of the deserted typewriter had made me feel sick, or maybe I had just eaten too much. I hoped Domingo would have no occasion to use his gun. He might be a famous guerrilla fighter, but he was also close to seventy. Dennis—or Win D'Angelo—ought to hire a security service and send Domingo off to his niece.

Those were my first reflections. After that I started imagining what Domingo's life had been like, serving the

136

whims of a wealthy, arrogant man, which was what Llewellyn had been, however charming. Domingo's eyes had lit up when he spoke of his new business venture. I wondered how long the restaurant had been on the books.

Llewellyn's death had freed Domingo, or would free him, to pursue what was plainly a cherished dream. Had he perhaps shortened the waiting period by slipping a little juice of larkspur into the Campari?

After all, Domingo was a chef, with access to a stove and a food processor, and thus a more logical suspect than Miguel. Perhaps Miguel had decamped because he was afraid of Domingo.

I did not recall seeing Domingo on the lawn after the Fourth of July dinner, but I hadn't been looking for him either. And he was capable of violence. He had said so, and I believed him.

"Yoo hoo!" Mother was standing on the veranda waving at me. Time to go.

We said good-bye to Domingo. Ma gave him a peck on the cheek and told him to keep her posted about his restaurant. She would tell her friends about it.

He pressed a bag of fresh brioches on me—for Jay, he said—and reminded me to tell Dennis to call him. We left.

Mother was still making great plans for the lodge when we reached the outskirts of Monte. She had fallen in love with the place. I did not doubt she would be writing there herself the next summer—or teaching a workshop. I said nothing to dissuade her, but I wasn't filled with delight at the thought.

The highway passes a nursery with a small flower shop. Ma broke off her speculations when she saw the sign and told me to pull in and find a plant for Angharad.

At that I balked. "I've got a nice book in mind for her. She can't read at the moment, but she's not allowed to have a plant either. If I'm supposed to make a futile gesture, the book will do."

"What is it?"

"A do-it-yourself divorce manual."

Ma gave an exasperated cluck. "That's sick, Lark."

"Anyway," I added hastily, "it's time for lunch."

"But we just stuffed ourselves with brioches."

"True. I have the bookstore to see to, though, and you're supposed to meet D'Angelo in half an hour. I'll run you out to his place and pick you up later."

"You ought to visit Mrs. Peltz."

"I will if you'll lay off."

Ma compressed her mouth into a tight little line, but she withdrew from the battle.

In spite of the fact that we were ten minutes early, D'Angelo opened the door for us before we had a chance to knock. He looked harassed and anxious, but he offered me coffee. I declined and left Ma inspecting the heap of notebooks and papers on his coffee table.

I drove straight to the bookstore. The press siege was over. The murder was then a week old, and nothing startling had happened since Miguel's disappearance. The stringer had moved his camper, and the rubbernecking kids had gone on to better things.

I pulled boldly up to the front entry, hopped out, and bonged my little bonger myself. I had missed it.

"Oh, wow, Lark!"

"Good heavens, Annie, what is it?"

Annie finished ringing up a customer's purchases, then ran from behind the counter. "I tried to call you. Ginger hasn't showed up and I'm on at the liquor store in fifteen minutes!"

No rest for the wicked. "Don't forget your handbag," I called as she dashed for the door. I hadn't meant to work that afternoon. Mundane chores like laundry and grocery shopping had piled up. I hoped Ginger's car hadn't broken down again.

She drifted in half an hour later as I was showing a retired professor our selection of California history. Jay had helped me stock the regional history shelf and I was proud of it, so I took my time selling the man a new account of the Donner party. When he left, I found Ginger drooping over the poetry with a feather duster in her hand and a vacant smile on her lips.

"So how did you do while I was gone? Did you have time to shelve the mysteries?"

"Uh, no. It was fine. Dennis says I'm supposed to give you notice."

"What!" Fortunately the store was empty of customers. I probably shouted.

She beamed. "We're getting married."

"Oh . . . well, great. That's wonderful news." It was awful news. Horrible. Revolting. Annie hadn't read a book since high school, and never voluntarily. I needed a clerk who thought reading books was an acceptable human activity—a clerk who knew what was in stock, a clerk who knew how to order what wasn't, a clerk who did not chew gum on duty. I needed Ginger. "When?" I croaked.

"August fifteenth." She sounded definite.

"I thought you were opposed to marriage."

"That was before Dennis asked me," she said simply. "He was so sweet, Lark. He took his mother home from the airport and came over here and proposed. Right here in this very store. There were two customers looking at maps."

"Did they applaud?"

The goofy grin again. "I invited them to the wedding. You'll come, won't you? And Jay? I want you to be my maid of honor."

"You can't get married, Ginger," I said firmly.

Her eyes widened.

"Not until you find me a replacement, and I don't mean Annie."

She laughed. "You're so funny. Dennis says you have a great sense of humor."

"I love Dennis, too," I said hollowly.

"Will you?"

"What?"

"Be my maid of honor?"

"If you want me to." This was noble self-sacrifice. I am a

139

head taller than Ginger and we weigh about the same, so we were going to look like Laurel and Hardy. "Tell me about it."

Between customers—there weren't as many as there had been but there were more than before the murder—Ginger told me all about her upcoming nuptials, which were to take place in a forest glade near Lake Alice. Shades of the '60s.

Dennis had resigned from the Forest Service. While he waited for the lawyers to prove the will, he was going to enroll in business classes at Humboldt State. He would have to learn how to manage, or at least understand, all that money. I was surprised Dennis had so much common sense, but I had the wit not to say so.

"I suppose you'll take some classes, too."

Eyes shining, Ginger clutched the feather duster to her shirt. "I'll be able to go to school full-time, and I can major in lit or art history—or whatever I want to. Oh, gee, Lark, I don't believe this is happening to me. And he's going to adopt the kids!"

We both got teary at that point. The customer who entered looking for *Pet Sematary* must have thought we were crazy. When he left, I let Ginger lyricize. It was awhile before either of us mentioned Denise. Somehow I didn't see Denise as the step-grandmother type.

I finally got brave. "Has Dennis told Denise?"

Ginger's face clouded. "Yeah, on the plane. She wants me to go out and see her—'call on her,' for Godsake, like some kind of old movie. I'm scared of her, Lark."

"What can she do to you? Dennis is a grown man, and he's the one who inherited. She wasn't even mentioned in the will."

"That's true." Ginger brooded. "And right now Dennis is mad at her—for not telling him about his father. Dennis is so softhearted, though. He'll forgive her, Lark, and then what'll I do?"

"Tell Dennis to give her the town house and pension her off." I described Llewellyn's San Francisco house in lavish detail to distract her. I could see the idea taking hold. It wasn't a bad one, even from Denise's viewpoint. Besides, I couldn't imagine either Dennis or Ginger living comfortably in a city.

A flurry of customers interrupted us. As they were leaving, I happened to glance at my watch. "Lord, it's two-thirty already. I'm supposed to go over to the hospital and visit Angharad Peltz. Do we have any wrapping paper?"

Ginger thought taking a book to a person with a fractured skull was a weird idea, but she helped me rustle up some white tissue paper and lace florist's ribbon left over from the opening. I didn't have greeting cards, but there were a couple of boxes of notepaper with noncommittal pen-and-ink drawings of Mt. Shasta. No saccharine verses. I broke one of the boxes open, wrote a get-well-soon message, and signed my name.

I didn't actually have the bad taste to give Angharad the divorce manual, though it was what she needed. A craftsy, small-press selection of Emily Dickinson's poems seemed like a suitable, if uninspired, gift for an English major. I wrapped the book and poked the card under the ribbon. "Back in half an hour."

"Lark . . ."

"What is it?"

"Will you go with me to see Denise?"

"What . . .Oh, no, not me. Not on your life."

"Please. Dennis says I have to see her, and she scares me."

"Make *him* go with you."

"She wants to see me alone. I mean without Dennis."

The better to eat you. "One of us has to run the store."

"Annie will be here tomorrow afternoon. We could drive out then and stay fifteen minutes. She wouldn't do anything awful with you there."

I thought of Denise at the cathedral, playing to the galleries. "Don't count on it. That lady likes an audience."

Ginger's eyes filled with tears. "Please, Lark. I'm scared."

"I'll think about it." I slid out the door and escaped.

I had had occasion before to visit County Hospital. Afternoon visiting hours were from two to four, and strictly enforced. Intensive care was on the third floor. I rode up in the elevator with a worried man in photogray glasses and an orderly pushing a cart of clean laundry.

The floor nurse informed me that only close relatives could visit intensive-care patients. That was a relief. I turned to go, but honor made me ask her where they had stashed Angharad.

"Mrs. Peltz is stable. She's been moved to a private room." She told me the number. It was on the second floor.

Foiled, I hung around waiting for the elevator though I could easily have trotted down a flight of stairs. Another thought occurred to me. I went back to the nurse. "Do you have a Ted Peltz on this floor?"

Her mouth tightened. "Are you a friend?"

"No! I just wanted to know if he'd been released."

Her mouth eased fractionally. "He was removed in the custody of two sheriff's deputies before noon. I believe he's being kept at the county jail."

"Good. Thanks." I caught her smile as I headed for the stairs. Ted must have been a wonderful patient.

Angharad's room lay at the end of a long corridor of four wards. County Hospital is not a luxury facility, but there are a couple of private rooms available at a hefty surcharge. I clutched my absurd gift and walked slowly. It was only three.

The door to the room was open but a pale-blue ribbed curtain shrouded the bed. At first I thought nobody was there. Then I heard low voices from the far side of the enclosing curtain. When I peered around the edge a man and woman looked up, frowning almost identical frowns. I recognized Angharad's parents from the memorial service.

I introduced myself and handed Mrs. Jones the slim packet. "For later. I know she can't read yet."

Mrs. Jones said something polite. Mr. Jones shook hands.

The room was, naturally, filled with flowers. I spotted a large bouquet of Lydia's delphiniums and a vase of gorgeous pink tea roses I was willing to bet were from D'Angelo.

Mrs. Jones was explaining her daughter's condition.

". . . and they had to operate to relieve the pressure on the brain. However, she regained consciousness this morning."

"Good. That's wonderful." Now what? "I'm awfully sorry it had to happen."

"They cut off her hair," Mr. Jones shook his head. He had tears in his eyes.

"It didn't *have* to happen," Mrs. Jones said sharply. "She could have left him."

My words exactly. I shivered.

"Now, Ann."

"Well, it's true. I don't understand Angharad. I never did. We have three children, Miss Dailey. The others never caused us a moment's trouble."

"Ev wrecked the BMW," Mr. Jones interposed, mild. "Be fair."

Mrs. Jones took a breath. "I am trying to hold on to my sanity here, George, and you're talking about BMWs."

Her husband wisely said nothing.

There was a moan from the bed. Mrs. Jones opened the curtain and was at her daughter's side in one movement. "What is it, Angie? Water?"

I looked at Angharad. Her head was swathed in a turban of gauze, and tubes dripped into both arms. She lay very still. All that I had expected. What I didn't expect were the black eyes.

Both her eyes were swollen shut. Blue and green bruises, hideous against her pale skin, turned her face into something from a horror movie. The left side of her jaw was swollen and bruised, too.

"They cut off her hair," her father whispered.

Angharad sighed and slipped deeper into her sleep, if it was sleep. Mrs. Jones smoothed the coverlet and came out again, closing the curtain.

"She looks awful," I muttered. A dumb thing to say, but I was shocked.

"The doctors think she'll heal without brain damage," Mrs. Jones said flatly. "But they're not sure."

143

"I'm sorry." I wanted out of that room in the worst way.
"She should have left him."

I shifted from one foot to the other. "Look, that was my first reaction, too, but what if she was trapped?"

"She could have come home."

"Could she? Maybe she didn't know that. Maybe she felt trapped." Shaky ground. I rushed on, "Being angry is natural, but shouldn't you be mad at Ted Peltz?"

"She chose him."

"Well, he probably didn't say to her, 'Hey, I want to turn you into a punching bag . . .'"

"She knew he was scum." Mrs. Jones was turning her anger away from Angharad, all right. Onto me.

I kept my mouth shut.

Mr. Jones said awkwardly, "We did warn her, you know. He wasn't her kind."

"We gave that girl every advantage," Ann Jones said through gritted teeth. "And I don't just mean money. Attention. A good, stable home. Principles. She's a graduate of Mills, for Godsake, not a high-school dropout. She threw all that down the toilet. I'm angry. I have a right to be angry."

At that point a sharp rap on the door frame made all three of us look around. Jay was standing just outside the room. He looked marginally better than he had that morning. His lip was healing. The contusion had turned green. I wondered how much of the conversation he had heard.

Mr. Jones took a step toward him. "Come in, Dodge. How's the hand? I won't offer to shake again." He gave an uneasy laugh. "Any word?"

Jay made no social gestures except a brief nod in my direction. "Ted Peltz was charged about half an hour ago. The judge will set bail Monday."

"Good, that's good." Mr. Jones was trying to sound hearty, but his eyes flicked from Jay to his wife to the closed curtain.

"How is she doing?" Jay nodded toward the bed.

"Sleeping."

"I wish you'd reconsider."

"No." Mrs. Jones folded her arms across her Liz Claiborne jacket. "We're taking her home. When she's well enough, she'll file for divorce. We'll protect her. She will not be dragged through a lawcourt."

"Do you think it's in her interests not to press the assault charge? Psychologically . . ."

"I thought you said *you* were going to charge him."

"I have," Jay said dryly. "With aggravated assault, assaulting an officer, and resisting arrest. But without your daughter's testimony, I'll be the only witness on the aggravated assault charge. I guarantee you he'll get a slap on the wrist for that, if anything, and probably six months real time on the other charges. That will give Mrs. Peltz a breather, maybe time to divorce him. Then he'll be out rampaging around the country again."

"Let him." Ann Jones's jaw stuck out. "He won't get at Angie."

"Are you going to keep her prisoner the rest of her life?" Mr. Jones made a rumbling protest.

"And what about the other women he'll victimize?"

"We're responsible for our daughter's well-being."

Jay shrugged. "Good luck. Lark?"

I went to him and we walked to the elevator in silence. Just as the door opened, Mr. Jones caught up with us.

"Listen, Dodge, right now Ann's scared and confused. I'll talk to Angie when I can. If she wants to press charges, I'll back her."

Jay nodded.

"And I've notified the lawyers . . ." Jones flushed. "The ones we hired for them when the government brought the drug charges. I told Ted's attorney we wouldn't underwrite his defense."

"A wife can't be compelled to testify against her husband."

"She can if she wants to, though."

"She'll be afraid to testify. I won't badger you, Mr. Jones, but I think she should be encouraged to press the assault charge. If you try to pretend it didn't happen, that's another way of saying you think he had a right to bash her head in. She'll internalize that—and she'll go right on being a victim."

"The scandal . . ."

"Spouse abuse is pretty widespread, Mr. Jones. In the best families."

Jones shook his head. "Well, we'll see. Ann doesn't want . . . there's this murder, too. Her uncle was enough of an embarrassment when he was alive. Now he's dead . . ."

"That case is still wide open," Jay said coolly. "If it turns out that Peltz killed Llewellyn in the belief that your daughter was going to inherit, she *will* be dragged through the courts. Probably as an accessory. The sooner she distances herself from Peltz, the better."

The whites of Mr. Jones's eyes were showing.

"Good afternoon." The elevator door had opened. Jay shoved me in and stepped in after me, jabbing the lobby button.

Neither of us said a word until we reached the parking lot. Jay had parked the Blazer beside my Toyota. He had put his sunglasses on and his face looked like Mt. Rushmore. Blank and forbidding.

"They're crazy," I burst out. "How can they? Ted Peltz ought to be prosecuted to the limit of the law. It's not right."

He didn't say anything.

"Did you expect that?"

He shrugged one shoulder. "Pretty much. They're respectable people."

"They're irresponsible morons. It's not fair to Angharad. My God, you saw her face." That was stupid. I bit my lip.

"I'm going to go out to the house tonight, Lark. I'll call you tomorrow."

"Jay . . ."

"I'm out of clean shirts."

"Mother wants to meet you."

"Yes, well, later. How's the store?"

"Ginger gave me notice. She and Dennis are getting married."

He stopped with his car keys halfway to the lock. "What does Denise have to say to that?"

"Call me tomorrow and I'll tell you," I said coldly. "I'm supposed to chaperone Ginger when she goes out to receive the maternal blessing."

He took off the sunglasses. His eyes were dark as a bog. "No shit? Take care of yourself, Lark."

"Why do you say that? It's Ginger who needs a backup."

"Ginger, too. That is one dangerous woman."

Having seen Denise in action at the memorial service, I had to agree. All the same, Jay's withdrawal hurt me. Had I or had I not lathered the man all over his body only that morning? "I hope you ate something," I muttered.

"Blueberry yogurt."

"Wonderful. Good-bye." I got into the Toyota and started the engine. For once it caught smoothly. I pulled out of the parking lot while he was still climbing into the Blazer.

I picked my mother up at half past five and showed her my apartment, refrigerator and all. She told me I ought to buy a box of Arm & Hammer.

We had dinner at La Casa Verde. The fashion for Mexican food had transformed it from a grimy cantina into a ferny grotto with real tablecloths. Fortunately the menu hadn't changed much.

Ma tried the salsa, blinking back involuntary tears. It was hot stuff. "Where's Jay?"

"At the courthouse, or at his place washing shirts and eating yogurt."

"Yogurt?"

"Because of the split lip and cracked ribs."

She blinked. "Inconvenient. Is he avoiding me?"

"Probably." Or me.

She brooded. I brooded. Our food came and we poked at it. The waitress, a bubbly blonde, asked us if something was wrong with our dinners. We reassured her.

I dipped a prawn into the spicy sauce. "Did you and Win D'Angelo work out a plan of action?"

Ma sighed. "We spent an hour or so talking about Dai's work. D'Angelo is knowledgeable. Maybe I said something that led him to believe I doubted his credentials, though. He told me a tale about Dai breaking up his marriage."

150

"I thought he'd probably get to that."

"You know about it?"

I described the Thursday night confessional.

Ma took a sip of Dos Equis. Beer is the appropriate liba-
tion for Mexican food unless you're into margaritas. "I'm
afraid I believed him."

"Afraid?"

"Dai was not always scrupulous."

"I'll say he wasn't. Seducing undergraduates while they
were enrolled in his classes! These days he'd find himself in a
sexual harassment suit so fast he wouldn't know which way
was up."

"I suppose so."

"For Godsake, Ma, that's gross abuse of power."

"It used to be fairly common, at least between male professors and female students."

"That's a justification?"

"Students have always had crushes on their professors."

"But most professors show a little restraint. Llewellyn
used his position to create a harem."

Ma cut a bite of grilled chicken breast, *pollo asado*. "I said
he could be unscrupulous."

"It does cast light on the problem of literary influence."

"Whereas the wonderful world of sports is pure and free of
corruption."

I had to concede the point, though seduction was less
common among athletes than bribery.

Mother poked at her rice. "Granted Dai used D'Angelo,
didn't that give D'Angelo a motive to murder him?"

"A fairly strong one. But everyone who was at the lodge,
except Janey Huff and Jay, had a motive to murder Llewellyn,
though I wasn't sure Domingo had one until today."

"The restaurant?"

I nodded. "The media folks suggested *I* did it to publicize
my bookstore. Or didn't you notice?"

Mother looked depressed. "You know I don't watch TV."

"Are you going to be able to work with D'Angelo?"

"Yes, but I'm worried about the foundation. He has the directorship sewed up for five years. He could wreck Siskiyou Summit permanently."

"I think he wants to make it work."

"Probably, but can he?"

"He's been running the English department at Monte for a long time."

"It is not the same thing."

"No, it's a lot more difficult. The governor just sliced the education budget again, the federal administration cut student loan funds, displaced homemakers and unemployed loggers are beating at the doors, and professors are moving east to greener pastures as fast as they can. In spite of that, the department has a reputation for being tough but fair, and D'Angelo has managed to keep some good faculty. Running a fat private foundation that will pamper a dozen hand-picked poets will be duck soup after that."

"You're mixing your metaphors."

"That's what comes of a public education."

"I have never understood your defensiveness."

"Nope," I said, cheering up, "you never have." Bennington, Mother's alma mater, is now the most expensive college in the nation, including Harvard.

"Ohio State was your choice, and we let you make it."

Under protest.

Standoff. We declared an unspoken truce and Ma changed the subject. "How's the bookstore?"

I polished off the last prawn. "Ginger gave notice."

That made her sit up. "That's unfortunate. Did she say why?"

"She's going to marry Dennis Fromm."

Ma stared. "I must say, she lost no time."

"He lost no time," I corrected. "Which is to his credit because Ginger is the best thing that ever happened to Dennis, including the inheritance. They're going to spend their honeymoon at Humboldt State."

Ma blinked.

"As far as Ginger is concerned, going to school full-time represents the height of decadent luxury. By this time next year she'll know better, of course. Dennis is going to take classes, too. He wants to learn how to read stock reports and hire slick tax lawyers."

Ma took a swallow of beer. "Doesn't his mother object to the marriage?"

That reminded me of my semipromise to go out to Denise's house with Ginger the next day. I told Mother about Ginger's plea.

Her eyes gleamed. "Take me with you."

"Ma," I said patiently, "I'm fond of Ginger. I want to help her."

"I do, too." Mother looked bland and benignant.

"You don't give one small damn about Ginger. You just want to see the fireworks."

"I'll have a moderating influence on *la belle* Denise."

"Don't count on it." The waitress removed our plates.

We declined the deep-fried ice cream. While we waited for our coffee, I thought Mother's proposition over. Her presence would provoke Denise to a bravura performance, but it would also give Ginger status. A little exercise in class warfare.

"All right." I stirred my coffee. "You can come if you promise to sit there and look poetic."

Ma beamed at me.

"One o'clock. Have you driven your rental yet?"

"No, but it's an automatic. I won't have any trouble." She sipped. "Do we rendezvous at the bookstore?"

"Yes. Annie comes on at one."

"Excellent. Now," Mother said demurely, "I want you to take me out to Jay's house."

I protested, but she had made up her mind, so we piled into the Toyota. Jay lives a fifty-minute drive from the courthouse, but only twenty minutes from Eagle Cap Lodge.

I was hoping he wouldn't be home yet, but the Blazer sat on its gravel patch by the back entry. I gave a toot on the horn by way of warning. He might have been in the hot tub we had

153

installed just before the snows came, though it wasn't hot-tub weather.

Ma was frankly gawking. "Some log cabin."

I knocked. As I was about to knock again, Jay opened the door.

"What the hell, Lark . . . oh."

"Sorry to intrude. My mother wanted to meet you."

"Hello, Jay. Thanks for the daisies," Ma chirped, sticking out her hand.

He shook it, wincing, and showed us in without visible enthusiasm. He was wearing cutoffs and an unbuttoned shirt, which would have been sexy except for the Velcro corset.

Jay's house *is* a log cabin. Each timber is squared and notched to fit with the others so tightly that no insulation is necessary even at that altitude. It has skylights and double-paned thermal windows all over the place, and there's a gleaming Franklin stove in the living room. The effect of diffused sunlight on all that exposed red cedar is friendly rather than rustic, and the whole layout is very modern.

The house was a kit. Jay and his brother put it together themselves. Jay is secretly proud of it, so I thought he'd get over his snit faster if he gave my mother the grand tour. I told him I'd finish his laundry.

While I tossed underwear into the washer and hung shirts fresh from the dryer, I could hear their voices. Ma is always interested in how things are made. I thought she'd like the crisp, tiled kitchen, and I knew she'd get a kick out of Freddy's room, which is a loft over the kitchen reached by a cleverly hung ladder. It's Freddy's to use whenever he visits. He takes his computer up there and plays games.

When I heard Ma's voice ten feet above me, I knew I'd guessed right. I paired socks, then sneaked into the bedroom in case it needed tidying. Except for the stacks of paperbacks on the headboard, it was neat, but everything was covered with a week's worth of dust. I plumped a pillow on the futon and decided to let the dust lie.

Jay stuck his head in the door. "You want a glass of wine?"

"Sure." I was too relieved that my strategy had worked to gloat. He sounded about twenty degrees warmer.

By then it was sunset and the sea breeze stirred the air enough to make sitting on the deck pleasant. Ma was leaning back in a lawn chair, drinking in the view of the lake.

It is not a lake in the Llewellyn sense. It's a glacial tarn, small, deep, and dotted with boulders, one large enough to be called an island. The light that bathed it was pink-gold and the air was full of birdsong. A riffle of wind moved over the water.

Jay came out with two glasses of white wine and a beer on a myrtlewood tray.

Ma smiled up at him as she took her wine. "It's a lovely place, Jay."

"Hell to get in and out of in winter." He served me, set the tray down, and took his beer to the rail. I think it hurt him less to stand than to squat on one of the lawn chairs, which were K-Mart specials and inclined to collapse. He leaned against the rail. He had buttoned his shirt.

Ma said, "I thought we ought to meet before I leave."

Jay nodded.

I sat up and the plastic webbing creaked. "Leave? When?"

"Tuesday morning."

Three more days. I sipped my wine and leaned back. The end was in sight.

"I had to see the lodge and get to know D'Angelo," Mother said earnestly. "I owed it to Dai."

"Yes, ma'am."

Ma made a face. "Good heavens, do people out here really say that?"

"Yes, ma'am." Jay smiled a split-lip smile. "Especially cops."

"Well, try Mary next time. Do you have any idea when you're likely to find the murderer?"

The smile went. "We have a warrant out for the chauffeur's arrest. No leads worth a damn. I was hoping the state lab could give me something on the poison, but they tell me it was made from a variety of larkspur that grows wild in this area."

"Frustrating."

"I'm up against a wall. Unless something gives soon, I'll have to put the case on the back burner. I have half a dozen others pending."

Ma frowned over her wine. "You mean give up?"

"I'm not likely to give up on a murder I was forced to witness." Jay wiped the condensation from his beer bottle on his shirt and drank. "I just won't be able to spend a lot of time on it. We're understaffed."

Mother sipped, still frowning. "Isn't this Ted Peltz a likely suspect?"

"Yeah, though he's not very subtle. He could have planned it, I suppose. He's in custody, but he'll be out as soon as he can make bail."

"On the wife-beating charge?"

Jay said flatly, "There won't be a wife-beating charge."

Ma was shocked and said so. I could feel the tension level rising again.

"People like the Joneses don't want their names dragged through the courts." Jay took a swallow of Henry Weinhardt's.

"But the young woman was almost killed."

Jay took another swallow. "They'll protect her and buy her a divorce."

"Leaving the son-in-law free to prey on other women?"

"They don't give a damn about other women. That's a trend," he said dispassionately. "You can really see it in Beverly Hills. Private cops. Walled estates. They build themselves a castle. Then they pull up the drawbridge, and to hell with the peasants outside."

"They?"

"People like the Joneses who think they can buy justice." He finished his beer and set the bottle on the tray. "Sometimes they're right."

"You don't like that."

He stared at her. "My liking it or disliking it doesn't

change the way things are. The Joneses will see that their daughter doesn't press charges."

"I'm sorry," my mother said gently.

Jay looked away.

Ma rose. "You'd better drive me home, Lark. It's getting late."

"Okay." I rummaged for my keys while my mother and Jay exchanged politenesses. As I rose to go he said, "Thanks for doing the wash, Lark."

"You betcha." I was still a little steamed. Also worried. However, the meeting with Mother had gone off smoothly. No casualties. I was glad it was over.

Jay watched us go from the back porch.

Three-quarters of the way to the turnoff to Eagle Cap, Ma said, "Are you going to marry him?"

"The question has not arisen."

"Perhaps not orally." Did I say my mother is shrewd? "Do you want to marry Jay?"

"Yes."

"Good."

I must have driven three mile without registering a thing, so profound was my astonishment. I almost missed the turnoff.

It was a night for surprises. When I got back to Monte I drove to the bookstore to help Ginger close up. I told her Mother and I would go with her to beard Denise in her den. Ginger was pathetically grateful. When Dennis came she told him, and *he* was pathetically grateful.

I chugged to the apartment, my mind on Denise, and nearly rammed the back of the Blazer. Jay had parked in my slot.

I took the stairs two at a time, then stood outside my door for a minute to calm down. It would not do to appear too eager.

Jay was standing by the window eating my last pint of yogurt. He waved a spoon. "Hi."

"Hi, yourself." I set my handbag down on the coffee table. "Ma approves."

"Did she like the house? That's good."

"Of you, idiot."

He scraped at the last morsels of yogurt. "I thought I was a surly sonofabitch, myself."

"Maybe she likes Heathcliff types."

He took the empty carton into the kitchen, came back, and gave me a nice yogurt-flavored kiss.

"Yum. What was that for?"

"Bribery. You're going to have to put me to bed again."

So I did.

We had maybe three hours of harmonic vibrations, sleep, to put it another way, when the telephone rang. Jay didn't wake immediately, as he usually does. I answered. It was Kevin Carey.

"You'd better put Jay on the phone. We found the chauffeur."

"Where is he?"

"Where was he," Kevin corrected.

"Is he dead?"

"Very dead."

Jay muttered something.

"It's Kevin. They've found Miguel's body."

He lay very still. "Shit." He didn't sound surprised.

I handed him the receiver and lay back, listening to a series of glum grunts. Finally he said, "Okay. Half an hour," and hung up.

The news had begun to register. I was near tears. "I'm sorry."

"Yeah. I can't drive, Lark." He had taken pain pills.

"I can." I slid from bed and gave him my hand. We got him dressed, I jumped into a pair of jeans and a sweatshirt, and we took off.

"Where?" I revved the Toyota's engine. It's a cold starter.

"South. That road that cuts off toward Weed through the high country."

"Why there?"

He leaned back, eyes closed. "No idea." We rode in silence.

We found the crime scene easily enough. Kevin had already sent the evidence team out.

The Mercedes had been parked in one of the big sheds the county uses to shelter its snowplows in winter. Piles of gravel and cinder had hidden the car from the road, and it would not have been visible to the helicopter crews either.

I pulled in behind one of the county cars. Its blue light whirled and the headlights stabbed at the highway shed. The lights from two other cars and a couple of floodlights assaulted the darkness. Deputies, some in uniform, some not, moved in and out of shadow. Barricades already blocked access to the turn-around area behind the shed.

Jay opened his door and swiveled sideways. "You'd better go home, Lark. Thanks."

"Thank *you*," I said crossly. "I won't get underfoot."

"I don't think it's going to be real appetizing after a week of hot weather."

"Oh." I had no desire at all to see Miguel's body. Or smell it.

Jay pulled himself to his feet. I got out the other side and we looked at each other over the roof of the car.

"I'll be here until sunrise at least. You'd better go home."

"Why sunrise?"

"They'll be taking tire casts, combing the weeds for evidence. I can't tell them what I want until I see the area."

"Okay." I started to say I'd go home.

"Dodge?" Dan Cowan strode up looking self-important. "You better talk to the guy who found him. Oh, hi, Ms. Dailey."

"Hi. How's Fern?" Fern was Dan's wife.

"She has hay fever real bad. I sent her to her sister in Fort Bragg." Cowan turned back to Jay. "Transient. I picked him up about half a mile down the road trying to thumb a ride. He says he was going to call us from town, but I doubt it."

"He touch anything?"

"I don't think he did much damage. Too freaked out."

"Okay. Where?"

"Back of the patrol car."

"I'll take a look at the body first." Jay's voice sharpened. "They haven't disturbed anything, have they?"

"Waiting for you. Secured the site. Gunshot wound to the head. Looks like suicide."

Jay took a deep breath, a mistake, and clutched at his side. "Karl here yet?" Karl was the medical examiner, Dr. Holst.

"On his way."

"Okay. Show me." Jay had forgotten my presence. I didn't remind him. He and Dan moved off toward the heaps of cinder. They were going to approach the shed from the far side, to avoid trampling on tread marks and footprints, I supposed.

I closed the passenger door and got back into the car, turning off the lights. I closed my door, too, but I rolled the window down. I was upset, puzzled, and wide awake.

I could see Miguel stealing the car and trying to get away. I could also see Miguel committing suicide if he had killed Llewellyn and been overcome by remorse. He had been an emotional young man. What I didn't understand was why he would steal the Mercedes, gas the car up and have the oil checked, drive south of Monte fifteen miles or so on a back road, and *then* kill himself. Why not do it at the lodge? And where had he got the gun?

I ought to have gone home. Dan, or one of the other cops on the scene, would have given Jay a ride back. My presence was superfluous and not in the best taste, but Miguel's death was going to hit Jay very hard. I wanted to be near him and I wanted to leave. In the end I just sat. It was as if I had no will.

I brooded, drowsing a little until some movement or voice from the scene would rouse me. I was at the scene, but not of it. No one came near me. I couldn't see the Mercedes from my position behind the patrol car and the cops were careful not to trample the access lane, so most of the coming and going happened on the far side of the shed. It was all very distant and surrealistic, like seeing *film noir* at a drive-in.

When Dr. Holst came his crew took their stretcher around the far side of the shed, too. I watched them carry Miguel to the ambulance in a body bag. It was an ordinary ambulance, like the one that had taken Llewellyn from the lodge. No reporters had showed up.

Bill Huff's paper was a weekly. I doubted his reporters stayed up all night listening to the police band. The stringer for the *Chronicle* lived in Weed. The TV station was up in Oregon. There didn't seem to be any neighbors either, so I was the only ghoul on the site. Not a very alert ghoul. After the ambulance left I drowsed and, finally, slept.

"Lark!"

I jolted awake. My neck was stiff.

Jay was leaning against my side of the car looking down at me. It was daylight. "I thought you were going home."

"I fell asleep," I said sheepishly. "What's happening?"

"I'm waiting for Kev. You might as well hang around and drive me into town."

"Okay. What time is it?"

"Six." He walked stiffly around to the other side and got in, leaving the door open. "I'm too grogged out to do much more here."

"Pills wear off?"

"Yeah." He shut his eyes. "Jesus, what a time to be crocked up. I wish I could swallow a couple of gallons of coffee."

"Was it bad?"

He grimaced. "I tossed the yogurt."

"Ugh. Did I hallucinate or was that a CHiPs car I saw around four-thirty?"

"State car. I had them take the gun to the lab in Sacramento. I need the report on that before I can do much." A car drove up at high speed, light revolving. "That'll be Kevin."

The county car wheeled neatly in behind me, boxing the

161

Toyota in. Kevin jumped out and Jay stood up again, clutching at his ribs. I got out, too. I needed to do something to get my circulation going.

Kevin did a double take when he saw me.

I gave him a smile. "Taxi service."

"Oh, yeah. How're the ribs, partner?"

"I have eaten tastier," Jay said with dignity.

Kevin grinned. He is a slender black man, not very tall, with a neat beard and glasses. He and Jay work well together. Kevin's wife teaches sociology at the junior college and yearns for the big city, but Kev is a fanatical skier, so she's probably stuck in Monte.

Considering that Jay was brought in from the LAPD over Kevin's head, it's a tribute to Kev's good nature—and maybe to Jay's—that they've become friends.

Jay said glumly, "You were right. I should've taken the kid into custody. If I had, he'd still be alive."

"I wonder why I don't feel a lot of satisfaction."

Jay sighed. "It's murder."

"No possibility of suicide?"

"Well, you have a look."

"The body's gone."

"Yeah. Have a look at the car, though. He was shot with the windows open. Then the killer closed 'em . . ."

"Electric windows—engine running?"

"Either that or the killer turned on the ignition after Miguel was dead, closed the windows, turned the refrigeration up, and left the engine on. Car's out of gas."

"Refrigeration? Shit. That's going to blur the time of death."

Jay shrugged and winced as the incautious movement pulled at his sore ribs. "That's going to be foggy anyway. He was probably killed within an hour of the time he left the Chevron station on Grand. Proving it . . ."

"Excuse me," I interrupted. "I know it's none of my business, but how could you tell he was killed with the windows open?"

Jay looked at me. "We haven't found the slug. It may be lodged in the upholstery. Still, the window on the driver's side wasn't smashed. And it was, uh, smeared but not . . ."

"Splattered," I finished, sick.

"You get the picture. Also, we're going to find blood and, uh, so on, on the grass when it's light enough."

"I'm sorry." I kept saying that futile little phrase. I was sorry. For Jay, who was obviously blaming himself, but especially for Miguel. I had liked Miguel.

". . . some attempt to make it look like suicide," Jay was saying to Kevin. "If the killer had left the windows open, I wouldn't be so damned sure it wasn't."

"Weapon?"

"A Beretta. Automatic."

Kevin groaned. "Common as blackberries."

"It's a .380."

"That'll help some."

I wondered what kind of gun Domingo had showed me, not that it mattered. It was obviously not the murder weapon. I also remembered Bill Huff's arsenal. Unfortunately, that wasn't worth much as evidence. Northern California was NRA territory. A lot of people collected guns.

". . . prints?" Kevin was asking.

"The gun was lying by the gearshift, near Miguel's right hand. His prints, pretty blurred."

"Any others?"

"It was clean—too clean. So was the ignition. I sent the weapon and the brass to Sacramento."

Kevin shoved his glasses up the bridge of his nose. "You in a hurry?"

"Yeah."

Kevin was squinting at him in the sharp morning light. "You look like hell, Jay. I can take over here. Get some sleep and I'll call you when the lab report comes in from Sacramento."

Jay frowned. "What about the press?"

"They'll be stirring around soon. I called the sheriff right after I called you. He'll make a statement."

"Give him something constructive to do," Jay said gloomily. "Can we maybe not mention that it's murder?"

"No sweat. The sheriff will give them the guy who found him."

Jay winced. "Poor bastard. Okay. And the bare facts. Dead at least five days. Single gunshot wound to the head."

"Shit, man, I could write a three-column story from that with one hand tied behind my back."

"So what are you doing working for the county?" They grinned at each other—tight, sour little grins.

"Go home," Kevin said.

"Okay. You'd better relieve Dan Cowan, too." They walked slowly over to the shed, skirting a pile of cinders, and Jay came back alone fifteen minutes later, feet dragging.

I drove carefully, eyes on the road. There was no traffic. Jay leaned back. His eyes were closed, but he wasn't sleeping.

I stopped where the county road intersected with the state highway and turned onto it in the wake of a log truck. "Bill Huff collects guns."

"Yeah?"

"Mostly hunting rifles. I didn't look closely. I think he had a couple of handguns, though."

Jay grunted.

"And Domingo showed me a gun yesterday."

"Old Colt .45. He has a permit."

"Did Ted Peltz . . ."

"I don't think Peltz did it."

"Why not? He's vicious enough."

"Wrong kind of personality. Too direct. This killer likes embroidery."

I shifted down for the traffic light where the county highway crosses Highway 99. "You mean embellishments?"

"Like the larkspur. And the trick with the refrigeration."

"Maybe that wasn't deliberate."

"What do you mean?"

"Maybe the killer left the engine running because he wanted you to think Miguel had been driving around a lot. And the refrigeration just happened to be on."

"The windows were open when he was killed."

I turned up Main Street, driving slowly. A teenager not much younger than Miguel zoomed by me on the right, driving a low-rider. "Was Miguel trying to blackmail the murderer?"

"That's the logical conclusion."

"But he was a nice kid!"

Jay wriggled his shoulders. The seatbelt cut across his ribs. "He was also facing unemployment, and he had a big family to feed back home in Baja."

"What will happen to them?"

"I suppose they'll get the legacy eventually."

I pulled into the lot behind the bank. It was seven-fifteen. The town was already stirring, and I had to open the store at ten.

I fed us scrambled eggs. Jay took a pain pill and lay down. When I left he was asleep and Kevin had not yet called.

I left for the mall early enough to run laps at the health club. When I had showered and dressed I felt as if I might be able to handle the rest of the day without real sleep. I kept thinking about Miguel.

The news story broke around eleven, according to Ginger. She heard it on the car radio on her way to work. Wasn't it sad, but suicide was a kind of confession, wasn't it? I said um.

Ginger was dressed to the eyeteeth for the encounter with her future mother-in-law, and her mind was on that. Otherwise she would have grilled me. I had forgotten Denise. At noon I dashed home and changed into a dress and sandals. Jay was gone.

Ginger was fuming when I got back. "I called Denise. She said a friend was coming over for lunch and not to show up until two. Of all the nerve."

"Now, Ginger."

"Like I was trying to sell her Tupperware or something."

"You should be relieved."

"You're kidding. The sooner I get this over with the better. Will your mother mind waiting?"

"Oh God, Mother. I should have called her about Miguel. Did Denise say anything about the m . . . about Miguel?"

"No. Geez." Ginger was still fuming and didn't catch my lapse.

I reached for the telephone. "Oops, too late." I could see Ma's rental car making its tentative way across the parking lot. She'd come to town early.

She was wearing the faille suit. I was touched that she had brought out the heavy armor on Ginger's behalf. As Ma locked the car door and turned to cross the few yards of asphalt to the door of the shop, a radio reporter, mike in hand, materialized from behind a Winnebago. I froze where I stood.

Ginger was muttering about Denise. I watched Ma. I could tell from her blank stillness that she had not heard the news. She said something quick and definite, and moved to the entrance with the reporter trailing her.

I unfroze, opened the door for her, and pulled her inside. The damned bonger bonged.

"My God, Lark, why didn't you call and warn me?"

"I should have." I whisked her behind the counter and into the back room as the reporter charged through the door, bonging. "I'm sorry."

"Then it's true?"

I nodded. "Let me get rid of the press. Be right back." Ma sat at my desk looking dazed.

I no-commented until the reporter gave up. A customer entered. I let Ginger show her the hiking maps and went back to Mother.

"I'm sorry," I repeated. "I wasn't thinking." And I gave her an edited account of the discovery of Miguel's body. ". . . so I'm a little disoriented."

"You might have phoned me, all the same." She brooded. "Shouldn't we put Denise off?"

I explained Ginger's nerves. "Anyway, Denise put *us* off—for an hour. We'd better do it today, before Ginger chickens out."

Ma thought. "You're probably right. You ought to close the store again, though. Until the press storm blows over."

"For Godsake . . ." I started to protest. I hated to do that to Annie and my real customers, but it made sense. "Today and tomorrow?"

"Yes. I'm surprised you opened at all, Lark. Bad taste." At least she didn't blame my misjudgment on Jay.

I took the criticism meekly and went out front. The customer was deliberating between the Pacific Crest Trail and Siskiyou Pathways, two of my better maps. I turned the Closed sign around while Ginger dealt with her. She finally left.

I was explaining why we were closing to Ginger when Ma came in.

"When does Annie show up?"

"Anytime now."

"We'll take her to lunch. Where do you suggest, Ginger?"

Ginger was flattered at being consulted, and they deliberated over restaurants while I lettered a sign with felt marker on the back of a promotional poster: "Larkspur Books will reopen Monday, July 15." What was it about July 15? Something. It wouldn't come. I was even groggier than I had thought I was.

Annie bounced in the back door and had to be comforted with the promise of compensatory hours the next week. She cheered up when Mother announced we were lunching at Wind Song, a posh place that overlooked Beale Creek. Annie had never eaten there.

Lunch was not jolly. Ginger poked at a salad. Ma was concerned for Domingo and worried about what a new wave of sightseers and souvenir hunters might do to the lodge. I kept thinking about Miguel. Annie ate a lot of manicotti.

We dropped her at her car and headed back out Beale Creek Road. Denise's small house lay about halfway between Winton D'Angelo's apartment complex and the Huffs' rural enclave. A side road wound uphill and dead-ended in a paved turnaround. Three driveways gave onto the cul-de-sac. One led to an unfinished cabin, one to a new three-level executive palace, and the third, rather narrow and overhung with evergreens, to Denise's hideaway. I could hear the high whine of a power saw from the direction of the cabin. Otherwise there were no signs of life.

Denise had bought the house when it was just an isolated farmhouse. The construction was new. I think she had subdivided the property, though I'd heard her complain that her neighbors violated her solitude.

I parked in the paved driveway by her small, shedlike garage, and we got out. She had had the good sense not to modernize the house. It was a classic frame farmhouse with a wide, roofed porch. She had had the house painted an uncompromising and correct white with gray trim. Nasturtiums and snapdragons rioted along the walk. Baskets of fuchsias in full bloom hung from the roof of the porch.

Ginger wanted to lag. I made her go ahead of us and ring the doorbell. We stood. No answer. Ginger rang again. Silence.

Ginger's mouth quivered. "She's doing it on purpose!"

"Lydia Huff said something about a new gazebo around back. If Denise fed her friend lunch, maybe she's out there cleaning up."

There were tears in Ginger's eyes. Ma had drifted over to look at the porch swing.

"I'll go see if I can find her, Ginge. Cheer up. You don't want to let her see she's upset you."

Ginger sniffed.

"And ring the bell again. Lean on it."

"Okay."

I followed the porch around the side of the house. Steps led down from a side door to a flagged footpath. I walked on around the back.

The Chinese delphiniums caught my eye. Denise had planted them in solid masses to hide the concrete base of the gazebo. The tips flared deep blue against the unweathered russet of the redwood structure.

"Denise?"

No answer.

A pure-white cat stalked around the edge of the steps. The movement startled me. "Hello, puss. Who's here?"

The cat gave me a cold stare and stalked off.

171

I squinted into the folly. Denise had already trained a vine up the trellised side. I thought I saw a patch of the flowered fabric of her lounging pajamas. As I opened my mouth to call to her again, a tiny breeze puffed and I smelled something fetid.

I didn't know what was wrong, but something was. My pulse hammered. "Denise . . ." I took the steps in single stride.

She was lying behind the small redwood table at the center of the gazebo, an overturned chair beside her. I took another step and saw her face. It was dusky with suffused blood, and her tongue protruded. In the moment of death her body had voided. I caught the stench full force.

I took two cat steps backward and bumped the trellis. My mind had gone so still I could not have screamed, and I think my heart stopped. Then it thudded into action and the adrenaline started to flow.

I thought of the two women waiting for me on the porch. I did not want them to see this horror. And part of my concern was that the crumpled body violated everything Denise had been. It was obscenely graceless.

I backed down the stairs and stood on the flagged walk, breathing through my mouth. The white cat crossed intensely green lawn. A bee bumbled past. I walked, stone by stone, around the house, and I took the steps to the porch leaning on the rail like an old woman.

"What is it?"

"She's there. Dead."

I remember their eyes—so wide they were rimmed white. I was still holding the rail, and a good thing, too, because I almost passed out.

I breathed in, held it. Light returned. "Denise was strangled. It's . . . ugly. Don't go back there!" That to Mother, who had risen from the swing. "Both of you stay right where you are. I'm going to have to call the sheriff's office." I hoped Jay was in.

Ma and Ginger exchanged looks. Ginger whimpered.

"But shouldn't we . . ." Ma started.

"No. Don't move. Maybe the door's unlocked." I tried it, and it opened easily. "I'm going to call."

Denise's salon—more than a living room—was superbly furnished in antiques, mostly rosewood, with a soft, pale-blue rug on the polished hardwood floor. The phone sat on a whatnot table. I picked up the receiver, got a dial tone, and went blank. Finally my fingers poked 911 and I heard myself asking for the sheriff's office.

Beth, the dispatcher, recognized my voice. When I had croaked out an explanation, she agreed to transfer me to Jay while she sent a call for one of the patrol cars. Denise's house was deep in county territory, at least ten miles outside the city's jurisdiction.

Jay answered on the third ring.

"It's Lark. Denise has been murdered."

"What . . . where are you?"

"At Denise's house. Beth's sending a car. Please come. I'm scared. I have Ginger and my mother with me."

"You're sure Denise is dead?"

"Oh, God, Jay, her face is purple." I swallowed hard. "And she stinks . . ."

"Don't touch anything, Lark. I'm on my way."

"Th-thanks." I hung up. I was going to cry or be sick, and neither would do Denise any good. I wondered if I was allowed to throw up in her bathroom and decided that if Jay didn't want me to touch anything, I'd better not. When the nausea subsided, I went back to the porch.

Ginger was sitting on the porch swing, crying on Mother's faille shoulder. Ma didn't look so good herself.

"He's coming?"

"Right away. The patrol car should get here first, though."

We stared at each other.

"The chauffeur didn't kill Dai, did he?"

I shook my head. "Miguel was murdered, too."

They gaped at me. Mother cleared her throat. "She . . . Denise was strangled?"

"With the scarf of her lounging outfit."

"Like Isadora Duncan. No, not exactly . . ."

"Jay says the killer embellishes."

"Jay's sharp, isn't he?"

That was kind. Jay might be sharp, but he was going to feel stupid that he hadn't been able to prevent Denise's death. Stupid and sick.

Ginger sobbed, and Mother patted her shoulders. I sat on the edge of the porch, dangling my legs in the snapdragons, and tried to think. The white cat nosed across the lawn. It was pursuing a butterfly.

The patrol car came within fifteen minutes. I didn't recognize the deputy, but he seemed to know who I was. He took my name for his incident report, and I introduced my mother and Ginger.

Ginger had gathered herself together. "Somebody ought to call Dennis."

"I'm sure they will, Ginge. Where is he?"

"Dennis?" the deputy asked.

"H-her son," I swallowed. "Dennis Fromm."

"He's at work." Ginger's mouth trembled and she bit her lip. "He only has three more days."

"I'll call the number in when I've seen the victim," the deputy volunteered. He was blond, about my age, and wore glasses. "They'll send somebody to tell him."

Ginger thanked him. Mother patted her arm.

"Now, Miss Dailey . . ."

I led him around back on the flagstone path, stood on the grass, and pointed. "She's in the gazebo behind the table. I'm not going any closer."

"You touch anything?"

"I brushed the inside of that trellis with my shoulder. I was dizzy. I didn't touch her . . . the body."

"You sure she's dead?"

Jay's question. "Go see for yourself," I snapped.

174

He set his jaw. I could tell that he was nerving himself to go up the redwood steps, and I was ashamed of my momentary annoyance. I didn't have to be told that cops were human, did I?

Nothing would have compelled me to go back into the gazebo. I waited on the grass.

When the deputy came back to me he was green. "Okay, Miss Dailey. Now I guess I'd better fill in my report."

"Let's go around front. My mother . . ."

He shoved his glasses up on the bridge of his nose. "I ought to stay here. Guard the body."

"Who's going to disturb her . . . it?"

He peered around. The yard was completely enclosed by a tall redwood fence, older then the gazebo and weathered. Roses climbed the boards, and salal and ornamental evergreens around the perimeter were relieved by carefully placed boulders. A towering cedar shaded the gazebo. In the northeast corner of the yard, Denise had planted an herb garden. Everything was very still. Eerie.

I shivered. "Can't we go around front?"

"No!" His color had come back. "I ought to keep the st . . . body in sight. I can take your statement here, though."

My memory was starting to function. "She had to be alive around twelve-thirty. She called Ginger . . . Ms. Gates. Said somebody was coming for lunch."

"Are you sure of the time?"

"No. It was after noon. Better ask Ginger."

The deputy and I stood on the flagstones while he took down the basic information. Afterward I went back to Ma and Ginger, and he went back to the gazebo to guard Denise's body from passing butterflies. There was no gate in the wooden fence that surrounded the area. I supposed neighborhood kids, if there were any, could have climbed over the fence, but it didn't seem likely.

Ten long minutes later, Jay drove up in the Blazer trailed by another county car. He had a word with the evidence crew.

175

Then he came straight to me. He held me and I think I cried a little. Neither of us said anything. One of the deputies cleared his throat. Ahem.

"Where's the body?" Jay asked me.

"Around back. There's a garden house," I said into Jay's shirt. "I couldn't stand it back there."

Jay stroked my back. "Go get things started, Mike." Mike went.

I didn't particularly want to move, but I knew I was being self-indulgent. I took a long breath and straightened.

Jay kept his hand where it was. "Mrs. Dailey, Ginger, I'm afraid you'll have to hang around for a while. When I've had a look at the scene, I'll want to talk to both of you. Lark, too. I've sent for Dennis, Ginger."

"Th-thanks. Can I use the bathroom?"

Jay hesitated. "If there's one upstairs."

"Denise had a guest coming for lunch," I interposed. "That's what she told Ginger."

"Then the guest may have gone inside. Don't touch anything downstairs, Ginger."

Ma said, "I think I'll accompany her, Jay, if you don't mind."

When they went in Jay took me over to the porch swing and sat me down. "Are you going to be all right?"

"I'm fine. I'm sorry to be such an idiot."

He bent and kissed me on the forehead. "Shock. Remember? Sit there and dredge up every damned thing you can recall about this, starting with why you and your mother came with Ginger. I'll be back when I've had a look around." He straightened, rubbing his ribs.

"There's a maniac loose, isn't there?"

"Not in the usual sense of the word," he said slowly, "but yes, I think so. Madness, or at least obsession. That's assuming the same person killed Llewellyn, Miguel, and Denise."

I stared up at him. The contusion had faded and slid down his cheek and he was wearing sunglasses. I wanted to see his eyes. "Surely there's only one killer."

"I hope so."

"But who would kill . . . oh, no, not Dennis."

"Or Ginger."

"She couldn't have! She's been with me since eleven, and Denise called the store after twelve."

"Were you there when the call came?"

"No. I went home to change. For Godsake, Jay, that's too crazy. Ginger?"

"It's not very likely. But I want you to remember that anyone can kill, given the right provocation. And Denise was being difficult about the marriage. Be careful who you confide in."

I gaped at him.

"Ted Peltz is clear on this one. He's still locked up."

"God, then the Huffs . . ."

"And Domingo. And Professor D'Angelo." Jay touched my cheek. "I'll be back. Will you help Dennis?"

"If I can."

"Keep him here in front when he arrives."

"Okay." My stomach churned. Dennis was not a mother's boy in the usual sense of the phrase, but his relationship with Denise had been strange, to say the least. I did not want him to hurt any more than he was going to have to hurt.

Dennis drove up in the Forest Service pickup while Jay was still inspecting the gazebo. The deputy on duty blocking the lane waved him on down.

Dennis pulled in on the grass in front of the house. The ambulance was waiting in the driveway by then, but they had not yet removed Denise's body. Ginger ran to him.

"Where is she?" He sounded hoarse.

I walked over to him, too. "She's in the gazebo, Dennis. Come and sit with us . . ."

"No, I have to see her."

"Dennis," I said desperately, "believe me, you don't want to."

He stared at me, mute and dazed.

"Come to the porch. Jay will be with you in a few minutes. In fact, I'll go get him."

Ginger took his arm and led him to the porch swing. He sat and put his face in his hands. Ginger and Ma bent over him.

"I'll get Jay . . ."

"Please tell me, Lark."

I licked dry lips. "She was strangled."

"God . . ."

"We came out because she wanted to talk to Ginger . . ."

"I know that."

"Around noon she called Ginger and said we should wait until two, that a friend was coming to lunch. I guess Denise was going to serve the meal in the gazebo because the table was set for two. But there wasn't any food. Just luncheon plates and silver, glasses, cloth napkins. The table looked untouched. She was lying behind it, and one of the chairs was overturned. I . . . I didn't go very close."

"Why didn't you go to her, help her?"

"It was clear she was dead, Dennis. I called the police immediately. I am so sorry."

His face crumpled and he began to sob. Ginger hugged him. Ma looked at me.

I shook my head, helpless. "I'll go for Jay."

I wanted to return to the backyard about as much as I wanted to kill a whale. As I rounded the corner of the house, I could see the photographers' flashes popping in the gazebo. I thought I heard Dr. Holst's voice. The m.e. must have come in the ambulance. He liked to view corpses in situ.

The ambulance crew stood on the grass looking patient. One of them was smoking a cigarette. Jay came as soon as he spotted me.

"Dennis?"

"Yes. He wanted to see her."

Jay took my arm again. He's not much of a public toucher ordinarily. I appreciated the gesture. I probably clung.

Jay took Dennis into the house, leaving Mother and

Ginger and me out front. We stared at each other. Ginger's
eyes were puffy. Ma looked very tired.

"Are you okay?"

Mother nodded. "There's a cat."

"What? Oh, the white one." It was lying couchant in the
shade of the ambulance.

"Somebody will have to take care of the cat," my mother
said stubbornly.

"I'll tell Dennis," Ginger said, still confident that Dennis
could take care of anything.

A car barreled down the lane and pulled up on the far side
of the ambulance.

We all got to our feet, including the white cat. The
ambulance driver stepped out. "Lady, you can't come in here."

It was Lydia Huff. She slipped by the man and came
toward us at a half trot, her chunky beads bouncing. "What is
it? What's the matter? Is Denise . . . ?"

"Denise was murdered." I was past tact.

"Where the hell are the barricades?" Jay roared from the
house, yanking the front door open and stalking out onto the
porch.

The cat padded over to Lydia and made a noise—prrrt?

Lydia fainted. Just like that.

She dropped where she stood. I was so unprepared, I
didn't even move to catch her.

A uniformed deputy came trotting down the driveway.
"Man, I didn't have a chance. She just wheeled right past me
on the shoulder." He was puffing from the short run.

Jay and the ambulance driver knelt by Lydia. "Get back
up that lane," Jay snarled. "I don't want any more tourists."

"The ambulance . . . ?"

"It'll be leaving soon. When it goes, put the fucking car
across the entrance if you have to. Block it."

"Okay." The deputy receded.

"Is it her heart?" I took a step toward Lydia.

"Pulse's strong." The driver got up and went to the
ambulance.

I knelt by Jay and straightened Lydia's homespun skirt. One of her slip-ons had come off. Blusher stood out on her cheeks like a clown makeup, but she was stirring. The cat had disappeared.

The driver returned with a blanket and some kind of smelling salts. He and Jay swaddled her and the driver stuck the salts under Lydia's nose. She sneezed and her eyes fluttered open. She focused on me. "L-lark."

"It's okay," I said stupidly.

"I thought . . ."

"Yes. It's Denise. Somebody . . ."

Jay's hand clamped on my arm. "I'm afraid she's dead, Mrs. Huff. Can you sit up?"

"I . . . yes. I'm all right. I never faint." The light-gray eyes were dull, but her voice sounded almost normal. The blanket slid off her shoulder like a toga as she struggled to one elbow and sat up.

Jay touched her arm. "All right?"

Lydia nodded. "Help me up."

I gave her my hand. Hers was cold. She groped for the shoe with her foot, leaning on me, and straightened. "I'll just go sit on the porch with Mary for a moment. Sorry to make such a fuss."

Jay got up creakily, holding his side. "What brought you here, Mrs. Huff?"

"I was just driving home from town. When I saw the patrol car I had to find out what was wrong. She's . . . she was one of my closest friends." Her voice faltered. "I think I'd better sit down." She tottered up the front steps, and Mother and Ginger helped her to the swing.

Jay followed. "Will you go in to Dennis, Ginger? He's in the living room."

Ginger nodded, wide-eyed, and went into the house.

"Now, Mrs. Huff . . ."

"For heaven's sake," Lydia said brightly. "That's Ethel White."

We stared at Lydia.

She half rose, and the swing creaked. We turned. The white cat had nosed around the edge of the flower bed again. It yawned and turned its back on us.

Something clicked in my mind. Two cats, one ginger, one white, chasing each other on the Huffs' lawn. Ethelred and Ethel White. "Your cat?"

Lydia fell back. The swing creaked again. "I don't know how Ethel got here. Of course we're only half a mile away."

"The cat was in the backyard when I found the body."

Lydia's gray eyes glinted.

Jay walked to the edge of the porch and snapped his fingers. Of course the cat ignored him.

"That's not the way." I walked to the flower bed and squatted. "Nice Ethel." I broke off a stalk of snapdragon and wriggled it. "Nice kitty."

She was watching the flower.

I trailed it on the grass. "Nice Ethel."

She crouched and began a leisurely crawl my direction. "Kitty, kitty."

She pounced on the stalk and rolled. I tugged. The snapdragon shed petals all over the place.

Fairly soon she was butting her head against my hand and sniffing my fingers. I picked her up, smoothing her coat. She was a sleek, well-fed short-hair with green eyes. Her flea collar was working loose.

I showed it to Jay.

His mouth set in a grim line. "More embellishment. No, don't take it off. Let me." While I held Ethel he undid the buckle, touching it on the edges. She jumped down and stalked off.

Jay took a Baggy from his jacket pocket and slipped the collar into it.

"Cats wander," Lydia said flatly. "We don't keep them indoors."

Mother said, "We once had a striped tiger that followed us home from Lake Cayuga. Remember, Lark? It took him a week."

181

Lydia smiled her gratitude.

Jay ignored Mother's cat saga. "Did you have an appoint-ment with Denise today, Mrs. Huff?"

"I called her around eleven. When I heard about Miguel."

"What was her state of mind?"

Lydia was rapidly regaining her air of command. "Really, Mr. Dodge, I'd be guessing, wouldn't I? I'd say she was relieved. Sad, of course, but relieved. If the boy committed suicide . . ." Her face went blank. Miguel's "suicide" didn't mean anything with regard to Denise's death. Lydia was not a stupid woman or easily discomposed, so her pause was interesting.

"And?" Jay prompted.

"We didn't talk long. She said she'd sent for Dennis's girlfriend. There was some nonsense about marriage. Denise wanted to set the woman straight."

"Did Denise mention that she was going to have someone over for lunch?"

Lydia shrugged. "She may have said something. This Ginger . . ."

"We'd like to know who Denise was expecting for lunch. The table was set for two."

"I . . . really, I've no idea. I know she was expecting the girlfriend this afternoon."

"She didn't ask you to lunch with her?"

"I told you, no. I called about Miguel. We talked maybe five minutes. She was concerned about her son . . . good God, Mr. Dodge, someone ought to inform the son. He works for the Forest Service . . ."

"Dennis is in the house, ma'am. That's his pickup in front of you."

"Oh. Well, I'll go to him, shall I? The poor boy . . ."

"Ginger Gates is with him. We'll see to Dennis."

"Then if I can't be of any use here, I think I ought to go home. Bill . . ."

"Mrs. Huff, you came down here of your own free will. There's an investigation in progress. I'll have to ask you to stay for a while until I have a better idea of what happened. I need to talk to you about Denise, since you knew her as well as anyone except Dennis. Right now, I want to see to the removal of her body. Will you stay?"

"Why . . . well, yes. If you want me to."

"Thank you." Jay went back inside the house.

Ma and Lydia exchanged unhappy smiles. They were sitting side by side.

My mother was definitely beginning to wilt in her faille suit. Fortunately the porch lay in shade. "I could use a drink of water . . ."

Dr. Holst came around the corner of the house. "Where the hell's Dodge? Beg your pardon, ladies."

Lydia's gray eyes narrowed.

"In the house with Dennis Fromm." I gestured toward the door.

Karl wheezed. He has asthma. "Tell him we're ready to move out, will you, Lark? I'll see to the ambulance crew." He stumped back the way he had come.

I entered the house again, blinking as my eyes adjusted to the dimness.

Jay was in the living room. At first I thought he was talking to Dennis. Then I saw that Dennis and Ginger were sitting together on the horsehair settee and Dennis was crying.

I averted my eyes.

Jay was talking on the phone.

". . . pick him up at the newspaper office. Yeah, question him before she has a chance to talk to him. And send Cowan out to the lodge. I want him to bring Domingo in."

I cleared my throat. Jay and Ginger looked at me.

"Okay," Jay said into the phone. "Sure, the girl, too. You've got D'Angelo? Fast work. Thanks, Kev." He hung up. He had taken his sunglasses off, and his eyes were shadowed with sleeplessness. "What's the matter, Lark?"

"It's Karl. He says he wants . . ."

"Okay." He glanced at Dennis, shoved himself to his feet, and came over to me.

"And could we please have a pitcher of water and some glasses? It's hot out there on the porch."

He frowned. "They haven't finished in the kitchen yet."

"Why . . . oh, you think maybe the killer was in there?"

"It's an outside chance. Tell the ladies half an hour and they can come inside."

"Okay." I blew Ginger a kiss. She gave me a wan smile and patted Dennis's back. I slid back out the front door.

Ma and Lydia were playing with Ethel White and talking about the foundation. Lydia was babbling something about a commemorative volume of Llewellyn's poetry, an art book with line drawings and tributes from friends. I thought it would probably sell as many copies as Llewellyn had had friends.

When they brought the stretcher bearing Denise's body around to the ambulance, Dennis stormed from the house and demanded to see her. Ginger and I begged him not to, but he was adamant. He blocked the rear of the ambulance and wouldn't let the paramedics load the stretcher.

To my horror Jay said merely, "It's his right."

The results were predictable. Dennis threw up on the snapdragons and Dr. Holst had to tranquilize him.

Ginger was furious. While the ambulance drove up the lane, she sat on the porch steps and held Dennis to her. "I'm taking this man home with me right now, Jay Dodge, and don't you try to stop me."

Jay took off the sunglasses and rubbed the bridge of his nose. "I'm sorry, Ginger. He had a right to see his mother."

"You could've said no. I'm going. I'll drive the pickup." She dug in Dennis's pockets and came up with the keys. Dennis was weeping quietly.

Jay rubbed his forehead and put the glasses back on. "All right. Just one thing. When Denise called you, did you get any impression of who she was expecting for lunch?"

"No!"

"Come on, think. Male or female?"

"A woman."

"Did Denise say so?"

Ginger was beginning to cool down. She stroked Dennis's hair, frowning. "No. I guess I just assumed it was a woman. A lady Denise's age, when she has a man call, she's apt to sort to capitalize the word *friend*. D'you know what I mean?"

"Tell me."

"Well, she would have said . . ." Ginger screwed up her face. "'I'm having a Friend to lunch.' What she did say was 'a friend of mine is coming to lunch.' Like that."

Jay stared at her a long moment, silent, then nodded. "Okay. Take him home, Ginger. I'll have to talk to him later. Call your kids."

"What?"

"Tammy and Larry. When the story breaks, they'll be worried."

"Oh, okay. Thanks." She bit her lip. "I'm sorry I yelled but you shouldn't have done that to Dennis."

Jay didn't defend himself. He and I helped her get Dennis into the passenger seat of the pickup. Ginger turned the truck around on the lawn and chugged off.

One of the technical crew came up and asked a question. Jay answered absently, hand on his side, and the tech went off.

Ma and Lydia had watched the entire scene from the porch. Lydia was outraged.

She stalked over to Jay. "I'm going to report you, Dodge. That was inexcusable. The boy will have nightmares the rest of his life."

Jay stiffened, but he didn't answer her.

Ma touched her arm. "Dennis didn't believe his mother was dead, Lydia. And he's not a boy."

I was standing beside Jay. I felt rather than heard him expel a breath. He spoke to Ma, half apologetic, "I thought nightmares would be better than delusions." He turned to Lydia. "If you'll come with me, Mrs. Huff, I want your statement now."

Lydia followed him into the house, muttering.

"Th-thanks, Ma," I sniffed.

Mother said wearily. "Some people don't have common sense. Come and sit with me, Lark. This is all very hard to bear."

We sat together on the porch swing and didn't even talk. I have seldom felt closer to my mother.

Jay must have taken Lydia through her story several times. It was a good hour before she came out, spots of indignation bright on her cheekbones.

She said good-bye to Mother rather formally, ignoring me, got into her car, and backed up the lane. Jay was slow coming out to us. Maybe he had another phone call to make.

He took us into the living room together and went through our accounts of the afternoon almost mechanically. He dredged from my recollections the state of the table in the gazebo and the fact that the front door had been unlocked. We went over the cat's presence several times. He got me to narrow down the time of Denise's phone call to Ginger, though he was going to call Ginger later.

He switched off the recorder. "Okay, I guess you can go."

Ma stood up. "That's it?"

"For now." Jay stood, leaning heavily on the oak table he had appropriated for his recording gear and notepad. "Thanks. I'm sorry you had to deal with this. Lark . . ."

I stood up, too. We had been sitting around the table.

"Are you going to be all right?" He rubbed his forehead.

"I'm fine. How much longer?"

"God knows. Kev interrogated Bill Huff and D'Angelo. I want to go through those reports, and I'll have to get onto the lab again. And Karl will be doing the autopsy on Denise . . ." His voice trailed, as if finishing the sentence would take too much energy.

"When?"

"Maybe eight-thirty, nine. Don't wait dinner."

"All right." I kissed his cheek. "Take care."

When the deputy had waved me past the barricade and I

turned the car onto the main road, Ma said, "I think I need a stiff drink. What do you have?"

"Wine and a six-pack of beer."

"Stop at a liquor store. I don't want to go to a bar."

I bought a bottle of gin, some tonic, and a lime, and we both collapsed on my sofa over the drinks.

"The damned rental car is still at your store," Ma murmured into her glass.

"Lord."

"I'd better phone your father. He'll worry."

"Okay. What about dinner?"

"Ugh."

"My sentiments, more or less. Ma . . ."

"What is it, darling?"

"I'm sorry."

"My dear, so am I sorry. Denise was a remarkable woman, whatever her faults. Your Ginger is a remarkable woman, too. I think Dennis will be all right."

"I hope so. He's a sweet guy."

"So's Jay."

"What?"

"Don't you worry about him? He looked like hell, not to mince words."

"Yes, I worry, but it doesn't do any good. And, as you said of Dennis, he's not a boy."

Ma got the phone from the kitchen and settled in to tell my father all about it. I took a shower.

The stinging hot water woke and soothed me at the same time, but I could have used another long run. I was tired but restless as Lydia's wandering cat. Lydia had driven off in such high dudgeon she forgot Ethel White. So did we. I hoped the beast would find her way home.

Mother finished her drink while she was talking. When she hung up she looked at me. "Squeaky clean. I envy you."

"Want a shower?"

"Show me the way."

While she showered I found a shortish skirt and a T-shirt

189

for her. She looked ridiculous in them. The skirt reached her ankles. But she said she felt almost energetic enough to get the car, so we bundled her suit and panty hose into a paper bag and drove over to the mall.

Ma got out. "Is that a Chinese place? Now I'm hungry." It was seven.

"It's not great. Strictly Cantonese."

"I could probably eat shredded wheat."

"Say no more." We got takeout stuff and I bought Jay a bunch of steamed rice, and a chicken and pea-pod stir fry I thought he could probably eat. Then I took the food home, Mother following in the rental, and we ate.

"Who killed Denise?" Ma dipped a spring roll in hot sauce.

I choked on a bite of lemon chicken. "How would I know?"

"Jay has no suspicions?"

"Lots." I was beginning to think. "Maybe Domingo . . ."

"No."

"Why not?"

"He would never have killed Dai. And he's basically a gentle man. Maybe we need one of those charts."

"Charts?" I was completely at sea.

Ma sighed. "Have you never read an old-fashioned mystery?"

"I read science fiction."

"I refuse to comment. Forget the chart. Start with the obvious premise. If there's only one murderer, what's the sequence? X kills Dai by poisoning the drink. Miguel sees something and tries to blackmail X. X meets Miguel, shoots him, and manages to make it look like suicide . . ."

"That's just the press interpretation." I took a forkful of fried rice. We hadn't bothered with chopsticks. "Jay never had any doubt it was murder."

"Why not?"

I explained about the windows of the Mercedes.

"All right. The blackmail attempt occurred when, Saturday?"

"Probably."

"The murderer must have felt fairly confident at that point. A week elapsed during which the bombshell of Dai's will exploded. Ted Peltz came back from San Francisco and beat his wife . . ."

"And Jay."

"So Peltz is in jail and his wife is in the hospital. Then this morning, just after the news of Miguel's suicide is broadcast on the radio, Denise calls Ginger. She has a guest coming to lunch and postpones the interview with her future daughter-in-law . . ."

"What about Lydia?"

"Yes, somewhere in there Lydia called Denise. If Lydia's telling the truth, it was probably before Denise called Ginger, because Denise didn't say anything to Lydia about another guest coming."

"That's doesn't mean anything. Maybe Denise just didn't mention the luncheon."

Ma sighed. "We're hypothesizing."

"All right, all right. Denise heard from her 'guest,' who was a close enough friend that Denise invited her—Ginger said it was a woman—to lunch on very short notice. Then Denise called Ginger. The murder must have occurred right after that. Denise had time to set the table, but not to put the food out. She was strangled in the gazebo. And Lydia's cat witnessed the killing."

"Then we drove up and you found the body, perhaps an hour or an hour and a half later. Who?"

I said slowly, "Lydia."

"Why?"

"I think she was lying about the phone call. And she could have faked the faint. The medic said her pulse was strong."

"If it's Lydia, she has nerves of steel. All that chat with me about the foundation and the book of Dai's poems."

"The murderer is a smartass."

"What?"

"A sick joker. Look at all the little extras. The larkspur.

Lydia came into the store almost as soon as I got the invitation and urged me to go to the lodge. I suspect inviting me was her idea. So she could have brewed up the poison well in advance. Then in Miguel's case the trick with the windows and the refrigeration. It wasn't necessary, but it did blur the time of death and create a cute little puzzle."

"But what about the gun?"

"What about it? Bill Huff has a roomful of guns."

"Would Lydia have incriminated her husband?"

"Maybe they were in it together. The bequest to the Huff Press was small, relative to the size of the estate, but Llewellyn forgave two large loans. The book side of the business isn't profitable."

Ma munched. "I don't like two murderers."

"Ma," I exploded, "I don't like any murderers. How can you be so detached? If you'd seen Denise's face . . ."

Ma sighed. "I'm sorry, darling. I know it was awful for you. I'm upset, too, and you know me. When I'm disturbed, I verbalize. Bear with me."

"It's okay," I muttered.

"You said cute touches. Jay said embellishment. I suppose the cat is the unnecessary complication in Denise's killing, but it implicates Lydia. Why would she do that to herself?"

"Maybe the cat was accidental. Maybe it followed her car." That was dumb. Ethel was a cat, not a dog. It could have been there for its own reasons." Something tugged at my mind. Two cats . . .

"A coincidence?" Ma shook her head. "Well, maybe. The question is, why was Denise killed? I don't see her as a blackmailer somehow."

"I have a hard time seeing Miguel as a blackmailer. Denise might not have wanted money, but she liked to bully people, control them." I thought of poor Dennis. And Ginger. "And she would have relished a dramatic confrontation."

"I suppose so. We're assuming the mysterious guest was the killer. Who, then? Winton D'Angelo?"

"Ginger said a woman . . . but if it *wasn't* the

guest . . ." In one of those flashes of insight that change the way you see things, like a twisted kaleidoscope, I suddenly saw a new pattern. Llewellyn and Denise. Both successful artists, full of renown. There was an element of gratuitous spite in those killings. And Miguel might have been Llewellyn's latest lover. "Ma, you can't go to D'Angelo's for cocktails tomorrow. I won't let you."

"Let me? We have important things to discuss."

"Look, you're a prominent poet. So was Llewellyn. Denise was a famous dancer. If D'Angelo's gone off the rails, he could be doing in every successful artist within range."

Ma broke open a fortune cookie. "That's not very likely."

"Nothing about these murders is logical."

"I disagree. I think it's a straightforward case of greed, followed by blackmail. I grant you the fancy touches, but it's possible to be greedy and imaginative. My money is on the Huffs. I don't like Lydia."

We drank green tea and polished off the fortune cookies in silence. Finally Mother stood up. "I'd better go, darling. Give Jay my love, and tell him I'm betting on him."

I saw her off. When she left, we embraced with unusual energy. We needed the contact.

Jay came in soon after that.

I fed him pea-pods and rice.

I was tidying the kitchen and he was sipping his gunky herb tea when he said without preamble, "When did your mother leave?"

"Half an hour ago, maybe forty-five minutes. What's wrong?"

He had gone out to the phone in the living room and was punching in numbers. "Just checking."

I watched him, bewildered.

"It's okay." He waved me off. "Yeah, can I speak to the manager?"

I went back to the kitchen and ran the garbage grinder. I think I was brain dead by then.

Jay came back. "Your mother picked up her room key five minutes ago. She's okay."

I stared at him. Why should she not be? I felt a chill. If Jay's suspicions were anything like mine, I wanted a twenty-four-hour guard on my mother. I almost said so, but the last stirrings of common sense told me Ma would be all right until morning. She always bolted hotel-room doors. When I considered what might have happened to her on the way out to the lodge—on that steep, winding road—I had to drink a cup of herb gunk to calm down.

By that time Jay and I were somnambulating. We fell into bed within half an hour. No conversation.

I had a nightmare, of course.

When I finally battled my way to consciousness the details had mercifully receded, except for Denise's gargoyle face. I lay as still as I could so as not to wake Jay, but the vision of Denise seemed to float in midair, bloodshot eyes reproaching me. My stomach rebelled.

I bolted for the bathroom and threw up. No more Cantonese dinner. I crept back into the darkened bedroom, shivering and half crying. I did try to be quiet.

"Nightmare?"

I started. "What else?"

Jay's voice was drowsy. "'Lectric blanket."

"What!"

"'Syour electric blanket still hooked up? Turn it on high."

It was July, but such is my attention to housekeeping detail the blanket was indeed still hooked up. I fumbled with the controls and slipped back into bed. My teeth were rattling in my head.

Jay took my hand. "You know it's not your fault." He sounded wider awake.

"I should've gone out earlier. Ginger was supposed to be out there at one, originally." I was quaking like an aspen, but the blanket was starting to warm up.

"Denise told Ginger not to come at one."

"Yes, but what if we'd gone out anyway?" We were at Wind Song, pigging out, while Denise was dying.

Jay ran his thumb in a slow circle over the base of my hand, massaging, unclenching my fingers. "You couldn't have known she'd be killed, Lark."

"Okay, true, but . . ."

He was talking softly about bystander reaction, telling me how none of it was my fault or Ginger's or Ma's or Denise's—or anybody's but the killer's. His thumb moved in firm circles, kneading. I suspect he was talking just to talk. He told me how clear and cooperative I'd been, the ideal witness.

Gradually my shivering eased. I drowsed, conscious only of the soft rumble of his voice, concentrating on it as noise because I didn't want to think.

As I inched closer, I was vaguely aware of the cracked ribs and the Velcro contraption that kept us on our own sides of the bed. The electric blanket was helping me, but warm flesh would have been better. Jay was saying very good things that had nothing to do with Denise's murder.

I suppose I murmured something.

". . . and I think you'd better marry me," he was saying. "Are you going to?"

"Yes, of course." I gave a muffled squawk and sat up. "What!"

He made a noise that started as "phew" and ended in a grunt of pain.

I fell back onto the pillow. "Did you or did you not just propose to me?"

He chuckled. "Yes, and you said 'of course.' I'm damned flattered, and I'll hold you to it."

"I can't be blamed for anything I say under hypnosis." I was reaching for him, trying to find his face. I connected with his sandpapery chin.

He nibbled my fingers.

"Hey! Of course I'll marry you, but why ask me now? The time is hardly auspicious."

Jay took another finger nibble. "You taste good."

195

"It's not exactly romantic."

Jay sighed. Not deeply. Deep sighing would have been a bad idea. "I wanted to ask you starting around the middle of last August. But it wasn't the right time. Then you moved into your own apartment."

"I needed room . . ."

"Not the right time," he agreed, mocking but not harsh. "It was never the right time, Lark. I was going to ask you when we went out to Llewellyn's lodge. I was working up to it . . ."

"Definitely not the right time. Okay, but why now? I just threw up, I feel rotten, I can't even hug you . . ."

His voice roughened. "I asked because I felt about as low as I could, and I figured if you said no, I couldn't feel much worse."

"Oh. Gosh, Jay, how could you doubt . . ." I sniffed a huge sniff. "I love you."

"I guess you must."

"When?"

"What?" His turn for confusion.

"When do you want to get married?"

He laughed—or started to and groaned. "Anytime. Except today. Give the ribs a chance to heal."

I was beginning to feel good and, unfortunately, amorous. I raised up on my right elbow and kissed him—delicately so as not to undo the split lip. "I suppose we can talk it over later."

"That's right."

I squiggled up against the Velcro.

"Don't get too comfortable. I need another pain pill."

I got it for him. He went to sleep almost at once, but I turned the redundant blanket off and lay awake awhile entertaining visions of orange blossoms. I'm ashamed to admit Denise hardly crossed my mind.

I woke next morning to the sound of Jay yelping in the shower. I dashed to the bathroom and pulled the shower curtain open.

"I thought that would bring you," he said complacently and gave me a wet kiss. "Come on in, the water's fine."

We had a pleasant interlude, cautious but satisfying, in the shower. In the course of our slippery conjunction, we managed to assure each other that he had indeed proposed and I had indeed accepted and neither of us had been hallucinating.

That was about as far as our nuptial planning got, because Jay was on his way to work. Kevin had called him with word of a possible make on the gun that killed Miguel. They had found a thumbprint, very old, on the clip, and the state lab's new computerized scanner was going to try to find a match.

"It'll turn out that the gun was stolen from some blameless citizen five years ago." Jay was trying to fit his .38 into the holster at the back of his waistband. Ordinarily he wore a shoulder holster, but the cracked ribs made that impractical. He grumbled and winced and finally got the gun fitted in where he could get at it in a pinch. Then I helped him into his jacket and he was off.

I phoned Ma.

It was not yet eight, so I had the satisfaction of waking her up. Revenge is sweet.

"Uh, you what?"

"I'm getting married!"

"Unh?"

I took pity on her. "We decided last night. I thought you should be the first to know."

"Er, that's wonderful, darling." But what do you want me to do about it at this hour? She didn't say that, but I could hear her thinking it.

I grinned at the phone. "Never mind, Ma. We'll just pop over to Reno and get it over with quick. Tell Dad when you call him." I hung up and went into the kitchen, chortling.

Ten minutes later the phone rang again.

"Just kidding!" I caroled, cradling the phone on one shoulder and picking up my coffee cup.

"Lark?"

197

Oops. "Oh hi, Ginger. How are you? How's Dennis, more to the point."

"Awful. He had an awful night." I could hear her swallow. "Listen, Lark, can we come over?"

"Now?"

"Dennis wants to talk to you."

"Jay . . ."

"Not Jay. I mean not yet. It's . . . well, it's strange."

I scowled at the phone. If Dennis had information, he ought to take it straight to Jay. I thought of Dennis's shock and misery the day before—and Jay's role in it—and I had to soften. "Well, okay. Jay's already at the courthouse. I'll make a pot of coffee. Did you eat breakfast?"

"No, yes, it doesn't matter." She was distracted by something and turned from the phone. "He's gone to work," I heard her say. She covered the receiver with her hand. Conferring with Dennis. She turned back to the receiver. "Fifteen minutes?"

"Okay."

She hung up.

I prowled around tidying the living room. I defrosted a coffee cake in the microwave and fixed coffee. I was out of cream, but it didn't matter because westerners drink theirs barbarian black. I was wondering what Dennis had thought of, of course, and curiosity and apprehension coiled my insides like a watch spring. I needed a good run.

The bell rang just as the microwave bonged. I flipped it off and went to the door.

Ginger and Dennis were leaning on each other, looking as if neither of them had slept. I ushered them in and poured them coffee without making small talk.

When Ginger had taken a couple of sips and looked as if she might live I said cautiously, "Did you get hold of the kids?"

"Yeah. Larry wanted to come over and mount guard." She sniffed. "Tammy was ready to quit work."

"Great kids."

She sniffed again, teary-eyed.

I let them drink their coffee. They sat next to each other on the sofa, but they weren't quite touching. Not a good sign. "More?"

Dennis nodded, still mute, and Ginger muttered something that might have been "yes," so I went for the pot. I also cut the coffee cake into wedges and grabbed some paper napkins. When I'd set the cake on the coffee table and poured, I took the pot back to the kitchen to brew refills. I returned to see Dennis absent-mindedly ingesting a wedge of cake, so he was probably going to be all right.

I plunked down on the rocker. "What did you want to tell me?"

He finished chewing solemnly and patted his mouth with a napkin. Ginger and I watched him put his brain in gear.

He was a big, slow man—not stupid, slow. He almost always came to reasonable conclusions, but his thought processes were tortuous. I could see he was working something through in his head.

I leaned forward and the chair creaked. "I ought to warn you that I won't withhold evidence from Jay. Neither should you."

He sighed. "The thing is, see, I don't know if it's evidence. I called . . . Mother yesterday around eleven-thirty. I was worried about her and Ginger meeting, see?"

"Yes."

Ginger took a sip of coffee and didn't look at him.

"See, the thing is, we quarreled." He swallowed hard, and there was a long pause.

I waited.

"I was trying to tell her how wrong she was about Ginger. I said some things." He cleared his throat and went on doggedly, "I said some rotten things to her and she kind of . . . well, I think she was sort of teasing me."

Torturing him, more likely. I nodded.

"She told me she was going to call and put Ginger off because this friend was coming to lunch. I blew up. I didn't listen real close. I was mad." He twisted the paper napkin in his big hands. "I told her she'd better see Ginger that afternoon or she wouldn't be seeing *me* and she teased at me some more and then when I said some other things, she said she'd see Ginger at two. I told her she'd better and hung up. I was steamed." His voice shook. "And that was the last time I heard her voice."

"Oh, Dennis."

Ginger sat very still.

Dennis cleared his throat again. "I think she told me who was coming to lunch. I think she said it was Lydia."

"Lydia?" I felt a chill along my spine. "Are you sure?"

"I thought about it, Lark. I don't know. I saw Lydia at the farmhouse when . . . when I got there, didn't I? Maybe I just imagined my mother said it was Lydia. I wasn't listening to what Denise said. I don't want to get anybody into trouble . . ."

"But if Lydia killed Denise . . ."

"If she killed my mother, I want her to suffer."

A long silence fell. I sank onto the rocker.

Dennis's face crumpled. "I wish I hadn't said all those things to Denise."

For the first time, Ginger put her hand on his arm. She looked at me.

I swallowed. "But you were right, weren't you? That she was being unfair to Ginger. And besides, she . . . your mother was teasing you. Neither of you would have said what you said if you'd known what was going to happen. She loved you, and she knew you loved her."

That started Dennis crying again. Ginger comforted him. I went back into the kitchen to collect my wits. When I returned, they were looking a lot more comfortable with each other.

Dennis gave me a wavering smile. "What do you think I should do?"

"Talk to Jay." When he frowned I went on, "He won't assume Lydia's guilty, you know, and he needs all the help he can get."

Ginger stirred. "Does Dennis have to . . .?"

I turned to her. She was looking uncharacteristically vague. "Have to what?"

"Have to mention that he and Denise quarreled?"

"He'll think *I* killed her," Dennis said miserably.

I sat down again, and the rocker creaked. I wasn't sure Dennis was wrong. "You may have to go over the conversation a couple of times, Dennis, but Jay doesn't go off half-cocked. He wants this killer. So do you. Why not help him?"

The phone rang. I dashed back to the kitchen. It was Mother. She apologized for not congratulating me with the proper fervor and begged me almost tearfully not to run off to Nevada.

"I was pulling your leg, Ma." I craned around the corner. My guests were showing signs of restlessness. "Look, I can't talk now. I've got company . . ."

"At eight forty-five on Sunday morning?"

"Ginger and Dennis."

"Oh. Tell Jay . . ."

"He's already at the courthouse."

"Well, darn it, Lark, I want to talk this over. It's important."

"Lunch?"

We agreed that I'd drive out to the lodge for lunch. Ma wanted me to bring Jay. I said I'd try but not to count on it. Ginger was up and pacing by the time we'd settled everything and hung up.

"Come to the courthouse with us." Ginger planted her feet on my granny's carpet and raised her chin. Her face was flushed. "Jay will listen if *you* explain about the quarrel."

That was nuts, and I told her so. Jay was a pro. He'd probably have someone else question Dennis anyway, and he'd dislike my intrusion.

Ginger dug her heels in.

We dickered. Finally I gave up and agreed to drive to the courthouse with them. The phone rang. Janey, wanting to get together with me. She was leaving for Oregon on Monday. She sneezed. Allergies. Did I want to go for a run?

I did but I put her off, hung up, and phoned Jay to warn him we were coming. He sounded distracted. He could not lunch with Ma. I was disappointed but not surprised.

I decided the session at the courthouse might take awhile, so I went into the bedroom and changed into a skirt and top that might pass muster at the dining room of the Eagle Cap Lodge. We didn't reach the courthouse until nine-thirty, and we drove in separate cars.

The Monte County courthouse is a stolid late-Victorian structure with a jail, circa 1970, tucked around back. Jay's office was on the third floor of the main building. He met us in the hall, which smelled of wax, room freshener, and ancient crime.

He gave me a brief kiss and shook hands with Dennis and Ginger.

"Dennis has something to tell you," I prompted, feeling like a fool.

Jay said easily, "I was going to come over to see you later, Dennis. I thought you needed a little time. Your memory was bound to be loused up yesterday." Not for nothing was Jay trained to negotiate with hostage takers. I practically felt Ginger relax. Dennis still looked apprehensive, but he had stopped twisting his hands.

Jay led us in through the main office with its bull pen of desks. A bored deputy was reading *True Detective* at the booking station and Carol, the dispatcher, gave me a smile from her communications board. Kevin wasn't at his desk. Probably at church. He was a devout Methodist. I flipped Carol a wave and followed Ginger into Jay's office. It was kind of crummy—badly in need of fresh paint and furnished in New Deal leftovers—but it had a corner window with a spectacular view of the Siskiyous.

Jay was making preliminary rumblings. Time for me to

bow out. I was about to say so when the sergeant on duty entered with her notebook, looking trim and official, and Ginger grabbed my arm.

"Don't leave us," she hissed.

I rolled my eyes at her.

Her perm was particularly electric that morning, and her eyes pleaded.

Jay and Dennis were looking at us, Jay frowning.

"Dennis remembered something that may be important," I said, resigned to my role as go-between. "But he and Denise had a disagreement over the phone, and he's sure you'll arrest him for murdering Denise if he tells you about it."

Jay turned to Dennis. "I can't make promises, but we're pretty sure you're clear on the first murder, Dennis, and I think there's only one killer."

Dennis and Ginger sighed in unison.

To my surprise Jay took Dennis through his story then and there, though they went out with the sergeant when Dennis said he was ready to sign a statement. When they returned, minus the sergeant, Dennis looked almost tranquil. I heard Ginger expel a long, relieved breath as she rose to go.

Jay kept us a few minutes while he told Dennis about the state lab's computer search for the owner of the partial thumbprint they had found on the gun that killed Miguel. Dennis got interested in—or perhaps distracted by—the technicalities. If my mother had been murdered, I wouldn't have been able to listen, which may be one of the differences between men and women. I think Jay was trying to give Dennis the illusion of progress.

Dennis and Ginger went off hand in hand. I looked at Jay. "Are you going to arrest Lydia?"

"Not yet, but you can bet I'm going to question her."

"Any other developments?"

The mustache whiffled. "Have you no faith?"

"In you, yes. In your gizmos and gadgets, very little. I'm going to lunch with Ma. Any messages?"

"I won't be married in a monkey suit."

"How about gorilla?"

"Ha." He kissed my cheek, a chaste and proper office-type kiss, and escorted me to the elevator. "We may have a witness at that construction site above Denise's house. Kev's looking into it." So Kevin wasn't at church after all.

I punched the down button. "I heard a power saw when we first got there. Do you think Lydia . . .?"

"Hush. Time will tell." The elevator door opened and disgorged half a dozen scruffy citizens, two I recognized as reporters, and a female deputy who smiled at Jay. We both smiled back.

I got into the elevator. "I'll call you when I get home."

Jay blew me a kiss and turned back to his office as the elevator door closed. Both reporters followed him.

I reached Eagle Cap Lodge about half an hour before the appointed time. I could have gone up to Ma's room, but I needed a moment or two to sort out my thoughts. She was going to want to talk Wedding. I walked around back and admired the gardens. The patrons looked very expensive.

When we finally went down to lunch, Ma did talk Wedding. The fashion for bloated formal ceremonies, grotesquely expensive and full of *Bride* magazine ideas of Meaningful Symbolism, was then at its height. My mother is not a slave to fashion, so I was a little surprised that her plans leaned in that direction. I put both feet down hard. I also pointed out that Jay had been married before and was not, as it were, a virgin. That distracted her from visions of color-coordinated tuxedos, as I had hoped it would, but she grilled me on the marriage so mercilessly I took refuge in fiction. I didn't know the details. Jay and I hadn't got around to discussing them. So I made up a plausible and dignified scenario. I think Ma believed it. I also resolved to cross-examine Jay as soon as possible.

Mother refused to see me wed in a forest glade near Lake Alice, though I catalogued the advantages of a double wedding with Dennis and Ginger, only half joking. We finally settled on a small, private ceremony in our backyard in

Childers, New York, and even set a date in August. I could see Ma was mentally reviewing her roster of caterers and judges, so I mentioned the partial thumbprint on the Beretta.

She leaned forward over her crab Louis. "Will a partial thumbprint show anything useful?"

I paraphrased Jay's description of the lab's new computerized matching system.

"Heavens. Does Jay think an arrest is likely?"

"I don't know, Ma. He did say there might be a witness near the farmhouse."

"Do you think the killer was Lydia Huff?"

I took a bite of asparagus. "It seems more and more possible. She has to be at least a material witness." Neither of us, oddly enough, suggested Bill as the killer.

"That's a strange family," Ma observed.

"How so?" I thought the Huffs were depressingly normal.

She buttered a bit of her roll. "It feels as if it were straining to fly apart. Bill is very unhappy."

"Very sloshed."

Ma chewed. "That's a symptom. And Janey's a puzzle."

"I should go running with her today. I suggested it while we were at the lodge, but I keep putting her off."

Mother regards voluntary physical exercise as a fly-by-night fad, so she ignored my mild guilt. "What does Janey do for a living?"

"Works in a public library up in Oregon. She's a librarian, not an aide, so she probably makes a living wage. What I don't understand is why she's staying with Lydia, whom she obviously despises."

Ma paused to appreciate a chunk of Dungeness crab. "Perhaps she's trying to protect her father."

"Protect?"

"The children of alcoholics are often very parental. Is she an only child?"

"Yes." I sipped my iced tea. "But Lydia's the parental one—toward Bill, I mean. She's a classic enabler." I described how Lydia had intercepted Bill that first night at the lodge and sent him up to sleep off the booze. And how she had hovered over him the next morning, talking baby talk, when he was hung over.

"How did Janey react to that?"

I didn't remember Janey reacting at all. Janey was beside the point, anyway, if Lydia was on the verge of arrest. It was true that Dennis's "evidence" was shaky and uncertain. I could see why Jay hadn't sworn out a warrant, but if he found the smallest fragment of corroboration, I knew he would act.

"Are you going to that cocktail party at D'Angelo's apartment this afternoon?"

"Certainly." Mother took a last blissful bite of crab. "We have to look at the notebooks again, talk things over."

"I wish you wouldn't go."

"Why?"

"Lydia's bound to be there." If she wasn't in custody. "I don't trust her an inch." I folded my heavy cloth napkin. "I don't trust any of them. Not after yesterday."

"Yes, I see your point. Nevertheless," she said, signing the check and writing in her room number, "I *am* going. I'll see you at ten tomorrow morning, darling." She was going to drive in to the bookstore and we would have lunch again before she drove the rental car to the airport. She was flying out north, via Portland. "Keep me posted, and tell Jay I want to see him before I leave."

I wondered how Jay felt about August weddings. I would find out.

The phone was ringing as I came in the door. I kicked off my shoes and padded over to it in time to hear Jay leaving a message on the answering machine.

I interrupted him as he finished. "Have you had lunch?"

"Lark? Did your mother go to that cocktail party at D'Angelo's?"

"Should be there by now."

"Who else was going?"

"Martha, Win, the Huffs." I carried the phone over to the refrigerator and started poking in the freezer compartment, looking for something to nuke for dinner. Fish? Chicken Cordon Bleu? Weight Watchers' Lasagna?

I heard Jay draw a long breath. "We've got an awkward situation here."

"No kidding?" He'd been in an awkward situation since the discovery of Miguel's body. "Give."

Hesitation. "Will you just go on over there and keep an eye on your mother?"

"Crash the party? Come on."

"The thumbprint on the clip was Bill Huff's. We got a match."

I shut the refrigerator door and leaned against it. My brain kicked in. "Then, if it was Bill's gun . . ."

"All we know is he loaded the clip. Probably not recently. The gun was unregistered."

"Then how . . ."

"We took his prints at the lodge. The army had them, too, but it takes time to pry information from the feds, so we just sent what we had down to Sacramento and told them to cross-check the suspects. We couldn't tell for sure that the print matched, but the new computer came up with Huff on the first try."

"Impressive."

"Yes. Will you go on over to D'Angelo's? If Janey is still at the Huff place, we'll try to execute the search warrant and she'll probably call Bill. When he comes to the house, we'll take him in for questioning. Meanwhile, someone should keep an eye on Lydia."

"Haven't you questioned her yet?"

"We only got the good word an hour ago. I phoned and asked to see her at seven. She said she was gong to the cocktail party first and I needed more evidence anyway, so I decided to delay . . ." His voice trailed, then came back strong. "I may have made another mistake. I don't want any more victims."

I got the point. My pulse was racing. I envisaged Lydia's square, craftworker hands twisting the scarf around Denise's neck.

"You'll have backup, but I don't want to alarm the suspects. I'll send a car to D'Angelo's. Check in with the deputy when you get there."

"Who?"

"Dan Cowan."

I refrained from groaning. After all, Cowan had saved Jay's bacon two days before. "I'm on my way."

"Lark?"

"What?"

"Take care."

"You, too," I muttered. "I love you." I hung up, dashed into the living room, and scuffed back into my shoes, grabbing my purse. I locked the door behind me out of pure habit and clattered down the back stairs to my car. I don't remember the drive to the apartment complex. I probably broke all kinds of speed laws.

I wheeled into a spot marked "Visitors" and jumped out. As I did, a marked sheriff's car, no siren or lights, nosed into the lot. I stood on the curb until Cowan saw me and rolled down his window.

"Evening, Ms. Dailey."

"Hi, Dan."

"Which unit is it?"

D'Angelo lived in a two-storey town house, two bedrooms up, at the edge of a grassy common that led to the swimming pool. Rose bushes in full flower lined the short walkway to his door. I pointed. "Over there."

"Okay. If you need help, open the door and yell. I'll sit where I can keep an eye on it." Dan was chewing gum and sounded bored.

"Thanks." I jogged across the lawn and up the walk. I hadn't seen Ma's car in the lot, though that meant nothing. It was an undistinguished vehicle, and the lot was nearly full. I leaned on the bell.

Martha Finn opened the door almost at once. When she saw me her eyes widened briefly, but she was an actress. She gave me her number-two smile, gracious welcome to interloper. "Hello, Lark. What a nice surprise." She was wearing a cool lilac-and-pink striped caftan that looked like I. Magnin.

I hoped my skirt wasn't too crumpled. I had given no thought to the tale I'd have to spin either. I presumed Jay didn't want me alerting Bill and Lydia before he had a chance to put his deputies in place at their house. "Er . . . ah, is my mother here?"

"Surely. Come in, Lark. Win and Mary have been sorting papers, but we were about to have a drink. I hope you'll join us."

"Ah . . . thanks." I followed her solid, graceful form down the hall and stopped dead in the archway that opened onto the sunken living room. All four occupants of the room gaped at me—Ma, D'Angelo, Lydia, and Janey.

"Hi." Confusion set in. Where was Bill? "Did you get your run in, Janey?"

Janey twitched a brief smile. "Couple of miles at the high-school track." She looked relaxed, as if she'd had a good workout and a cool shower. She was wearing a long-sleeved pink T-shirt and a pair of pants made out of pink sheeting fabric.

All four of them were seated around the low myrtlewood coffee table, Janey and Ma on cushions on the carpet, D'Angelo and Lydia chummily together on an oatmeal-colored sofa.

"What are you doing here?" Ma put the question the others were probably too polite to ask. The table before her was covered with neat exercise books, the kind with marbled cardboard covers. She squared one of the piles.

"Jay's on duty. I got scared all alone in that apartment."

This was truly feeble taradiddle at five in the afternoon, but for some reason everyone fell for it. Martha practically shoved me into a low-slung chair, and everyone clucked. It was all so innocent and kindhearted I began to feel like a paranoiac. Lydia told a crisp little tale of being left alone while Bill attended a reunion. She got scared and almost shot one of the cats, she said. Ho, ho. I didn't ask her with which gun.

Martha had gone off toward the kitchen to fetch munchies. Janey followed her. D'Angelo rose and went to a small cabinet on rollers that was stocked as a bar.

I looked at Ma. She was frowning slightly. I cleared my throat. "Get all the papers sorted?"

She tapped the pile of notebooks. "What we had to. Did something happen?"

Unwilling to lie to her, I just shook my head. I turned to Lydia. "I thought Bill was coming. Too bad he couldn't make it."

She gave a brief, tinkly laugh. "Oh, you know Bill. He deputized Janey, said he had business calls to make for the paper. I think he wanted to loll around and watch the Cubs on cable." Her eyes glittered. They were the color of gray that sometimes seems incandescent. I had noticed the glow before, but I didn't know what it meant. She didn't say a word about her upcoming interrogation.

She trilled another laugh and rose. "Let me help you, Win. What do you need?"

D'Angelo was setting out glasses. "Poll the company. Gin and tonic, right, Mary?"

Ma nodded.

"Me, too," Lydia echoed, giving a little nervy bounce. She trotted off toward the kitchen.

"Lark?"

I started. "Just ginger ale, Win. Thanks." I wished Jay would hurry up. If Bill were home Jay would probably do his search, take Bill in for questioning, and stop for Lydia on the way. The ordeal began to stretch before me forever.

I wasn't keeping much of an eye on Lydia.

Guilty and a bit scared—what the hell were they doing in the kitchen?—I got up. Ma was still watching me, still frowning. Apparently D'Angelo had noticed nothing strange in my behavior. He had gone off into a discussion of the early notebooks, rattling glasses and ice cubes while he talked.

Ma answered him absently. She was watching me. I grimaced and rolled my eyes kitchenward. Ma's frown deepened.

As I began to move back toward the hallway I heard the three women erupt from the kitchen on a gale of giggles. Lydia's rather shrill. I moved up to the arch and waited for them.

Martha led the way, bearing a tray of canapés on which peeled shrimp figured largely. Janey was carrying a bowl of salsa and a basket of assorted crackers. Lydia brought up the rear, empty-handed. When she spotted me she trolled out gaily, "Were you about to send a posse for me? Two white wines, Win. One with spritzer." Innocent as a newborn babe.

"I had to stop Janey from pigging out on the crackers and salsa," Lydia added with one of her malicious grins.

Janey scowled at her and put the crackers down on the

coffee table. Ma was setting the neat stacks of notebooks on the carpet beneath the table to make room for the goodies.

Everyone fluttered and settled, so many doves in the cote.

Lydia—could she not sit still?—jumped up again and danced over to D'Angelo. "Oh, gorgeous. Lime slices. I'll take the tray, Win. Mix yourself a nice gentlemanly scotch and let me be your cupbearer. Lark?" She thrust the tray out at me.

I took my tall ginger ale glass and a paper napkin. The two gin-and-tonic glasses sat smugly and identically beside each other. My stomach twisted. Surely Lydia hadn't had a chance to lace Ma's drink. Or mine.

The phone rang.

"Damn," D'Angelo said mildly. "Can you get that, Martha?"

Martha popped a prawn into her mouth and looked around.

"Over by the fern."

"Right." She rose, in no hurry, and caught the phone on the fourth ring.

My hand was clenched around the cold glass so hard it was a wonder I didn't shatter it.

"Hmm? Oh, hi."

D'Angelo brought the wineglasses to the table and went back for his scotch. I was still frozen in the doorway. Ma and Janey were dipping prawns in the fiery-looking salsa.

"Sure, Bill. I'll get her." Martha turned. "Lydia, it's Bill."

Lydia made a face and trotted over to her, taking the receiver. It was one of those portable phones that always sound tinny. "Thanks. What is it, darling? We're . . . what?" Her voice rose.

I was watching her closely. She went so pale I thought she was going to faint.

"No. No, look again. I'm sure I saw it . . ." She clung to the receiver. "Try the cabinet."

I took a step into the living room, the better to see her face.

"Right. Yes. Let me know." She hung up slowly. Her

color was coming back, She met my eyes, hers glittering. Her lips moved on a single syllable, but I couldn't read them.

"What did Daddy want?" Janey, wineglass in hand. She took a sip.

"Just looking for something he misplaced." Lydia moved slowly back toward the table. "Men. They can never find anything. Why is that, Win?" She settled on the oatmeal couch.

"Dunno," D'Angelo said cheerfully. "I can. Maybe it's because I put everything where I *can* find it." He sat beside her and swallowed scotch.

Lydia reached for her gin and tonic and took a large gulp. She glanced up at me as I made my way back to the low-slung chair. Her eyes glinted. "And how are the local Gestapo doing?"

I misstepped. Ma drew in a sharp breath, and all of us stared at Lydia.

A hectic flush reddened her cheekbones. She finished her drink in a second large gulp and got up again. "I need another. Do you mind, Win?"

He gaped at her. "Feel free."

I reached the chair and sat slowly. So Jay was at the Huffs' house, probably searching it. Why wasn't Lydia proclaiming the fact at the top of her lungs? Gestapo indeed. Was Bill under arrest? If he were, surely he would have told Lydia so and set her to stirring up his lawyers. At the very least, she should leap up and fly to his side. But she didn't.

I suppose my confusion was mirrored in my face.

D'Angelo said mildly, "I haven't found Dodge overbearing, Lydia. Aren't you being unfair?" I gave him a grateful smile.

Lydia poured a little tonic into her gin and stirred vigorously. "Probably. Sorry. I'm jumpy today."

Ma rose from her squishy cushion and took her own drink to the bar. "Needs freshening," she murmured.

"What did Daddy lose?" Janey inspect another prawn, dipped it carefully in the hot sauce, and took a bite.

216

"Never mind," Lydia muttered.

Janey chewed and swallowed. "Maybe I could help him find it."

"I don't think so." Lydia made her way back to the couch. "I don't really think so, Janey."

The interchange was peculiar, to say the least. Clearly it baffled Janey. She sipped her wine. "Is he . . . has he been drinking?"

Lydia stared down at her, mouth tight. "For Christsake, of course he's been drinking. Bill drinks. Sometimes he drinks himself under the table, in case you hadn't noticed. For what it's worth, he isn't drunk yet."

Janey's mouth set in a prim line. "You shouldn't talk that way about my father."

"I am your father's wife," Lydia said coldly. "I'll talk about him any way I damned well please. I'm sick of covering up for him, sick of sparing your feelings and his feelings and everybody's feelings but my own. He's an alcoholic, and the sooner his nearest and dearest admit it the better."

"I used to attend Al-Anon meetings," Martha observed. She spread cream cheese on a Triscuit. "My mother drank. They've very helpful. Isn't it interesting how many different kinds of support groups have developed over the past twenty years?"

Ma clinked a spoon on the ice in her drink. She picked up Martha's cue. "So kind and practical. A solution to the modern loss of neighborhood. People used to talk their problems over with their next-door neighbors. Now we have little hypothetical neighborhoods, some of them linked only by technology. A friend of mine has started a support group for poets through one of the larger business networks."

"Is that on Compu-Serv?" D'Angelo wasn't slow either. He got up and gave Ma his place on the sofa.

They were soon deep in an amiable but very abstract discussion of synthetic communities. Gradually Lydia's flush faded. She set her drink on the table.

Win eased to the carpet between Janey and me. Ma set her

drink down untouched. When a pause in the discussion gave her the opportunity, she suggested to D'Angelo that he purchase a modem and a personal computer for the foundation.

They began to bicker in a cheerful way over Macintoshes and IBM PCs—familiar territory. I threw in my two cents' worth, though my head spun from the unreality of the conversation. Janey ate another cracker. With cheese. At that rate she'd have to run ten miles a day. She kept glancing at Lydia, glancing and munching.

Lydia said nothing. She didn't look particularly embarrassed. In fact she looked absent, as if she were brooding over the preservation of Patagonian plant species, or something equally remote.

Lulled by the chatter and the lack of incident, I got up and went to the bar myself. The ice cubes had melted in my ginger ale. I poured the watery slop into the bar's tiny sink. When I got back to my chair they were still chattering, this time about the foundation. Win was hugging his knees in a boyish way that should have stirred up any latent rheumatism in his spine. He and Ma were trying to decide whom they should invite for the inaugural summer session of Siskiyou Summit, and Martha had wandered vaguely to the window.

Because of Win's position on the carpet, I could no longer see the surface of the table. Janey was still hunched over the goodies, and Ma had her eyes on Win. She reached for her drink.

I sat up and craned. Her drink and Lydia's had been sitting side by side, and I had lost sight of the glasses for a good five minutes. I didn't think Lydia had made a move, but I wasn't sure. I cleared my throat. "Uh, Ma . . ."

She looked at me, drink halfway to her mouth, the slight frown she used when my manners left something to be desired creasing her brow.

"Uh, don't drink it. Let me make you another."

"I just freshened it, Lark." The glass touched her mouth.

"Don't!" I got up. My face was probably crimson, and I felt everyone's eyes on me. Even Lydia's.

She stared at me without expression.

Ma set the glass down. "What in the world . . ."

Then Lydia did something completely off the wall. She picked up Ma's glass, eyes locked on mine, raised it, and took a large swallow.

Ma and Win gaped like gaffed flounders. Martha took a step toward us. I know I was staring.

Janey began to giggle.

"Shut up, Janey." Lydia's voice was almost dreamy. "Why don't you all shut up?" She raised the glass again and finished Ma's drink.

The doorbell rang.

We froze in a tableau. After a long pause the bell rang again, and Martha moved across the room to answer it.

My knees unlocked. I rose and walked around the sofa to stand behind my mother.

"What is it?" She swiveled so she could see me.

"I don't know. Something's crazy . . ." My voice dried up. Martha had returned, with Jay, Bill Huff, and Dan Cowan on her heels.

Jay gave me an unsmiling nod and looked at the others.

Beside him Bill was red in the face, perspiring. He took a a half-stumbling step down into the living room, leaving the others standing on the hall level. "Lydia?"

"They know?" Her voice sounded calm, almost serene.

He nodded, his face a mask of misery. "I'm sorry. I couldn't help it."

Janey was looking from one to the other, big brown eyes wide. Slowly her hand rose to her lips and she began to titter.

"Oh, don't!" Bill's voice rose. "Don't, Janey."

Jay said in undramatic, almost conversational tones, "Mrs. Huff, I have one question to put to you. If you prefer to come to the courthouse . . ."

"Ask me now."

Jay frowned.

Janey had both hands over her mouth. Her eyes were bright, and she emitted tiny snorts of laughter.

Jay ignored her, eyes still on Lydia. "I have reason to think you were the one Denise Fromm invited to lunch yesterday."

Wait a minute, I thought. He hasn't read her her rights. I opened my mouth.

"That's right," Lydia said flatly. "She was dead when I got there, and my cat was yowling by the gazebo. Denise gave us those cats. That was when I knew what had happened. I tried to shoo Ethel away, but she wouldn't go and she wouldn't let me touch her either, and then I panicked. I got in the car and left. I drove home . . ."

Bill groaned. "I wasn't there. She couldn't reach me. If I'd been there . . ."

Lydia shrugged. "It was too late, Bill. You know that. Janey was taking a shower. I waited for her. When she came out I asked her where she'd been. She said running. I knew she was lying. She was still wheezing a little, the way she does when the cats get in the house. After she dressed she went out to her car. I watched her from the study window. She took the cat carrier out of the front passenger side and put it in the garage."

Janey?

Janey's flush had faded. Her hands drooped to her lap. She was frowning at Lydia, but she looked more bewildered than angry.

Jay finally turned to look at her. "Jane Huff, you're under arrest for the murders of Miguel Sanchez and Denise Fromm. You have the right to remain silent. . . ." He finished the Miranda warning.

"Daddy?" Janey started to rise. She had been sitting so long in one position her legs probably cramped. She leaned hard on the coffee table as she struggled to her feet. "Daddy . . ."

Bill didn't answer. He wasn't even looking at her. His poached-egg eyes pleaded with Lydia.

Lydia said nothing. Her profile was stony, but her cheeks were flushed.

Janey turned on Jay. "You're wrong, you know. It's Lydia." She sounded reasonable, like a librarian explaining a fine. "It was Lydia all along."

"I don't think so, Miss Huff."

"But I don't have a motive."

"We have a witness, Miss Huff."

"Lydia would say anything. She hates me, she's always hated me, you can't . . ."

"An independent witness," Jay said gently. He sounded almost sorry for her.

So the power-saw operator had come through. Nobody moved. I was still trying to assimilate the idea of Janey as a cold-blooded killer.

"Are you going to take her to jail?" Lydia's voice was slightly slurred.

"As soon as the deputy arrives." Jay turned to look at Dan Cowan. "Kay's on her way?"

Dan nodded. He was chewing gum.

Bill looked at Janey for the first time. "I'll call your mother."

Lydia coughed.

"Call my *mother*?" Janey's voice rose. "Call Mommy to make it all right? Fuck you, Daddy dear. I want a lawyer, *your* lawyer, your nice expensive screw-the-wife-and-kiddies lawyer, and I want him now. I'm not going to take a fall for your artsy-fartsy wife."

Take a fall. I wondered what Janey had been reading. I wondered what the hell was happening.

Lydia coughed.

"Miss Huff," Jay said pleasantly. He's at his pleasantest when other people are screaming, a habit I'll have to watch out for. "Would you object to rolling up your sleeves?"

Janey gaped.

"Your sleeves," he repeated, mild as May.

"Janey!" Bill said sharply. Janey looked at him.

Lydia's cough turned into a choke.

I remembered Ma's drink. "Jay, she's poisoned!" I took Lydia's heaving shoulders. "Ma's gin and tonic."

My mother turned. "Lydia?"

Lydia began to retch.

It was a reprise—with embellishments—of our Independence Day nightmare. The ambulance came quickly, though. Jay monitored Lydia's pulse, while I stood by. Bill fussed and wept. The others looked on, more or less wringing their hands. Except for Janey.

She watched the procedures, jaw set, sleeves still down, and didn't say another word. Somewhere in the middle of the confusion, the female deputy arrived and took her arm. As the medics carted the gurney bearing Lydia out the door, Janey began to cry. Martha Finn went to her and held her by the shoulders. Janey wept on Martha's I. Magnin dress.

Bill had gone in the ambulance without a backward glance for his daughter. The rest of us, Jay included, stood in the shambles of the living room staring at the three women.

Martha patted Janey's shoulders and made soothing sounds.

The deputy cleared her throat. "Hadn't we better take her in?"

Jay said, rather sharp now that things were peaceful, "Search first. Ms. Finn . . ."

Martha regarded him coolly above Janey's honey-blonde flip, which was now rather rumpled. "What is it?"

"Will you accompany Miss Huff and Deputy Ryan to a bedroom? And stay with them while Kay does a body search?"

Martha grimaced. After a moment she nodded. "Come along, Janey."

Ma bent down and picked something up. "I think this is her purse." It was one of those small leather clutches, pink like Janey's outfit, and it was unzipped. Ma poked in it. "Is this what you're looking for?"

Jay was beside her in one stride. "Jesus, don't smear the prints." He whipped out a handkerchief and took a small brown bottle from her.

Ma backed off, still holding the purse.

Jay folded his handkerchief tenderly around the bottle and handed it to Dan Cowan, who was still chewing his cud.

Janey sobbed. Jay jerked his head at Deputy Ryan, and she and Martha took Janey out of the room and down the hall.

There was no further drama. The search went quickly and produced nothing new. Jay appropriated the purse and the glasses Lydia had drunk from. The evidence crew arrived and shoved us into the ferny corner of the room by the telephone, where we stared at each other and said nothing. Finally Jay, Dan Cowan, the woman deputy, and Janey left. Janey was not handcuffed, and she had stopped crying but she still had said nothing at all.

That left me, my mother, Martha, and Win in Win's trashed living room.

"I don't believe it," Ma grumbled, tidying the spattered and smeared hors d'oeurves' tray. "Not Janey. She was crying."

Martha took the tray from her with fastidious fingers. "Lydia upstaged her." There ensued a long silence. Martha went off to the kitchen.

Part of my mind agreed with Mother. The rest, sifting through the events of the previous ten days, began to see

Martha's point. She saw the killer in theatrical terms, and she was right about one thing. Lydia was always upstaging Janey.

After a while Win said from the bar, "I suppose they'll order a psychiatric evaluation."

"I hope so," Ma snapped. "It doesn't make sense, none of it. *You* didn't think Janey was the culprit, Lark. You warned me not to drink that gin."

"I thought it was Lydia," I agreed, unhappy, "but I was wrong. Janey makes better sense."

"She had scratches on both forearms and a bruise on one shin where Denise kicked her. She's guilty, all right. But why did Lydia swallow that drink?" Martha exploded. "That I don't understand."

None of us understood. It was crazy. I thought of Miguel, of Denise, her eyes bulging, tongue protruding, of Llewellyn dying as I breathed for him. Crazy was the word. Crazy and cold.

When we had restored the room to a semblance of order, I took my mother home to my apartment. We left the rental car in the parking lot. I think Win and Martha were glad to see us go.

Mother and I collapsed in the living room and stared at each other for a while. Finally I said, "We ought to call Dad."

"Yes." She didn't sound enthusiastic.

"What I need is a good, long run. I know that doesn't appeal to you . . ."

She gave a snort of laughter. "Whether it appealed or not, I couldn't. I'm an elderly lady with varicose veins."

"Now, Ma. How about a swim?"

"I don't have a suit."

"We'll find one for you at the health club."

She resisted halfheartedly, but I dragged her off. I swam laps, and she paddled around in a green tank suit somebody had abandoned. When we got out we looked like skinned rabbits—or March hares—but we felt better. At least I felt better, and Ma said she did.

My bookstore looked abandoned. No reporters or gogglers haunted the half-vacant parking lot. They would tomorrow, when I reopened. I wanted to get back to my books. Work was going to seem strange without Ginger.

The phone rang as we entered the apartment, and I caught it before my message tape kicked in. It was Ginger.

"Has something happened? I tried to call Jay. They said he was busy, so I called you and you were out."

I broke in on her reproaches and gave a terse account of Janey's arrest.

Ginger heard me in silence. When I finished she gabbled something at Dennis, then said into the receiver, "We're coming right over."

"But Ma's here . . ." There was no point in objecting. She had hung up.

Mother was poking in the refrigerator. When I told her Ginger and Dennis were on their way she just looked resigned. "Better send out for a pizza. I'm starving."

So we shared a vast mushroom-and-olive pizza and bottles of Henry Weinhardt's Private Reserve with Ginger and Dennis while we hashed everything over. Both of them were as stunned by the idea of Janey's guilt as I had been. It was my mother who pointed out that Janey had been charged only with the deaths of Miguel and Denise.

"You mean Jay still doesn't know who killed Dai . . . my father?" Dennis's big face flushed.

"Lordy," I muttered into my beer. "Maybe it was Lydia after all."

"Or Ted Peltz," Ma said darkly. She was still unreconciled to the fact that Peltz was going to get away with wife battering.

We finished the pizza, speculating wildly, and adjourned to the living room. It was half past ten by that time, and Mother remembered she hadn't called Dad. After some hesitation—it was one-thirty in New York—she decided to wake him up anyway and went off to the kitchen to call.

Ginger and Dennis and I talked about weddings for a while. I was relieved to hear that they still meant to go through with their sylvan ceremony and told them about my own plans. That necessitated a round of rearrangements so the dates wouldn't conflict and somebody could take care of the bookstore. We were trying to figure out how to time all the flying back and forth when Jay came in.

He took one look at Dennis and Ginger, groaned, and went to the refrigerator for a beer. Ma trapped him and made him say something to my father, so he looked harried as well as exhausted when he and Mother returned to the living room.

He creaked down on my second-best chair, an overstuffed 1950s armchair covered in brown plush, and took a long swallow straight from the bottle. We all stared at him.

When he rested the bottle on the chair arm I said, "Give."

He looked wary and said nothing.

"Who killed Dai Llewellyn?" Ma demanded.

Jay's brows shot up. "I charged Janey Huff with all three murders when we got to the courthouse."

"But you only arrested her for killing Miguel and Denise," Mother protested.

"That was before you found the poison bottle in her purse," Jay said reasonably. "I was sure she'd done it, but I only had hard evidence for the later killings at that point. The bottle—it still contained a trace of the poison, by the way— gave me enough to book her for Llewellyn's death, too. The bottle's just like the one we found at the lodge, and the one Cowan found in the glove compartment of her car about an hour ago. She must've brewed a big batch of the stuff. In Lydia's kitchen. Janey will go before the judge tomorrow." He took another swig of beer. "And that, friends, is all I'm going to say."

We all protested at once.

"That's not fair!" I got up and stood over him. "Come on, Jay. We won't talk to the press, and we have a right to know."

"Not the ghost of a right," Jay growled. "The alleged killer will be tried in a court of law. I am not going to say anything that can be twisted, misrepresented, or otherwise used to jeopardize a verdict." Very high-minded—or, more likely, paranoid.

It took awhile, but we wore Jay down. I suppose it wasn't fair, all of us jumping on him like that. When we had sworn not to discuss the killings with anyone outside the room and I had pointed out that Dennis, at least, had a right to know what kind of case the D.A. would be able to make, Jay sighed and gave in.

"I talked to Lydia."

"She's okay?"

Jay patted the arm of the chair and I sat on it. "Not okay, but definitely lucid. She wanted to talk. Bill didn't like that, and neither did the doctor. For that matter, I could have waited until tomorrow, but Lydia insisted on making a statement."

"Did she say why she drank the poison?" I had an inkling.

"She thought you suspected her of lacing your mother's drink and she started to panic. Janey had already directed suspicion at her with the cat. Lydia had some vague notion that drinking the gin and tonic would prove her innocence, at least to you. She hadn't seen Janey spike it, so she took a gamble."

"And lost."

"Maybe not," Jay said slowly. "Maybe not."

"Was she trying to protect Janey?" Mother's dark hair, curly like mine but gray-streaked, had dried in lopsided kinks and whorls. She looked tired, but not half as tired as Jay.

Jay said, "At first. Lydia didn't get along with Janey, but Janey was Bill's daughter, and Lydia has this habit of shielding Bill from life's little unpleasantnesses."

"Unpleasantnesses!" Ginger's perm crackled with indignation. Another woman into protecting her man.

Dennis was trying to puzzle it out. "But my mother . . ."

Jay sighed and rubbed the Velcro corset. "I'm sorry,

Dennis. I don't mean to trivialize your mother's death—or the other deaths. I was trying to give you Lydia's viewpoint. Denise apparently saw Janey put something into Llewellyn's drink. That it might have been an act of murder didn't strike her until the next day, when Lydia woke her up to tell her your father was dead. Lydia sedated Denise and persuaded her she must have been mistaken."

I got up and went to the front window. The street below was empty. Small-town Sunday evening. I sat on the wide window ledge. "I suppose Denise was too caught up in the . . . er, the developments about the will to brood over what she had or hadn't seen."

"We'll never know," Jay murmured, still watching Dennis.

"She was kind of moody the whole time we were in San Francisco." Dennis's voice cracked. "I thought . . . well, see, I was pretty confused myself. We didn't talk much about . . . about old Llewellyn's death. There was too much else to discuss. And there was the will and the funeral."

Ma leaned forward in the rocking chair, her eyes on Jay. "But when she heard about Miguel's death, Denise must have reconsidered."

Jay nodded. "She called Lydia as soon as the news broke. We had to clear that point up because Lydia had claimed she called Denise with the news of Miguel's death. Denise called, Janey answered and brought Lydia to the phone. Janey must have hung around and heard enough to suggest a plan of action." His face was grim. "Denise fought."

Ginger gave a single, satisfied nod. Dennis gulped, but he didn't say anything.

"The cat was an attempt to incriminate Lydia," Jay went on. "Or scare her. It's solid evidence of premeditation. One of the carpenters working on that cabin above Denise's place identified Janey's car. He was up on the roof eating his lunch and enjoying the view. Claims he can see Mt. Shasta from the ridge of the rafters. He saw Janey's car pull up, still with the sailboard on the roof. He was definite about that."

"Did he see Janey herself?" Ma wondered. So did I.

Jay took a swallow of beer. "Yeah. The guy saw Denise answer the door and let Janey in. He also heard her pull out, and looked over about five minutes later when Lydia drove up thinking she was going to eat lunch with Denise and talk things over. He just caught a glimpse of that, enough to notice that it was a different car. Then he got busy. He didn't see Lydia leave, though he did spot the Toyota, Lark. He remembers thinking it was unusual for Denise to have all those visitors."

We were all silent for a long moment. Poor Denise would have been safer in San Francisco, with one of the highest rates of violent crime in the nation, than she was in bucolic retirement.

I was remembering the scene in the gazebo a little too clearly. I got up. "What about Miguel?"

Jay frowned. "I guess he must have seen what Denise saw."

"Blackmail," Ma murmured.

Jay nodded. "Poor kid. I should've taken him in and sweated it out of him. I knew he was holding something back, but I thought it had to do with his relationship with Llewellyn." He finished his beer without looking at Dennis.

"Janey arranged a rendezvous with Miguel, took Bill's gun from the collection, got in the Mercedes with Miguel . . ." I was pacing and probably making my guests nervous, but I couldn't help it.

"He wouldn't have seen her as particularly threatening." Jay sounded almost apologetic. "A woman alone with a young man, way out in the tules—the flip side of machismo."

"So she shot him." I plunked down on the carpet by my mother. The rocker creaked. "But why the trick with the refrigeration? Why the cat and the larkspur?"

Ma said, "I'll lay any odds you like she's a compulsive reader of murder mysteries. Librarians often are."

I craned around to look at her.

She gave me a faint smile. "My contribution to the evidence. W. H. Auden wrote a good essay on the symbolic meaning of mysteries, but I don't know what he'd make of Janey's. I read them myself, and one thing I've noticed is the texture of their absurdity."

That interested Jay. He straightened in the plush chair, hands on the arms. "Absurdity?"

"The juxtaposition of wildly disparate elements that aren't inherently odd."

"Just odd in context?"

She nodded, approving. "Whether consciously—in an attempt to confuse the investigation and throw blame on Lydia—or unconsciously, Janey was trying to reproduce the absurd texture of the classic mystery."

"Life imitating art?" Jay sounded skeptical, as well he might.

Mother said gently, "Life often does imitate art, which is why art is such a heavy responsibility."

The rest of us, not being artists, had nothing to say to that. Ma was watching Jay. Finally she said, "Why did Janey kill Dai?"

Jay shook his head. "I'm not sure. She seems to have expected us to arrest Lydia for the first murder. Because of the legacy."

"The Huffs knew about the will?"

"I guess Llewellyn told them the day he arrived from San Francisco. Lydia was delighted. Bill hated the idea. They quarreled. The Huffs confirm that. Janey apparently imagined the bequest was an important part of the estate. Of course Dennis's inheritance was far larger—and far more of a surprise."

"She killed Dai to throw suspicion on Lydia?"

Jay said dryly, "She still wants to throw suspicion on Lydia."

Ma gave a rock and the chair creaked.

Jay added, "We didn't need motive to charge Janey. Just the witness, and the poison container."

The rocking chair creaked. "Is she talking?"

"Sporadically. Huff called the lawyer for her—Avram

231

Roth. He got to the courthouse around eight-thirty and ordered her to clam up. We won't be able to use anything she said before that." He leaned back and closed his eyes. "She kept insisting it was Lydia, that Lydia wanted Llewellyn's legacy for the Huff Press. It seemed to rankle Janey that Lydia's brainchild was making a splash in the publishing world. She wasn't very coherent."

I hugged my knees. "I thought Janey liked Llewellyn."

Dennis shifted on the sofa. "My father . . ."

We all started. I had half forgotten Dennis's presence, he had been so quiet.

Dennis flushed under our stares. "My father," he repeated, dogged, "didn't pay enough attention to Janey."

Ginger touched his arm. "When did you see them together?"

"Couple of summers ago. He liked people with brains, see, and talent, and he liked you to speak up. If you didn't . . ." He looked at his big hands. "See, if you didn't say something that interested him, he just ignored you."

"So Janey tried to be a part of that world, Lydia's and Llewellyn's world." Jay was wide awake, sitting up. "Bill's new world."

"And Dai shut her out." Ma rocked the chair. Her face was sad. "When did the divorce happen—how old was Janey?"

"Twelve or thirteen." Jay was rubbing his beer bottle between his palms, eyes narrowed to slits. He set it down. "A bad time to deal with divorce, especially for girls. She would have seen Lydia as *her* rival as much as her mother's."

"Janey spent her summers with her father," I said slowly, working it out. "And Llewellyn came to the lodge every July for the month. Glory time for Lydia, once the Huff Press came to his attention."

"So Dai was just a surrogate victim, a substitute for Janey's wicked stepmother." Ma sighed. "I almost wish Dai had done something to injure her. His death would make more sense."

"If he made her feel stupid, he injured her." I flushed

under Mother's stare and went on with less heat, "He probably didn't mean to, Ma, but when you're a teenager every little slight is magnified. And Janey never really grew up."

"She's childish for twenty-seven," Jay agreed. "I noticed that. I thought she was just trying to be cute and girlish, but maybe she *is* thirteen emotionally."

"And morally." Mother sounded grim. She looked tired, too. She had known Llewellyn a very long time, since she was a teenager herself.

"I think she was just crazy."

We all looked at Ginger, who blushed but held her ground. I was inclined to agree with her. We were theorizing too much.

Dennis was still brooding. "I suppose she'll, what d'you call it, plead insanity?"

"She may. The judge is almost sure to order a psychiatric evaluation." Jay leaned against the plush backrest. "But all murderers are at least temporarily insane. I think she'll stand trial."

Ma said, "I'm glad there was a resolution before I had to leave. Thank you for trusting our discretion, Jay." She got up. "Dennis, can I trouble you to drive me out to D'Angelo's apartment? I left my car in the lot, and I really ought to be off."

Jay said, "I'll drive you."

I said, "No, you won't. You're going to bed. I'll take you, Ma."

Ginger settled things. "She'll come with us." She rose, too, and pulled Dennis to his feet. Then she went over to Jay. "I think you're smarter than hell for figuring all that out. Thanks for telling us what happened." And she stuck out her hand.

Jay rose and shook it. "All right, Ginger?"

I wasn't sure what he meant, but she apparently was. She nodded emphatically and gave him a quick kiss on the cheek. Then she turned to me. "I'll see you tomorrow, Lark."

"You're coming to work?" Hope sprang like a green shoot.

"Sure. We have to start training Annie."

I hugged her. "You're right. We do." I kissed Dennis and my mother and verified Ma's plans for the morning. Finally they left.

I closed the door and went in search of Jay. He was in the kitchen making a turkey sandwich.

"I forgot to feed you!"

He turned and kissed me ferociously. "What am I, a bird in the nest, that you have to stuff my craw? Don't get stuck in Lydia's mode, darling."

"We had pizza."

"I can taste it." He's not supposed to eat pizza.

I put the kettle on and we sat down at the table. I watched him eat.

"This should put you in good with the sheriff."

He took a bite. "I quit yesterday."

He was chewing, so I took a moment to translate the message. "What?"

He set the sandwich down. "I resigned Saturday and told the dean at the college I'd take the director's job."

"Oh, wow." The kettle screamed. Distracted, I jumped up and made him a cup of herb tea of the kind guaranteed to put you to sleep. "Wow."

"You don't sound heartbroken."

I swallowed my relief and set the cup by his plate. "I'm glad because it will give us a lot more time together, but I'm not glad if it was because of Miguel."

Jay touched my cheek. "No. That was a bad judgment call, and I'll probably regret it the rest of my life. But I'm used to judgment calls. And to regret, for that matter. I quit because I lost my professional judgment with Ted Peltz." He took another bite, chewed, and swallowed, adding, "And because it's time."

"Time?"

"I've been a cop about as long as it's safe to be a cop. Time for a change. Time to start over."

I could have protested. He was a good cop. But starting over sounded very good to me. I told him so.